The Book of Polly

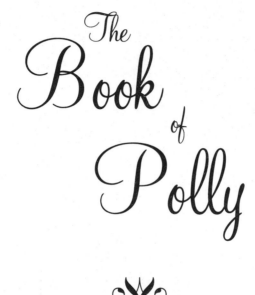

Kathy Hepinstall

PAMELA DORMAN BOOKS/VIKING

VIKING

An imprint of Penguin Random House LLC
375 Hudson Street
New York, New York 10014
penguin.com

A Pamela Dorman Book / Viking

ISBN: 9780399562099 (hardcover)
ISBN: 9780399562112 (ebook)

Printed in the United States of America
1   3   5   7   9   10   8   6   4   2

Set in Baskerville
Designed by Cassandra Garruzzo

To my mother, Polly Hepinstall,
precious cargo on the road of life.

Acknowledgments

Thank you, my true friend, agent, fellow kayaker, and stairwell safety inspector, Henry Dunow, who told me, "This is the novel you were meant to write."

Thank you, Pam Dorman, rock star of the publishing world, for finding Polly and using your editing brilliance to bring her to life.

Thank you, Brian Tart and Andrea Schulz. Your support means everything. Thank you, Jeramie Orton and Seema Mahanian for helping to shape and refine the manuscript. Thank you, Lindsay Prevette, Carolyn Coleburn, Mary Stone, and Kate Stark for all the time and effort you spent making sure as many people as possible heard about Polly. Thank you, Roseanne Serra for the stunning cover, and Cassandra Garruzzo for interior design that impressed my mother—no easy task. Thank you, Tricia Conley and Tess Espinoza for shepherding this novel through. Thank you to everyone on the sales team for their early and enthusiastic support, and especially Michael McGroder for the kindness, hospitality, and margaritas.

Thank you, Polly and Becky for being there from the beginning and offering insights, advice, and support. Thank you also to all the other family members and friends who served as early readers of this book. Your words and laughter were encouraging, and I am very grateful.

Thank you, Dallas Jones for dropping out of the galaxy one day in Maui, and for being a friend and an inspiration.

Thank you, Michael. I love you.

The Book of Polly

I'm not sure at what young age I became frozen with the knowledge, certainty, and horror that my mother would die one day. Spared the passing of my father, the Captain, by my status as a fetus, I was cowering in the womb when my mother found my father dead in his chair.

Polly told me the story when I was old enough to hear it. She was smoking a cigarette, a habit I feared and detested. One of my earliest memories was reaching up and trying to snatch a cigarette from her lips. Even then I knew my enemy. But she was too fast for me, and by the time I heard the story of my father's death I'd mostly given up trying. So I just sat watching the trail of smoke. "The Captain was once a navy man, you know that. Anyway, he got this wooden lobster from the Philippines when he met Ferdinand Marcos—another story—but when he died the lobster was sitting there in his lap. I guess he'd taken it down from the wall to admire it just before the stroke got him. And that's what happens when you die. It's no more complicated than that, if you're lucky."

She took a long puff and the smoke spiraled toward the ceiling, her eyes bright. My mother never cried, at least not in front of me. Instead, her green eyes got greener, more sparkly, as though the tears were fuel for that color and nothing else.

She had conceived me in something close to a bona fide miracle, when she and her soon-to-be-late husband of thirty-seven years consummated their love for the last time. From the absurdity of that union came the news that my mother received from her doctor three days after my father's funeral: Polly, in her late fifties, was due to have one more child in the year 1992.

Willow.

Me.

The doctor advised her to terminate the pregnancy. She advised the doctor to drop dead and mind his own business. Eight months later I was born, my family already gone like a train pulled out of a station: my father dead, my brother and sister grown and gone.

Polly was old and tired and cranky and yet she had to start over. A new generation of parents had moved into the neighborhood, remodeling the houses around her as hers fell apart. Old enough to be my grandmother, she brought me up with the same methods she'd used with her other children: folksy southern wisdom and distinctly custom-made punishments. Which explained why, on this brisk April morning, we were barreling toward my school in a two-tone Impala, Polly driving, me riding shotgun, and a falcon in a cage in the back seat.

Polly had found the falcon through an old fishing buddy of hers and had managed to procure its rental for free.

"Please," I begged Polly one last time. "I'm sorry. Don't go to school with that falcon."

I was ten at the time, and Polly sixty-eight. We were at a light. The brakes squealed a bit and she glared at me. She had on her Homeowners' Association power suit: a pale, pearl-colored dress with round buttons, a small silk handkerchief in the breast pocket, and medium-heel shoes—she'd rubbed them down with a cheesecloth earlier that morning to take out the scuff marks. She was a small, slim woman, petite, with a delicate face and remarkably smooth skin for a woman her age—the result, perhaps, of the homemade mixture of rosewater and black currant seed oil she faithfully slathered on at night.

She wore no makeup except for a burgundy lipstick, in the shade of a knowing glare. She had worn the same hairstyle for decades—a soft bowl around her head, and had kept her hair, more or less, the same shade of light brown, although she had dyed her hair the night before. Either through agitation or distraction she had left it with a certain orangey tone that she had noted with exasperation, but did not have time to address.

Orangey hair and red, red lipstick—they did not go together. Like two flowers that clash in a bouquet, the configuration was wrong and I was somehow to blame for it, too.

"Did you hear me?" I asked. "I'm sorry."

But she was unmoved. "No one calls my daughter a liar," she said, leaning on the word in a way that made me miserable because I was, in fact, a liar. And I had told some lies—and even worse, some truths—about my mother to my classmates. In my defense, she was great fodder, and this was years before she killed our neighbor.

I sighed, giving up. Once she had determined a punishment, she never deviated, so it was hopeless to ask. I turned around and looked at the falcon. Polly's friend had shown her how to take it out of the cage and wear the leather protector on her shoulder. The falcon had white feathers with brown spots, a yellow, world-weary head, and a dangerously curved beak. It stared back at me. The falcon, no doubt, was equally unamused by the situation.

"Just tell me," Polly said, "that saying I hunted with a falcon was the biggest lie you told."

It was not.

My elementary school had not been updated for decades and still bore that seventies school decor. We arrived right before school started, so the halls were crowded as Polly moved down the hallway with a purposeful stride, the falcon balanced on her right shoulder, perched on its leather protector, its right foot secured by a leather strap.

I followed her, wilting, horrified, as I'm sure she had expected. It was one thing to speak of her in fond abstractions, to tell both the tall tales and the truthful ones, and let my listeners sort them out, but here she was in the flesh, and kids stopped to gape as she passed by.

No insults or smart remarks or giggles of laughter. Just open wonder at the sight.

The falcon sat calmly on her shoulder, staring at the students as though sizing them up as prey, its eyes flat and dark. As shamed as I was at being part of such a spectacle, I could not help a creeping pride in my mother's regal manner, the way she glided along in that dress, with buttons carefully repurposed from another dress and sleeves she had pressed that morning with the tip of an iron. She did not speak to me. I quickened my steps to catch up with her and then entered the sphere of her fragrance, lilacs with an undercurrent of honeysuckle, the only gentle and forgiving part of her outfit, for it was the perfume she wore to church to be sniffed by her Methodist God.

My mother had made no bones about the fact that she had already raised two children in this school, both of whom had their own share of disciplinary problems—Shel, with his penchant for pocketknife flipping, and Lisa, with her proselytizing—and Polly's only wish was to lie low while the last, laggard child grew up without trouble. And here I was—in trouble.

Our school counselor, Ms. Jordane, used to be Coach Jordane back in my first-grade gym class. I remembered her as somewhat boyish and happy, her cheeks puffing out to release the shriek of a whistle lustily during dodgeball, her arms bare and thick with dark blond fuzz, and a single hair growing out of her cheek. Ms. Jordane had taken night classes, gotten a master's degree in psychology, and hoisted herself into administration, but even her name on the door seemed to evoke the hot, cat-tongue smell of that gymnasium.

Ms. Jordane sat behind her desk going through some papers when we entered her office. I hadn't seen much of her over the years, and up close, her appearance startled me. They'd tamed her, plucked the hair from her face, smoothed her arms, taken her out of gym clothes, and dressed her like a businesswoman. She sensed our presence and looked up, her face unguarded for a brief instant as she took in the sight of Polly with the falcon on her shoulder.

"Who's calling my daughter a liar?" Polly demanded by way of greeting.

She shook off her look of surprise, stood and extended her hand. "I'm Beth Jordane. And you must be Mrs. Havens. So nice to meet you."

I knew right then that she had lost my mother's respect. Even as Polly reached with equal politeness for the handshake, I could tell by the slight shift in her body language that she did not think much of Ms. Jordane's attempt at equanimity under the stern and humorless gaze of the falcon. Polly would have much preferred for Ms. Jordane to come out and say, "YOU HAVE A FRIGGING FALCON ON YOUR SHOULDER," even though she wasn't fond of that particular expletive.

My guidance counselor got right to the point. "Your daughter has been telling some pretty tall tales about you. Normally, we tend to think this kind of thing is harmless. But the stories have escalated. We have had some complaints from the parents of some of the more sensitive children."

"Wussies," Polly said under her breath.

Ms. Jordane's eyebrows went up. Her face was so smooth. They'd put makeup on her. They'd killed my gym teacher, stripped her boy/girl soul away. She looked down at her notes.

"Willow says she has an older sister who's with Jesus."

"Not a lie," Polly responded. She crossed her arms in satisfaction.

"You have a daughter who is deceased?"

"No, Willow was simply saying that her sister is on Jesus' team. Although, I might add, so am I, but sometimes I'm puzzled because her Jesus doesn't sound like mine at all. Hers won't let her drink margaritas or say *damn* or play slot machines. I don't know how she met this Jesus, but mine is much more fun to be around."

She blinked a few times. "Not dead?" she said at last.

"No, quite alive, but boring."

She picked up her black pen and jotted down something. I could feel a stream of cold air coming from the vent in the room. The falcon stared at the potted plant, or beyond it, as my old gym teacher's eyes moved down the page to the next item.

"Willow says you are the oldest living mother in the world."

"I am not the oldest living mother," Polly answered. "I've actually been beaten by mothers in South America, China, and even the U.S. I would call that a slight exaggeration, not a lie."

She sent me daggers with her eyes, as did the bird. My mother was somewhat sensitive about her age, and happy to look much younger. I sank down lower in my chair as the litany continued.

"You can make an obscene gesture with your toes."

"Yes, I can, with the left foot," Polly said proudly. "I would show you, but I've got hose on."

Ms. Jordane looked uneasy but she continued down the list.

"You shoot the squirrels in your garden with a shotgun."

"The gun is loaded with blanks," she snapped. "It just stuns the little bastards. Occasionally, I flip them off with both fingers and toes. Sometimes at the same time. Do you own a garden?"

Before she could respond, Polly answered for her. "Of course not. If you did, you would know that squirrels and other varmints are the enemy. They strip my peach trees and tear up my greens and steal my pecans. And just the other day I caught a squirrel dragging his butt between my cucumbers and sugar peas like a dog. That was pure spite."

Her interrogator's shoulders had begun to slump. She was used to dealing with truancy and bullying and low grades and boys fighting on the playground. Clearly my mother's game plan was way above her pay grade.

She looked at the list again. "You and your neighbor Mr. Tornello hate each other. You once paid a little girl to knock on his door and ask to borrow a cup of dumbass."

"True!" Polly nearly shouted.

She made one more weak, insubstantial volley. "Do you think it is a good example to a girl as young and impressionable as Willow to have feuds with the neighbors?"

Polly fixed her with a steely gaze. "We were all born into a world made of Hatfields and McCoys. And as you grow, you need to ask yourself: Am I a Hatfield? Or a McCoy? Because there is no middle ground. You are one or the other, and Willow's going to be the best she can be."

"It's just that these stories she is telling around school . . ."

"Are true. It's not my fault that the gray of everyone else's stories makes the color stand out."

Ms. Jordane looked like she'd give anything to be back in the gymnasium, in her tomboy clothes, blowing on the whistle with her tennis shoes squeaking and her single, long cheek hair growing wild from her face. There was still a whole list to go through and its sheer length seemed to make her weary. She started to put it away and then something caught her eye.

"You have a tail?" she asked in wonder.

Polly looked stunned. From the side, I could see her left eyebrow twitch—a sure sign of agitation. The pupil of the one visible eye darted over and shot me in the heart. That glance was a month of deportation out of the sunshine of her good graces, and I withered. She returned her gaze to Ms. Jordane, and I could feel the inner struggle going on inside her—to keep up the farce that everything I was telling was the truth, or to lose face and call me a liar.

Several more moments passed before she composed herself. "Yes," she said at last. "I have a tail. A very small, dainty tail. Barely noticeable, and certainly I don't go flashing it around. I wish my daughter would have been a bit more . . . *respectful* of my privacy. And yet, I'm proud of it. I'm proud of my tail."

The falcon was growing restless and so was Polly. She stood up, balancing the bird carefully, and held out her hand. "I appreciate you having me come in to discuss Willow," she said, saying my name as though it belonged to a horned, green worm attacking her tomatoes, "and I trust everything is fine now. I've already raised two kids in this school system, and I'd like to grow even *older*"—(another glance in my direction)—"and die without having to attend another meeting like this."

Polly didn't speak again until we were in the car and she had bucked it into reverse and then hit the accelerator, making me lurch against the seat belt as she careened out of the parking lot. In the back seat, the falcon's cage slid over the seat and it gave out a slight shriek.

"Mom," I said, "why are you so mad at me?"

Her face had turned a shade of red I'd barely glimpsed before. "How could you tell them I had a tail?" she demanded. "I am a *southern lady*. Ladies most certainly do not have tails!"

"But—"

"Now it's going to spread all around! Everyone in town will hear about the crazy old lady with the tail! The Homeowners' Association will find out! The Garden Club. The people at church. Mr. Tornello will use it against me. Maybe *Good Morning America* will do a special on it. Would you like that? A special on your mother's tail?"

She was nearly apoplectic with anger. She zoomed through a yellow light just as it turned red. "A tail!" she shrieked. "You're a liar and not even a good one!"

She didn't speak to me for three days. But that didn't stop me from talking about her. She was so much older than the other mothers, and I was determined to make her bigger than life so that she would never die. I couldn't let her die without knowing her secret. What had happened before she met my father? Something that made her vow to never return to her hometown in Louisiana. The story was a blank stare and I wanted it to blink.

☙

By the time I was born, all my grandparents were dead. Polly's only sister, Rhea, came to visit once, when I was very young. She was a small, kind woman with a head of black hair teased in all directions, with two fascinating streaks of white fanning out past either ear. Rhea and my mother called each other "Devil Cat." I wasted no time cornering her out in the backyard, where she was smoking one of my mother's Virginia Slims.

"I'm sorry, honey," she told me when I asked her what on earth had driven my mother from Louisiana, why she wouldn't return, and why she refused to speak a word of it. "I've been told to keep my piehole shut in no uncertain terms."

"But I want to know!" I shrieked. "I have a right to know!"

"How old are you? Eight, nine?"

"Seven."

"Jesus. Why are you so curious? When I was seven, I was wondering about the birds and bees and when I found out I was sorry I ever asked."

"I don't care about the birds and bees. I want to know about *her*."

My intense stare and fake, slow-forming tears never worked on my mother, but Aunt Rhea had a soft heart and a big mouth.

"Don't cry, honey," she said. "It was a terrible thing that happened. She was just eighteen years old. Wasn't her fault. There are people in that town who might very well shoot your mother if she ever showed up at their door. I'm here to tell you that her only crime was falling in love."

"With the Captain?"

"No, no, no. He came later, after the mess was already done. She was in love with a man named—"

The back door slid open. Polly had her own unlit cigarette in her hand. She looked at Rhea and then at me.

"What are you talking about?" she demanded.

"Nothing, Devil Cat," Aunt Rhea said innocently.

But I was young and stupid. That night when Polly was putting on her night cream, I approached her. "What happened in Louisiana?" I demanded.

She paused, midslather. "What are you talking about?"

"The terrible thing with the man you loved. What happened? What was his name? Did the Captain know him? Why does everybody over there hate you?" She turned to me, her eyes a suddenly bone-chilling green, and brushed past me out of the bathroom. Presently I heard a stormy fight erupt between her and Aunt Rhea. Shouting and then the slamming of doors.

Aunt Rhea left the next morning, and never came again. She and my mother eventually repaired their relationship enough to speak on the phone once in a while, but the lesson was clear to me: The mystery of Polly was not something that was going to be handed to me. I had to root around for it, dig for it, claw for it, snoop and lie.

And keep her alive.

I

Enemies of the Garden

One

What tormented me most, even more than Polly's secrets, were her cigarettes. I'd seen the black lungs in ads, and pictured Polly's lungs, already old, already threadbare, quivering in the smoky cloud of each puff like doomed soldiers in the trench of her chest. The cafeteria lady at my school loved Salem Lights. I'd see her outside in her smock, smoking up a storm. Then she got sick and left for a while. She came back thin and pale, hairnet pulled over a bald head as she served us spaghetti. Then one day she disappeared for good. They announced her death over the intercom, and everyone got free onion rings.

"A shame about the poor lady," Polly remarked. "You never know when the Bear might strike." Polly never used the word *cancer*. It was as if invoking it would be an invitation for it to slide under our door and slink inside her cigarettes. So she said *Bear*. People had lung Bear, stomach Bear, skin Bear, or worst of all (and she said this in a whisper) *hinder Bear*—or, colon cancer. "My uncle had the hinder Bear," she said delicately. "He shrank down to ninety pounds, poor fellow. But they cut it out of him and he was okay for a few years, 'til he had a heart attack while leaning over a rain barrel and drowned."

When I was eight years old, my third-grade teacher told us about the Great American Smokeout. If smokers could just quit for one day, the theory went, maybe they could quit forever. I stared in fascination at the charts showing circulation improving, lung function increasing, heart rate dropping like a sparrow from the sky.

The morning of the Great American Smokeout, an event that held zero interest for Polly, I hid her last packet of Virginia Slims. She discovered that fact just before the bus came.

Polly had worked as a cashier at Walgreens ever since my father died. She confronted me before school in her Walgreens smock, her name tag dangling from a cord she wore around her neck.

"Willow," she said. "Come here."

"Yes?" My hair was drawn into two ponytails. I had my prized lunch box and was ready to go.

"Where are my cigarettes?"

"I don't know."

Her eyebrow arched.

"Don't you lie, Willow."

I looked at her defiantly. "It's the Great American Smokeout."

"So? Some damn fool who doesn't even smoke made up a holiday? What if it was National Pee Your Pants day? Should I pee my pants, you think?"

"I have to go to school."

I opened the front door, letting in a fall breeze and the murmurs of the kids at the bus stop.

"You're not going anywhere," Polly said.

"But, Mom, I have perfect attendance!"

"Well that's your problem and you can fix it in two shakes of a rat's tail if you just tell me where you hid my cigarettes."

I turned around, but left the door open. We stared at each other. My lunch box dangled from my hand. A line had appeared in her skin between her eyebrows, like a twitching nerve rising to the surface. I could hear the bus rumbling down the block, coming closer.

The gauntlet had been thrown. I hated Polly at that moment, but not enough to capitulate. It was National Smokeout Day and I was going to save a fraction of her life.

"The Bear is going to come for you," I told her. "Just like he came for the lunch lady. Is that what you want?"

We held each other's gaze as the bus groaned to a stop and I heard the creak of the doors opening. Then with a hush, they closed. The bus eased away and there was silence.

"You know, in my day, girls who missed school grew up to be tramps. Got pregnant early," Polly remarked.

"You are so mean," I said.

"No!" she answered. "*You* are mean. Forcing your poor old mother to drive to the store and restock."

"I'm trying to keep you from dying!" I shouted, my voice full of righteous indignation.

The line between her eyes was back. "That's God's way!" she

shot back. "The parents are supposed to die before the child and everyone starts bitching soon as it happens. Now tell me where you hid my damn cigarettes!"

I stood perfectly still, stone faced, lest my body or expression give away when Polly was getting warm. I heard her back in my bedroom, swearing, jerking opening drawers. Next the kitchen, then the den. The cushions from the couch hit the floor. The magazine stand rattled. The wooden blinds thwacked against the window.

I was going to lose. This was nothing; it was only a desperate gesture of love and rage. It would not stop Polly, in the long run, from smoking or from getting older or from dying, but suddenly it meant the world to me. I wanted perfect attendance, but more than that, I wanted someone above me in the chain of life. I didn't want to be alone, a single blue egg in a crumbling nest.

"Damn it," Polly mumbled. "Damn it, damn it, damn it. You damn kid."

Finally she slumped down at the out-of-tune piano in the hallway. I glanced over at her and she stared back at me. Something in my posture or expression must have tipped her off because her eyes squinted and took on a hooded look and then she turned from me, gazing at the piano.

She struck the middle C and it clanged in its off-tune fashion.

I held my breath.

She struck D.

My heart began to sink.

E, F . . .

G was a muffled thud.

She perked up, struck it again.

"No, Mom," I said pleadingly, but it was too late. She jumped up and propped her knees on the bench so she could open the lid of the piano and peer inside at the keys.

"AH HA!" she shrieked. She stuck her hand in and retrieved a crumpled box of Virginia Slims, the one she'd opened the night before. She withdrew a bent cigarette and tried to straighten it, but gave up. "It'll do," she said triumphantly. She cast a glance at me, but something in my expression caused the glee to leave her face. The hand with the cigarette slowly fell to her hip.

"Ah, well, you tried, don't feel so bad," she consoled me. "I won't smoke this in front of you, okay? You are a good kid. Now come on, let me drive you to school."

⌒⌒

My fears about Polly's health and life span left me with a certain undercurrent of daily anxiety that ruined even good things for me: the upside-down Jell-O molds she'd make for me, holding more cut fruit than needed; the movies we watched together; and my favorite sound, that of a car door locking. It ruined the feel of guinea-pig fur and the crunchiness of popcorn. Ruined smooth, dark water and the stones skipping over it.

Polly didn't even know of the extent of my suffering; the way I'd stand over her at night and listen to her breathing, as though it might stop at any time, and I would be needed to start her old heart up again. I'd read manuals on resuscitation and practiced on a large bisque doll with a flat chest whose crystal blue eyes stared up hollowly as I counted the pushes.

"I don't think that's going to help," said my best friend, Dalton. He was small and lean, with expressive eyebrows, and longish hair he kept slicked back over his ears. He had two small dents on either side of his eyes due to a forceps accident at birth, where he was pried from the womb of his mother, who later ran off with a tour boat guide from Key West.

Dalton's father was very permissive and never seemed to notice him running around with dirty jeans and undone homework, and let him ride his bike all night if he wanted. Polly was oddly kind to him, in a stern sort of way. "It's not that boy's fault that his mama ran off on him," she said. "Take a look at what those forceps did to his face and you got to believe there was some hurting on her end, too. Not saying that's why she vamoosed. I've met his daddy a time or two and he's no prize. Anyway, not my concern." Dalton reminded her of another boy who had lived in the neighborhood years before.

"Name of Phoenix Calhoun. Parents acted like he wasn't even there for some reason. Goofy as hell, ran around barefoot in December. But he and your brother were thick as thieves, and Phoenix was loyal as a hound dog."

Dalton's dad had a series of live-in girlfriends who never stayed around for long. Thus my friend was philosophical on the subject of mothers.

"I can't let her die," I said. "She's so old."

He shrugged. "Things die. That's one thing I've learned. My dad says my mom's love for him died one day when they were arguing about who left the lunch meat out on the counter. Boom. Dead."

I looked back down at my doll. At the crystal blue eyes, the ridiculously long lashes. "Help me count pushes," I told Dalton.

The only time my mother seemed truly invincible was when she was in her garden, which encompassed most of our front and back yards. A nest of violets bloomed in her front garden, shadowed by the hedges of ligustrum and holly. Indian hawthorn, iris, and hydrangea, blue and pink. The backyard contained a fig tree, a peach tree, a satsuma tree, a pecan tree, and the vegetable garden, set into ten rows she had hacked and shaped herself. Tomatoes, cucumbers, yellow crookneck squash. Eggplants, new potatoes, Kentucky Wonder pole beans. Peppers, sweet peas. Strawberries. Greens. These were her children. These were the ones she tended and praised and criticized and brought to harvest unless the frost or the heat or the insects killed them dead.

"Varmints," she said, speaking of tomato worms, red spiders, leaf beetles, stinkbugs, and snails, but also raccoons, squirrels, possums, weeds, the neighbors' pets, and the neighbors themselves.

On the one side was Darcie Burrell—a reed-thin woman with a permanently conflicted expression, as though, deep inside her, someone was trying to bathe a cat. She attended our church, and was famous for praying over people who later died.

"The angel of death," Polly said. "Every church has one. There was one back home in Bethel. She had a goiter and blue toes."

Mrs. Burrell had two little twins, a boy and a girl. Several years younger than me, with horrific dispositions and a penchant for jumping up high enough on their backyard trampoline to flip us the bird over the fence, a gesture that Polly heartily returned.

"Mom," I said. "Come on. They're like five years old."

"Old enough to shoot the bird, old enough to be shot by the bird," she answered grimly. "I know the Good Book says not to hate anyone, but I hate those kids. They're not even human. They're like child/rodent half-breeds."

Mr. Burrell was an airline pilot and always traveling.

"Right," Polly said. "He's probably a shoe salesman who says he's an airline pilot and goes and sits at a bus stop all night so he doesn't have to come home to those brats."

"Mrs. Burrell says her kids are gifted."

"Oh, yeah, they go to that fancy school. Montosaurus."

"Montessori," I corrected. I had read about it in a magazine. I wanted to attend a Montessori school, moving from station to station, self-guided, a genius.

"Brat colony. That's what I call it," Polly said.

One morning we went out into our driveway and found our trash cans I'd set out the night before turned on their sides, and the twins going through the garbage.

Polly's shrieks brought Mrs. Burrell out of the house and made the children look up disinterestedly.

"What are you kids doing?" Polly howled. "Are you raccoons? Get out of my trash!"

"We were curious!" the boy said. Obviously, this was their go-to excuse for all their evil deeds, and Mrs. Burrell fell for it hook, line, and sinker. "I understand, but that's not the proper way to express your curiosity," she chided benevolently. "Jared and Madison, apologize to Mrs. Havens."

They smiled. "We're sorry," they intoned together.

"Like hell you are," Polly sniffed.

Mrs. Burrell looked aggrieved. "Mrs. Havens, I'd appreciate you not using language like that in front of the children."

"You've got to be kidding me," Polly shot back. "I've heard those kids say the 'S' word while they're out on the sidewalk pounding ants with a hammer."

"Go in the house, kids." She gave Polly a long, martyr's stare. "My kids are Montessori children and they've been trained to be open to new experiences. They just got confused about what's proper."

Polly was having none of it. "Why don't you leave them with me and I'll show them what's proper with a peach-tree switch?"

She gasped. "Violence is never the answer, Mrs. Havens."

We stood and watched without helping as Mrs. Burrell picked up the garbage herself.

"Don't forget to drag the cans to the curb," Polly reminded her. "And turn the handles to the street."

The twins weren't the only problem with the Burrells. Polly complained bitterly when their aggressive strain of Bermuda grass crawled under the fence and began bullying her more stately St. Augustine. Also, their gardener piled wood against the common fence they shared with Polly, causing it to rot. Polly suspected the gardener of using a kind of pesticide that took out the bees, too. Bees were the chosen insects of Polly's world. Almost biblical in their goodness, spreading mercy and pollen on their crooked little legs. The Burrells were bee killers and that was the worst crime of all.

"They have no respect for nature," Polly complained, ignoring the fact of her constant war on the varmints of various species who invaded her garden. "Of course, who knows how many critters those horrible kids have taken out with a claw hammer."

Old Mr. Tornello and his wife lived on the other side of us. They were stooped, reclusive people who let the neighborhood newspapers pile up on their driveway. Mr. Tornello was grouchy and slow-moving. His wife was small and quiet and almost always sporting a Band-Aid somewhere on her face.

"She's got the skin Bear," Polly said. "Too much time in the sun, I suppose. She was Miss Kansas back in the day. She's still real pretty, such a delicate face. A shame."

So Mrs. Tornello and her rotating Band-Aids had Polly's sympathy. Mr. Tornello and his heart problems did not.

"Listen, pure meanness is keeping that man alive," she said. "That old heart of his will still beat long after I'm toes to the sky."

Mr. Tornello's crimes: sawing off the limbs of her prize red-bud tree, which dared drop its blooms on his side of the fence; letting his dandelion scourge send its seeds over the fence every spring to take root in her backyard; and also owning the ominous one-eyed cat that perched on their common fence and stared at her.

Rain or shine, no matter the season, Polly fought the good fight against the predators of her garden, not just the neighbors, but the cold winters and the rains that, in high summer, scalded her tomatoes, and the funguses and blights, and the raccoons that crawled the fence and ate her figs, and, of course, the squirrels. The squirrels were the worst of all. They would strip her trees of pecans and peaches and tear through her garden, pulling down the delicate trestles she'd used for her climbing tomatoes. They'd crawl up the bird feeder and eat all the seeds. They'd gnaw on the lead skirt of her vent pipes, causing roof leaks.

Polly tried putting a rubber snake in the peach tree to scare off the squirrels. It was found belly up to the sky the next day. She tried a mixture of cayenne pepper, vinegar, and water, which she sprayed at the edge of her garden, again to no effect. She seemed especially distracted when the pecans began to mature and turn brown, pacing around and puffing a cigarette down to the filter while cursing the squirrels. Her shotgun, I knew, was loaded with blanks. BUT I hid my brother's old BB gun, afraid that she would grab it and shoot a squirrel with it.

"That gun is useless anyway. Your brother shot your sister in the back of the leg one time, and all she did was scream and call for Jesus. It's not gonna wipe the smirk off a squirrel or I would have used it by now."

She gave me a long, hard look. "And don't think I don't know whose side you're on."

Polly knew that I was traitorously enamored of all varmints

great and small, and once, after she caught me trying to feed a squirrel one of her prized pecans, I never heard the end of it. ("Not just a pecan!" she'd raged. "A *shelled* pecan!") But she did not know that Dalton and I had great plans for our animal friends: Someday we were going to pool our money and buy some acreage out past the old farm road, where land was cheap, and establish the Fur Good Animal Sanctuary. There we would coexist with our saved, spoiled creatures, living on cake batter and hot dogs, and let goats sleep in the living room.

Dalton's backyard was twice the size of anyone else's, and it was already a bit of an animal sanctuary. They had dogs, cats, rabbits, chickens, and a bullfrog pair that would hang out in the ferns behind the koi pond. Dalton's dad, Pete, was soft on animals, easy on rules, and mostly drunk, so the animals kept collecting, and that growing herd was responsible for driving off more than one of the live-in girlfriends. Pete was also in on Dalton's and my deepest, darkest secret.

Down on Allengrove Street, there lived a family who kept their poodles outside in the backyard and never paid them any attention. They were thin and their coats were dirty and tangled. Dalton and I would toss hot dogs over the fence for them. One bitter cold night in December, when the dogs were shivering outside, Dalton and I sneaked out of our houses, crawled over the fence, stole the poodles, and never brought them back. Instead, we gave them baths and trimmed their fur and toenails and they slept in Dalton's bed and were happy as clams. The family that owned the dogs put up posters everywhere, offering a reward for their return.

Polly didn't approve of anyone who neglected or abused an

animal. But still, I wasn't certain of what her reaction would be, so I decided to keep quiet about it. In the process I discovered that, although I didn't appreciate Polly's secrets, I really liked my own.

∾

When I got home from school one day in early September of fifth grade, I found Polly once again riffling through *The Farmer's Almanac*.

"Did you order some other kind of squirrel repellent?" I asked.

"The best repellent of all. The squirrel's natural enemy."

"You ordered a dog?"

"No, dummy." *Dummy* was a term of affection from her. She said it lightly and humorously, the way a grandmother would say *dear*. She cackled with delight when a package appeared on our front porch a few days later. It was a plastic owl, looking remarkably real, with a no-nonsense beak and a twisted head and beady yellow eyes that seemed to stare right through me, searching for squirrels in my rib cage. Polly set it on the kitchen table to admire it. "Looks a bit like Mrs. Burrell, does it not?" she mused. "And a bit like old Tornello around the beak." She propped the owl in the limbs of the pecan tree and patted its head. "I am going to have pecan pie this November, so help me God."

She waited by the back window and peered into the yard. A squirrel moved off the fence and approached the pecan tree, the nuts gleaming green. Blooming pampas grass moved in the wind. The sun was falling but Polly didn't move. I was afraid she'd freeze that way, a statue built of schemes and venom, but I stood beside her and waited with her.

"Look," Polly breathed. "The bastard's on his way to the tree."

The squirrel darted and stopped, darted and stopped, raised up on his little legs and stood staring at the owl.

The owl stared back. Polly tensed.

The squirrel darted away, jumping on the fence and disappearing into the gloom.

Polly was jubilant. "The owl did it! It was worth twenty-two dollars and ninety-nine cents plus three dollars and fifty cents shipping!"

The next morning, I awoke to a shriek. I jumped from bed and rushed to the living room to find her staring out in the backyard in her bathrobe, shaking her head and murmuring, "Sweet mother of a son of a bitch!" I followed her gaze, disbelieving. A fat squirrel sat on top of the owl, eating a green pecan. Its tail was draped sideways over the owl's head, as though the owl were wearing a Daniel Boone cap.

Polly turned and rushed into her bedroom. I heard a rustling sound and she came out holding her shotgun.

"Mom, you'll upset the neighbors again," I said, but I could have saved my breath.

She burst into the backyard, aimed the shotgun at the squirrel, and blasted away. The sound of the blank echoed in the quiet neighborhood. I imagined the world waking up to the acrid scent of black powder and gardener rage. The squirrel beat it out of our yard so fast it was just a blurred image, a contin-uum of fur and tail that made a quivering line to the fence and then shot up and out into the yonder. She was cursing now at the outer reaches of her cursing limit, *ass* and *damn* and *thieving bastard* and *big-balled son of a bitch.*

"Mom . . . ," I said. "It's Sunday morning."

"Jesus would understand!" she bellowed back at me. "Jesus threw a fit in the temple with the money changers; they were the squirrels of Jerusalem!"

"Hey!" called a voice from the other side of the fence. "What in the hell do you think you're doing?"

Our back gate creaked open, and there stood Mr. Tornello in nothing but his long nightshirt and his slippers. He had a hoe in one hand with yellow pieces of his damnable dandeli-ons stuck to the blade. His face was bright red and contorted with rage.

"Woman," he told Polly, "you use that shotgun one more time and I'm going to call the police!"

"It's loaded with blanks," she retorted. "And if your old cat was worth a damn, there would be no squirrels in my garden, nor yours."

"You leave Marty out of this!" Mr. Tornello shouted. He laid a liver-spotted old hand over his chest. "My doctor says this could go at any moment. I'm not supposed to get excited."

"She hasn't had her coffee yet," I mentioned in a weak, peacemaking voice.

He pointed a finger at Polly. "Mark my words. You're gonna kill me someday."

∽

Polly had one friend in the neighborhood: Mr. Chant, a bache-
lor who lived five houses down and worshipped her. He was a
shy, sweet man in his early fifties, slightly built, with bowed legs
and hairless arms. He was wistful and sad eyed, as though he'd
recently given someone unacknowledged flowers. In his spare
time, he painted.

"Is he any good?" I asked Polly.

"I saw some of his paintings when I went over there with
some canned summer squash," Polly said. "They are a little
strange. Hard to identify. I saw one that looked like a bird but
the rest lost me. I hear he's got a store on the Internet." Polly
doted on Mr. Chant, treating him like a son. In return, he'd
come over and have coffee with her and march obediently
around her backyard as she pointed out some damage by squirrel or nature with her lit cigarette. Four times a year, Mr. Chant
would drag the old ladder out of her garage and laboriously
haul himself up it and clean her rain gutters. In the summertime the mosquitoes always got him, and no matter what kind of
repellent he wore, he'd come down scratching the welts on his
arms.

"Now, Bob," she'd say. "The skeeters went and got you. I can
clean the gutters myself and those critters leave me alone."

"Oh, Miss Polly," he'd say. "I'd never forgive myself if you fell
off that ladder and hurt yourself."

One evening, just before Christmas, Dalton was over watching *Black Beauty*. We'd both been traumatized earlier that day

when Polly had taken us to the North Houston Aquarium, and an octopus had eaten his mate right in front of us. "That's how it was on the farm, too," Polly had told us dispassionately as she drove us home. "Peaceful and happy one minute, the next minute: *Chomp.* That's God's plan. Stay for supper, Dalton." Polly had let us eat rice and beans in front of the television, arching her eyebrows at Dalton's manners. "Is there no one home to teach that boy not to eat like a wolf?" she'd whispered to me in the kitchen. "You'd think one of his daddy's trampy girlfriends would show him how to hold a spoon."

"Mom," I whispered, "stop being mean. He tries so hard around you."

"Now how is that being mean?" she demanded. "He can't hear me."

Dalton and I lay sprawled on the floor in front of the gas fireplace, watching the magnificent stallion thunder down a beach, when the doorbell rang. "Could you get that, baby?" Polly called from the kitchen. "I'm sunk to my elbows in dishwater."

I found Mr. Chant standing on our front porch, his eyes shining, his face flushed, panting and holding a large, flat item in Christmas wrapping.

"Hello, Mr. Chant," I said. "What's that?"

"It's something I painted for your mother," he told me. "I just finished it." Indeed, he still had a fleck of rust-colored paint under his eye.

"Is she here?" he asked.

"Yes," I answered cautiously.

"Come in, Bob," I heard Polly say behind me. She brushed me out of the way and finished drying off her arms with a kitchen towel. "My daughter is rude to keep you standing there in the cold."

We went to the kitchen and Mr. Chant put the present reverently on the table. "It took me all fall to paint this," he said. "I hope you don't mind, but I used your Homeowners' Association photograph as a guide."

Polly stiffened. She hated that photo. But now she made a great effort to smile and say, "Why, what a lovely gesture, Bob."

She glanced at me. "Don't you have a horse movie to watch for the hundredth time?"

"Nah," I said. "This is much more interesting."

She gave me a chilly stare.

"Are you going to open it?" Mr. Chant asked.

Polly looked uneasy. "Okay, but first, let's have a margarita."

He smiled shyly. "Oh, Miss Polly, you know I don't drink."

"Well, I'll have one."

Mr. Chant began a story about his dog and kept right on going while Polly turned the blender on high and whirred up some courage.

"All right, then," Polly said after taking a healthy sip. "Let's see what you've got here." She set down her drink and carefully opened her present, revealing her image in all its glory.

I gasped. Polly was dressed regally in a high-collared Victorian robe. Her hair was a shiny rust cloud around her face, the same color as the splotch on Mr. Chant's cheek. Her jaw was frozen, her smirk terrifying. One nostril was bigger than the other. Her eyes were an unnaturally bright, satanic green, and she had very little neck.

She couldn't take her eyes off it. "Oh, Bob," she said at last, "it is absolutely gorgeous! I'm going to have a cigarette right now to celebrate." She fumbled in her purse.

"Do you really like it?" he asked. "I don't do lids very well."

"It's so lovely," she said, pressing the hand holding her unlit cigarette to her chest in a way that tipped me off immediately that she was being insincere. "This is so precious." She embraced him, and he held on a bit too long.

After Mr. Chant left, Dalton wandered into the kitchen. He stared at the painting. His ears moved back and forth slightly, always a sign of nervous excitement. We exchanged glances. I shook my head, warning him. Polly drained the margarita and took long, deep drags of her cigarette as we stood studying her portrait.

"Is one of my nostrils really bigger than the other?" she asked.

"No. I think that's a mistake." I leaned in close. "Looks like he got the nose hole crooked and then painted over it."

She swiveled her head suddenly and glared at Dalton.

"What do you think?" she demanded.

Dalton's ears moved again. He'd always found Polly extremely intimidating.

"Uh," he said. "It's nice?"

"Nice!" she barked and he began to shiver.

"Nice! I mean you're much more pretty, Mrs. Havens!"

She touched her own throat. "I have a neck, right?"

"Yes," he affirmed, with confidence now. "You have a neck."

"What are you going to do with it?" I finally asked.

She shrugged. "Hang it up in the sewing room."

"You're going to hang it up?"

"Look, he means well. And I need my gutters cleaned."

Two

Despite her tough talk, Polly had a streak of sentimentality that revealed itself in the way she left Lisa's and Shel's rooms exactly as they had been when they were teenagers. I found their music on dusty cassettes and listened to it on Shel's old boom box, wore both Shel's and Lisa's old clothes, and pored over their photos. I had made the Captain's old office my room so as not to disturb the shrines of my brother and sister, and because the smell of my dead father's pipe still lingered there. That odor was undercut by another—sweet and slightly medicinal—that I couldn't identify until the day I burrowed to the very back of the closet and found two bottles of Tanqueray gin, one full and one broken, with the rug a slightly different shade underneath it.

I asked Polly about the bottles, but she only nodded and said, "Uh-huh," with the same expression on her face she used when she tucked the corners of the sheet under the mattress.

Shel's room smelled of glue. "He loved model planes," Polly

said. "Got glue all over the carpet. Impossible to get out." Posters still hung on the wall of music groups that had come and gone: hair bands from the eighties, Duran Duran, David Bowie, the Rolling Stones. Inside his desk, notebooks were filled with algebra equations and sentence parsing and chemical combinations.

"Was he smart?" I asked.

"Smart as a whip. But bored by school. Just wanted to hang around with that goofy Phoenix boy and work on the Captain's boat with him. They'd work all day on that damn thing. Never figured out exactly what they were doing but that boat ran like a top. Then Shel moved away and the engine wore out and the Captain was going to fix the boat, but never got around to it. So there it sits, in the backyard. . . ."

Her voice trailed off.

"Why don't you sell it?" I asked.

"Sell it?" She seemed insulted by the very thought. "Shel and the Captain loved that boat."

Shel was married now and working in the ad business in Los Angeles. He didn't come home much, though he'd spent one Christmas with us and had brought his wife, Arielle, who was slender and lethargic and decorated her wrists in henna tattoos.

As Polly put it, Lisa's room held a lot of Jesus. He lived in that room in many forms—from terra-cotta figurines, a framed watercolor Jesus, a cross-stitch Jesus with a lamb in each arm, a charcoal drawing of Jesus ascending to heaven, and even a cluster of tiny plastic Jesus figurines, set together like army men on her chest of drawers, all of them wearing robes and crowns of thorns.

"She overdid it," Polly said. "She'd been a tomboy, catching bullfrogs, running around with a slingshot, and building tree houses, but Jesus came around and knocked all that fun right out of her. It was like she hit her head on the doorknob and started talking a different language."

One day I played Lisa's old ABBA cassette on the boom box, drawing Polly to the doorway to listen. The look on her face was both wistful and amused. "She dropped ABBA for Jesus. Said ABBA wasn't a Christian band because they dressed provocatively. I didn't understand what she meant. I mean, the women wore scarves a lot but that's not exactly tramp wear."

"I wish I'd grown up with them," I used to say.

"Oh, don't be dramatic," Polly would shoot back. "You came when you came because that's the way of God. I didn't understand it and I could have talked it over with your father but he'd gone belly-up by then. And I did not have a single margarita for nine months though God knows I deserved one."

"Did you smoke?"

"*Did you smoke?*" she mimicked in a high-pitched voice that was meant to be mine. "Hell, yes, I smoked like a chimney. You would, too, if you were fifty-eight years old with a dead husband and a baby on the way."

She was very open about memories of the family, and the Captain. I would ask, and she would answer everything I wanted to know—everything except about her life in Bethel, Louisiana. I tried. I pleaded, cajoled, manipulated, sulked. But she held

her secrets the way a cat cuddles up against a warm pile of laundry.

I lived for the rare visits from my brother and sister. Lisa was
kind and pale, long limbs and fingers and a delicate nose, blond
hair cut in severe bangs and long on the sides. She would sigh
slightly when Polly fired up the margaritas or lit a cigarette.
Polly would counter, "Everyone's got sins of the flesh, Lisa. Impossible to get rid of them. Like those M&M's you gobble down
like they're going out of style."

Lisa treated me with a formal affection, taking an avid yet
somehow distantly polite interest in my fascination with elec-
tronics, watching me as I showed her a circuit I had made out of
a battery, wires, a lightbulb, and the lid of a tin can. I pressed
my homemade lever and a weak light came on.

Lisa clapped. "Amazing," she said.

Equally amazing was my rendition of "Für Elise" I banged
out dutifully on the old piano. Lisa sat with her back straight,
raptly attentive, seemingly oblivious to the tuning and pacing
issues, and when I emerged from the mockery I'd made of the
arpeggio, she stood up and clapped. Lisa would make us hold
hands and pray before meals, her prayers long and sweet, en-
compassing everyone from our family to the poor kids in Africa
to the heathens still unsaved, to the air and the soil and the animals, and those who led our great nation, and those suffering
the loss of . . .

Blah blah blah, said Polly's tightening hand in mine. *Get on
with it, okra's getting cold.*

I liked Lisa, found her strange and kind. Told Polly so.

"I like her, too, damn it. She's my daughter. Are you saying I don't like her?"

Shel was handsome, blue eyed and dark haired, with broad shoulders and a penchant for sudden changes of mood; his long, intense monologues about U.S. imperialism and the dwindling middle class would give way to raucous laughter at Polly's impatient expression.

"You don't care about the world outside your neighborhood, do you, Ma?" he'd bellow. "So let's talk about that fascinating garden."

I pestered Shel and Lisa with questions about their lives, what Polly was like back then, life with the Captain, everything, seeking to fill in the details of a family that had lived and loved and fought and grown past its prime without me. "Lisa was so awesome at one point in her life," Shel confided in me once when she was out of earshot. "She could ride a bicycle without using the handlebars and skip a rock better than any boy I knew. And she could fight. One time this kid was bullying Phoenix on the bus. Just being a douche. I was too much of a wuss to step in, but Lisa did. She punched this kid in the face and broke his tooth." His voice held a wistful sadness when he spoke next. "Then Jesus got her. Happened at church camp. It was supposed to be a Methodist church camp but another Jesus infiltrated. Grabbed her at a sing-along. She was ten years old and was never the same after that."

I asked him about the Captain.

Shel shrugged. "I dunno. He was kind of a quiet guy. Loved dogs and basketball and reruns of *Gunsmoke*."

"But wasn't he heroic?"

"Like how?"

"Like when the neighbor's house caught on fire and the Captain battled it with a garden hose and made everyone move the cars so they wouldn't explode?"

"Yeah, he did that. Unfortunately, though, when he tried to move his own car he plowed into a tree."

"He did?"

"He was drunk, Willow."

I looked at him, shocked. "Drunk? Mom never mentioned that."

"I'm guessing she was embarrassed at that part of the story."

The Captain, in my mind, was a quiet Doberman who slept on the floor unless danger was near, then he turned into a hero, saving the world in slow motion, eyes of fire, paws of grace.

"Did he get drunk a lot?"

"You could say that, Willow. But listen, don't tell Polly what I told you. Let her remember him the way she wants."

Once when they had both come to visit and Arielle was talking about yoga to my bored mother, Shel volunteered to go to the store because Polly had forgotten the chicken broth. I jumped in the car with him, eager to get some more time to ask him the ultimate question, the impenetrable secret of Polly's early life. Shel had rented a Prius on Arielle's orders. "She doesn't like the poison gases regular cars emit. Priuses are a purer car, the way Lisa found a purer Jesus. My life has been full of women who think they're too good for the proletariat."

I wasn't sure, at the age of eleven, what the *proletariat* meant, but I sounded it out in my mind and resolved to look it up later.

We took the main parkway. Shel put on a classic rock station and eased the windows down. I was determined to find out as much as possible about Polly's past in the space of this errand. It was strange to my ears that he called our mother "Polly," but I played along.

"Did Polly ever talk about her childhood?" I asked.

He kept his eyes straight ahead. "Nah," he said. "Didn't come up, and when it did, she had nothing to say."

"Don't you think that's strange?"

He shrugged. "I have reached the age when I am grateful when women don't feel like talking."

"But don't you think it's strange that Mom—that Polly— won't talk about her childhood or anything that happened before she married the Captain?"

"Yeah, when we were kids we snooped around a little. This was back before Lisa found Jesus, who had a no-snoop policy."

We were now at the supermarket. Shel headed straight for the beer section and began looking over the selection. "Corona's too light for a day with the family," he muttered.

"So what happened? Did you find anything?" I persisted. The air from the beer was cold and I had forgotten a sweater, but I leaned in right next to him to remind him that among his beer choices was a living, breathing little sister who had to know.

"Well, we found some letters."

"Really?" I breathed. "What kind of letters?"

He selected a case of Heineken. "Love letters."

"From the Captain?"

He headed toward the checkout lane. "No," he said. "Not from the Captain."

"What did they say? Tell me, tell me!" I knew he'd forgotten the chicken broth but I didn't care, and I wasn't going to interrupt the conversation, not for that, not for anything.

"Calm down." He hoisted the beer onto the counter and rummaged through his jeans pocket, pulling out a ten. "Look," he said, turning to me, "we shouldn't have read them. They were sacred. Lisa said we'd go to hell if we ever told anyone. Not that I'm afraid of hell, because I've got a wife, but Lisa's right. It's up to Polly to share it."

"Did the letters say why she left Louisiana?" I persisted.

"Not directly. Something about a tragedy and how it wasn't her fault."

"What wasn't her fault?"

"I don't know. I was seven years old, Willow!"

We didn't speak all the way to the car. He grabbed a bottle of Heineken and flicked off the cap with a pocketknife. He sat there drinking the beer, staring into the distance.

"Suffice it to say," he said, "that she thinks she goes through life getting people killed."

That tantalizing story set me on fire with curiosity. I was determined to find those letters.

"Don't do it," Dalton advised. "I told my dad about it and he says leave well enough alone."

But I paid no attention. Instead, I put my crafty plan into motion.

The next Sunday, Polly stood in the doorway of my room in a blue dress that accentuated her small waistline. She had on a butterfly brooch, the closest she would ever get to letting a varmint ride around on her chest. Her hair was a soft, natural-looking shade of brown.

"You sure you're going to be okay by yourself here?" she asked.

"I'll be fine," I said weakly.

She came in and laid a hand on my forehead. "You don't seem too warm. That's good. I'm not sure I should leave, though."

"No, you go ahead."

She bent down to kiss my evil forehead. "Be good, brat. And call the church office if you need me. That preacher will probably be giving a sermon from Leviticus. You know I'm not fond of that book. Drags a little."

I waited for the back door to close, then crept out of bed and stretched my arms toward the ceiling, healthy as the day was long.

The doorbell rang and I jumped, startled. Who could it be? One of the irate neighbors on either side? Someone selling something? Polly herself, having figured out everything and deciding to make a grand entrance in a tornado of wrath? I stood there, uncertain. The doorbell rang again, and again.

Finally I opened the door. There stood Dalton. Barefoot, in a pair of dirty jeans and an Astros T-shirt.

"What are you doing here?" I demanded.

He raked his hair out of his eyes. "Today's the day you're snooping, isn't it? You need a lookout."

"No, I don't. Polly's at church."

"Just in case. I have twenty-twenty vision."

I gave up and ushered him inside. "Fine. Be the lookout."

We fueled ourselves with cold Snickers bars from the refrigerator, which Polly had hidden under the celery in the vegetable drawer.

"What's the signal?" I asked.

Dalton thought about this. "She's here!" he shouted.

"That will work."

I headed straight into her walk-in closet, crowded with clothes and coats and shoes, plus an old chest filled with items of God knows what. This is where my secretive mother no doubt hid her past. I opened drawer after drawer, rustling through them, finding treasure troves of forgotten things. Old book reports, Bible tracts, church bulletins, a mini-photo book of Christmas 1975, when Lisa and Shel were kids, staring up from their opened presents, and my father's slippered feet stretched out in the background. But no letters.

I stepped away from the chest of drawers feeling defeated. I looked around and picked up one of the shoe boxes, prying it open and peering inside to find a pair of leather church shoes. I began to pry open the other boxes willy-nilly. The sneakers of my brother, the tap shoes of my sister, the worn-out slippers of my father, scuffed and scratched and faded but never thrown away.

When I reached the last box, I knew something was different before I touched it. A warm vibration went into my hand and up my arm. I opened the lid and found a plaster of a baby's feet weighing down a stack of letters.

The top envelope had Polly's maiden name written in a distinct handwriting I'd never seen before.

Pauline Perkins

In the left hand corner was this return address:

#14576
Breezeway
Baton Rouge
Louisiana

Here was the treasure trove. The oil well that was Polly's history. Not just a trickle but a Texas sized gusher. I sat down cross-legged in the doorway of the closet, the stack of envelopes on my lap. I drew out the letter from the envelope on top of the pile, unfolded it, and glanced at the date: April 17, 1953.

Dear Polly,
Today is Tuesday and my thoughts turn to—

"Willow!"

A shock ran through me at the sound of her voice. I looked up and there she was, framed in the bedroom doorway, her purse still swinging from her shoulder. I could only watch as her look of surprise changed into Old Testament fury, made of betrayal and stones and heads on platters and devastating floods.

"What are you doing? What are doing?" she screamed at me.

"Why aren't you in church?" I asked weakly.

She barged into the room, flinging her purse on the bed. "Because I left early! I was worried about you! But instead I find you here, rummaging through my private letters. And you're not even sick, are you? Are you?"

"I feel a little sick right now," I said truthfully. I didn't know whether to stay where I was on the floor, my lap full of letters, or to stand up to face her.

"Ahhhhh!" Dalton shrieked from the doorway. "You came in through the back, Mrs. Havens," he added, his eyes wide with horror.

"Young man," Polly said severely. "Come here."

Dalton crept forward. His face was drained of color. His ears twitched frantically.

"Were you helping my daughter spy on me?"

"I . . . was just . . . just . . . ," he stuttered.

"ANSWER ME!"

Dalton threw up on her feet. In the pool of vomit floated two sections of the Snickers bar, still identifiable. He must have gobbled them down without even chewing.

He shot Polly a horrified look, turned tail, and ran. We heard the front door open and slam and then we were left alone, staring at each other. My heart was pounding in my chest. I wanted to jump up, follow Dalton, and live in his backyard.

Polly reached down and snatched the letter out of my hand. "What have you read?"

"Just the first sentence!" I wailed, tears beginning to fill up my eyes. "'It was Tuesday! His thoughts were turning somewhere!' That's it! I swear to God! I swear on your mother's grave!"

The words struck Polly. Made her blink. "Lying and snooping and looting Snickers bars on a Sunday," she growled at last. "May God have mercy on you. Now give me those letters."

I had no choice. I handed them over.

She whirled around and marched out of the room, leaving only her church scent behind.

"Mom!" I called, jumping up to follow her. "What are you doing with the letters? I'm sorry! I'll never touch them again!"

She had already entered the kitchen, opened the cabinet under the kitchen sink and removed a bottle of lighter fluid. She jerked open the drawer next to the stove and pulled out a box of strike-anywhere matches.

"Mom, no, don't!" I begged her, but she was in her own world, a Polly-world of black and white, a cut-off-your-nose-to-spite-your-face landscape scarred and damaged and flanked by burning bridges. You could not disturb her in this world, or lure her into softer pastures. You could merely watch.

The spring breeze hit me when I followed her out on the patio. The back lawn had grown lush and thick from the April rain, and the green beans were pushing up in the garden. The pecan tree waved in the wind and the wind chimes gave a merry little tinkle completely wrong for this moment. She knelt down and put the letters in a pile on the flagstone patio. "Mom," I pleaded, "if you burn them, you'll never get them back, ever."

But she was already soaking the letters in lighter fluid. Mr. Tornello's one-eyed cat, smelling my anguish like a hint of tuna, crawled up on the fence to watch. There wasn't a squirrel in the garden, though. Not a bird in the sky. Not even a lazily circling butterfly.

I shut my eyes. From inside my dark lids I heard the match strike and the small clack of it hitting the top letter and the whoosh of the flame. I opened my eyes and watched the fire, tears running down my face. A strong breeze came up and stirred the flames, whirling the ashes and dispersing them into the air. Just inside my field of vision, I noticed not just an ash but a small piece of a page, singed on one end and shaped like a triangle. I stopped crying and watched it, fascinated, as it whirled and danced and finally drifted over the fence we shared with the Burrells.

Polly didn't notice. She was staring down at the fire, her arms crossed. She said nothing and I said nothing and all hope was lost except for one shard of a letter that had somehow escaped into the sanctuary of our neighbors' yard.

A minute passed, two. Then it was over.

Just a heap of black ashes where the letters used to be. Sentiments, passions from another era, charcoaled down to carbon and the mute sounds of something that can never be spoken again.

◦◦◦

That night I lay in bed fully dressed, the covers pulled up to my nose. In the back of my diary I had written down, from memory, the address on the envelope:

> *#14576*
>
> *Breezeway*
>
> *Baton Rouge*
>
> *Louisiana*

I was thinking about the small triangular piece of paper, torn and singed, that had escaped the flames and leaped the fence and was now waiting to be rescued. When the house went quiet, I rose and crept to Polly's doorway, stuck my nose in the crack, and stood perfectly still until I could hear her measured breathing. I found a flashlight in the kitchen, tiptoed through the living room, and unlocked the sliding glass door ever so gently. It opened with a whoosh and the spring night came in, too early for crickets, the birds asleep, the world quiet except for a dog barking faintly somewhere in the neighborhood. The sky was cloudless and the stars were out.

I stuffed the flashlight in my belt and climbed the fence, my fingertips collecting pollen that had settled on the rails. I dropped into the yard on the other side, making no sound but the soft thump of my feet. I hoped the Burrells' old mutt was sleeping inside. My flashlight beam moved over the sparse Bermuda grass, but revealed nothing. I rummaged through a tangled mass of bougainvillea growing along their back fence, pushing my hand into the vines, parting them, training the circle of light on one space and then the next.

I was about to give up when I found it. I pulled a torn piece of paper from the vines and held my breath. There it was, caught between my fingertips, singed and flapping in the breeze. I held the scrap up to the light. A single moth buzzed the letter fragment as I read it in the dark:

We are too
I love you, Pol
Garland.

Three

Garland.

I had a name, an address, and the word "love." Polly had hosed the ashes off the flagstone but they left a dark stain in the shape of a spray of peonies. I should have just let it go. But I couldn't. There was this thing out there called the Internet, and though I had never been on it, I felt that it might hold the key to the mystery. I took the address over to Dalton's house the next Saturday. He'd been avoiding me since the Letter Incident, possibly over embarrassment at failing as a lookout, or the sheer humiliation of throwing up a Snickers bar at Polly's feet.

Besides all the animals, Dalton's backyard was host to four or five cars in various stages of repair, and a mechanical bull that Dalton's father dragged to the fairs in the summertime. It was fully functional, and had broken the arm of one of the more macho men in the neighborhood before being banned for neighborhood use by the Homeowners' Association.

The first animal that came rushing to meet me was Barney, the goose. Dalton's dad, Pete, had discovered him, a helpless gosling at the edge of the man-made pond in the back of the neighborhood, being taunted by a gang of small boys. Pete scooped him up and he and Dalton had nursed him into the terrifying, sullen creature that now swooped toward me, beak open for the bite. But I had learned how to intimidate the wretched fowl. I stood my ground, got up on tiptoes, raised my hands to the sky, and growled ferociously.

Barney stopped and stared.

"Barney," Dalton's father called, "stand down!"

The goose looked a bit sad not to be able to take a good nip out of me. His beak closed. His wings folded and he let me pass.

Pete was small and rangy, and his hair was longer and greasier looking than his son's. He had a beard long enough to get caught in the machinery of the cars he was working on. One time Dalton had to cut him free.

Now he glanced up at me, but Dalton kept his hands in the engine, working on something I couldn't see.

"Heya," called Pete. "Look who's here, boy."

The two happy stolen poodles ambled up to me in greeting, but Dalton kept working.

"Boy," Pete said, "get some manners. Drag yourself out from under that hood and go see your friend."

Dalton slunk over to me.

I finished petting the dogs and straightened. "It's okay. About the lookout thing."

"I failed you."

"No, Polly's like a panther. Sometimes she makes no sound. It wasn't your fault. And she's made me want to throw up, too."

He still wouldn't meet my eyes. Various pets came up around his legs, barking, pawing, clucking.

"Dalton, I need you for something."

"No!" Now he was looking at me, eyes wide, backing up. "I'm not gonna help you this time. I'm just gonna mind my own business."

"Don't be such a baby. I'm the one in trouble. I need you to show me how to use the Internet, that's all. You know how to use it, right?" I persisted.

"Yeah," he admitted. "I help my dad book appointments for his bull."

Ten minutes later I had cajoled him into his father's office, a cluttered room with bowling trophies crowding the desk and license plates nailed to the wall.

"I don't like this," Dalton said as he fired up the computer.

"Oh, come on. She's not God. She can't float around watching you."

"She scares me."

"Yeah, well, welcome to the club."

I opened my diary to the page with Garland's address on it and crossed my arms, looking out the window at the wild woods of the backyard. Dalton's dad had grown tired of working on the car and was now throwing a stick, trying to make the poodles fetch. They ignored him, rolling in the grass, pink bellies toward the sky.

Dalton's small yip brought me out of my reverie.

"Breezeway is a prison," he announced.

"What?"

"Was a prison." He pointed to the screen. "It closed in 1994."

"My mother was in love with someone in prison?" I marveled. "What's his last name?"

Dalton sighed. "The Internet doesn't tell you everything. It's not a magic wand."

"That number on the envelope—do you think that was his prisoner number?"

He shrugged.

"I have to find him!"

Dalton's hands left the keyboard. "Dead end," he said. He couldn't hide the relief in his voice.

But it wasn't a dead end to me. Only a dead beginning. I couldn't just let Polly be. It was bad enough that I didn't know my father, and barely knew my brother and sister, but I could not forgive that I didn't know her. To be sure, I knew her vagaries and favorite spices and swear words and songs, the way she brushed my bangs affectionately from my eyes before telling me I needed a haircut, her propensity for feuds and her way of moving one hand slowly to the sound of her classical music as she drove around in her old car. But I didn't know the loamy soil of the deep past that lived within her and that grew the varied crops of her life.

I didn't know that part of her and I needed to. If I knew her, then perhaps it would somehow make her eventual death more bearable.

She seemed subdued the rest of that April, tense, hostile at times, tending her garden maniacally against the bugs and varmints that came in to nibble upon and infest her growing crops, the dandelion heads that floated over the fence in a lazy, seed-bearing spray. She'd brought something new to her long-running battle with those squirrels. It looked like a plastic mat but it had wires on it and a little dial.

"It's a squirrel zapper," she said proudly as she wrapped it around her pecan tree. "It gives the bastards the shock of their lives when they try to set one sticky little paw on it." She touched the mat herself. She jerked her hand back and smiled appreciably.

"But Mom, the pecans won't even be ripe 'til next fall."

"Might as well start teaching them early!" she crowed.

"But it's not fair to kill a squirrel just because he's hungry. He doesn't know it's your garden. He thinks it's his garden!"

"Oh, don't be ridiculous. It doesn't kill the damn squirrel. Just teaches him a lesson."

"Just turn it down to two," I begged.

"Two? They won't bat an eye at two."

"Three, then."

"Eight!"

"Five."

And so it went. She turned it up, I sneaked out and turned it down, back and forth, like two roommates fighting over the thermostat.

One morning Polly went out and found yellow stains all over her mustard greens. She bent down, inspecting them. The ribbons from her straw hat twisted in the breeze. She sniffed, considered, sniffed again. "Some varmint has been peeing in my garden," she announced. She looked around and noticed the one-eyed cat sitting on the fence. "I bet that's it. That old cat. I've never known him to venture into my yard before, but maybe he's testing his boundaries."

It happened the next day. And then, four days later. And then, after three days of respite, again.

"I'm going over there," Polly declared. "My garden is not a litter box."

"I'll go with you. You're not very . . . diplomatic."

"What do you mean?" she snapped. "Do you remember me giving the old bastard and his boring wife a whole gallon of black-eyed peas from my garden? Did I ever receive anything in return besides a grudging thanks? Well, did I?"

But she let me tag along.

"Just be nice," I said before she rang their doorbell.

Mrs. Tornello opened the door. "Why, hello," she said. She had watery eyes and a thin, frail voice. "How can I help you?"

"I'll handle this," said a gravelly voice as Mr. Tornello emerged from the gloom of the foyer and stood beside her. "Delores, you go back to your crossword puzzle."

Mrs. Tornello wandered away.

"What now?" he demanded.

"It seems that your cat has been spending some time in my backyard, rummaging around in my garden and relieving himself on my greens."

He snorted. "Marty has been at the vet with an inflamed bile duct for almost a week. And the vet bills are adding up. So don't come here throwing around accusations at my poor sick cat."

"Oh," Polly said. "Couldn't have been him, then."

He shut the door in our faces and we stood there on his porch.

"Hmmmph," Polly grumbled. "Give me a trash can lid and I'd conk that old cat on the head. That would take care of the bile duct and the vet bills."

She went to make herself a margarita. A double. Then she went out to her garden and I saw the spiral of smoke rising over her head, an indication she had turned to her mentor and priest, Virginia Slims, to counsel her on this vexing matter. Eager to get back into her good graces after the Letter Incident, I resolved to stand guard that night over her garden, find the varmint, and somehow make it go away without resorting to violence. That night, I crept over to Polly's doorway, listened to her steady breathing, and then went out on the back porch and sat in her white wicker rocking chair under an extinguished light.

I waited.

The floodlight of the neighbors who lived behind us drifted through the cracks in the back fence, illuminating the garden with an eerie glow. I folded my arms. I was dressed in black pants and a black T-shirt, black socks and black tennis shoes. My brother's old black baseball cap was pulled low over my head. I was a ninja, the color of protection and stealth, as dark as Polly's history. The night air was warm and smelled vaguely of pollen. Summer was coming, meaning an entire three months in the dominion of Polly, and it was in my best interests that she not descend into madness.

I heard something.

A faint giggle.

I listened closely. Another one followed it. The sound came from the Burrell side of the fence. What were they doing up so late at night? I heard our gate open and the twins crept into the yard, giggling and shushing each other as they headed toward the garden. When they reached the mustardgreens, the girl pulled down her pants and the boy unzipped his.

"No," said the girl, watching him. "Pee like me."

"I'm a man!" he protested, "Men don't pee like that."

"Pee like me or I'm going home."

"Okay, okay."

A rage seized me. I could feel a line forming between my eyebrows, a Polly trench that signified a human being not fully in control of her faculties. I darted toward the back door, opened it silently, and ran into my brother's room. I returned outside moments later, armed with Shel's BB gun. I didn't think. Didn't plan.

The twins were crouched in the garden, their bare butts glowing in the light creeping out from the fence. Even from the porch I could hear the strong double stream of urine splashing on the leaves. I raised my brother's BB gun and fired.

"Ahhhhh!" The boy grabbed his butt. "AHHHHHHH! AH-HHH!"

"What the mat-AHHHHH!" said his sister as I shot her, too. They hurried out of the garden, their pants still around their ankles, falling, entangled, shrieking. Bee-stung by some unseen monster, they threw themselves on the back gate and, still chattering in consternation, finally hoisted it open and slammed it shut behind them.

I lowered my weapon, ashamed, jubilant, and turned back to the house.

I froze.

Polly stood in the doorway, her sleeping mask pulled up and sitting on her head like a pair of dark sunglasses. She stared at me as terror filled my body. "Get in the house," she said, her voice flat, the look on her face impenetrable. I followed her into the kitchen, a hard knot forming inside of me. "So let me get this straight," she began. "The Montosaurus twins were the ones peeing in my garden."

I nodded.

"And you took it upon yourself to shoot them."

"But they're okay!" I shrieked. "I don't think it broke the skin! I was all the way on the porch and—"

She held up her hand to silence me. "I have enough trouble with the neighbors without my own daughter becoming a deranged gunman. That is not a toy. Don't you ever shoot a BB gun at a human being again."

"I'm sorry, Mom. I was just trying to protect your garden."

"You leave that to me." She walked over to her purse on the counter, opened it, and withdrew a dollar. She came back over to the table and handed it to me.

"Oh, wait a minute, there were two of them," she reminded herself. And she went back to her purse and got another dollar bill.

Four

The first weeks of summer passed with a certain measure of peace. The twins kept their distance; Marty recovered from his bile duct attack and, after a brief convalescence, summoned the strength to hoist himself back on the fence, good eye glaring balefully at Polly; squash was plentiful, green beans, too; magnolias and hydrangeas bloomed; the garbage man came on time; and mosquitoes hovered but did not land. Mr. Chant cleaned the gutters and beamed with delight when shown his portrait of Polly hanging in the sewing room (which was draped with a tablecloth when he wasn't visiting). Polly and I worked side by side in the garden, weeding and planting and tending and singing. She sang when she was happy, and when she was happy so was I, although the mystery of her still gnawed at me, and sometimes, at night, I took that scrap of letter from its hiding place and read it again and again, trying to discern the story that lingered in the dark margins of those tantalizing words.

We are too
I love you, Pol
Garland.

I had been punished and warned. But I was a mosquito, muting my buzz but waiting for the right opportunity to sink my nozzle into the warm skin of new clues, should they ever present themselves.

Toward the end of June 2004, just after I turned twelve, a great storm came. Polly stood at the window, nursing a margarita, staring out at the pouring rain and wincing at the thunder.

"We had an old uncle used to live with us. Uncle Elmer. Used to pee his pants when it thundered, poor old fellow."

"What happened to him?" I asked as the lightning creased the sky.

"What do you think happened?" she said. "He got younger and got his mind back and won a bingo tournament. He died, you fool."

"My teachers would call that child abuse," I said darkly, "the way you talk to me."

"Well, why don't I send you to the Montosaurus school, where you can swing a puppy around by the tail while everyone claps?"

It was hard to sleep that night, with the thunder bellowing and the lightning flashing. It felt like the whole world was coming undone. The next morning, the backyard was in shambles and tree limbs were down. The bird feeder had been knocked to the ground.

"Damn storm," Polly muttered. "Worse than any varmint."

"I'll help clean up."

"That's sweet of you, baby. But you're gonna clean your room first, like I told you yesterday. I'll worry about the damn yard."

That very same day, Polly's strange behavior began. She kept going back and forth to her bedroom with a furtive look on her face. I narrowed my eyes. What could it be? When I walked into the kitchen that afternoon, I found her hunched over the phone. I hovered near the doorway, listening to her conversation.

"Yes, I have an eyedropper . . . bottle's almost empty. I'll clean it out . . . its eyes are open. Well, how do I know how its gums look? Esbilac powder, what the hell is that?"

I couldn't take it any longer. I didn't care if I was punished again. I ran into Polly's room, searching under the bed and sink, then finally went to the closet, the same one that had contained the secret letters. There I found an open shoe box. I drew closer and peered inside.

Swaddled in soft cloths, sound asleep, was a baby squirrel.

I could barely breathe. I leaned over it, stroking its nearly naked body, just a few tufts of fur, pink skin showing through. Its cheeks puffed and relaxed with tiny soundless breaths.

She was washing out an eyedropper bottle when I entered the kitchen.

"Aha!" I said.

She turned around and looked at me. "Don't you come sidling up here scaring me. Is your room clean?"

"Yes. My room is clean. How about your closet? Or does it have maybe . . . A SQUIRREL IN IT!?"

Her shoulders sagged and her expression darkened. "You are a snoop. You'd think you learned your lesson about rummaging through my closet."

"What are you going to do, set the squirrel on fire, too?"

"I don't need your sass, young lady. That little squirrel must have been blown out of its nest in the storm, and I watched it all morning and the momma's not around. What was I supposed to do, let it die out there?"

"But you hate squirrels! You said they were the devil's way of saying you shouldn't have a garden!"

"Well, I'll tell you what. I'll raise it until it's good and healthy and then I'll wallop it with a brick. Now get out of my way." I followed her into the closet and watched her wake and give the baby squirrel water, putting the eyedropper into its little mouth and cooing encouragement as it drank, its tiny black paws clinging to her index finger. Polly could not disguise the gentleness in her voice. I know being a squirrel hater was part of the face she showed to the world, and she did not like cracks in the armor, but she could not help herself. Her love of babies—baby humans, cats, dogs, deer, even varmints—was the trump card laid on top of the others, and I could not help but imagine her doting over me when I was a baby, everything harsh drained from her like wax running off a candle, leaving only this maternal wick from which a knot of warm flame burned without faltering.

"That's a good boy," she mumbled.

"It's a boy?"

"Yep. I turned him over and he's got the male equipment, 'bout the size of two sweet peas."

"What should we name him?"

"We? It's not *your* pet so don't go getting ideas. But *I'm* going to name him Elmer."

"After your uncle?"

"Yes, because the storm reminded me of him peeing his pants. Names come down out of the blue and there's no rhyme or reason."

Dalton hadn't mustered the courage to visit our house since the snooping/thrown-up Snickers bar incident, but news of Polly's tiny guest compelled him to come over, although he insisted on ringing the doorbell and waiting to be welcomed in. Polly beat me to the door and threw it open.

"Willow, come see!" Polly boomed. "It's the failed lookout!"

I found him shivering in the doorway, wearing his best pants and a white button-down shirt that either he or his father had attempted to iron.

"Hello, Mrs. Havens," he managed. His ears twitched.

Polly put a hand on her hip. "Let me ask you something, boy. Why did you steal a Snickers when a jar of pecan sandies was right there on the counter? You think a store-bought Snickers can beat my secret cookie recipe? Well, do you?"

"No . . . no, ma'am!" Dalton stuttered.

"Well, next time you throw up in this house, it better be something homemade."

He looked frozen to the spot.

She laughed suddenly and patted his head. "I'm joking with you, boy! Come in and see the varmint."

Elmer was a curious baby, and he had the run of the house, sitting on Polly's paper when she was trying to read, darting in and out of bedrooms, climbing up the curtains, and sleeping in the crook of her arm while she was propped in her recliner watching reruns of *Dr. Quinn, Medicine Woman*. At night we'd be awakened by the sound of Elmer creeping across the badly tuned piano.

But Polly never complained about him, even when she was on her hands and knees spraying Windex on his pee, or carefully collecting his pellets with a paper towel.

"I can't believe this," I told her. "It's like you're a different person."

"It's a baby," she said. "Can't help being born a squirrel, any more than you could help being born a brat."

"I think it's sweet," I said, "that you love Elmer."

"I do not love Elmer!" she answered hotly. But the tone in her voice said differently. "That is one smart squirrel," she said admiringly when Elmer figured out how to get into her bag of pecans, as the shotgun sat cold and lonely in the closet.

"Please," I begged in August, when it was hot outside and Elmer was a tween, with all the restlessness and darting madness of his age. "Please let us keep him."

"We can't keep him." She sounded a bit sad. "He belongs with his own kind."

We couldn't release him outside in the backyard, because Polly couldn't bear for Elmer to get shocked by her pecan tree contraption and yet couldn't bring herself to turn it off and let the other squirrels run rampant. And so came the day when we drove him out of the neighborhood, miles away to a well-kept park, where the pine needles were at a minimum and crape myrtle bushes were kept trimmed in tidy spheres.

"It's nice here," Polly said. "Old ladies will come and throw him nuts, and there's a leash law, so the dogs won't get him. There are plenty of other squirrels to make friends with here. He'll be happy."

Elmer was perched on her shoulder. He'd had several pecans earlier that Polly had shelled for him to celebrate his freedom. Polly stood very still as he looked around, evaluating his new home.

"Go on, Elmer," she said gently.

I began to cry. "He should stay with us! He loves us."

"And we love him. That's why we're letting him be a squirrel."

I stopped crying and looked at her in amazement. She said "love." I didn't know her. I didn't know her at all. I thought I did but I apparently only knew the surface of her, and here a scratch had just appeared in it. A scratch in the shape of a squirrel. I felt like an onlooker, perpetually kept in the dark.

"Go, Elmer," she murmured. A full ten minutes passed before he finally crawled down Polly, hesitated at her waistline, then continued down her leg and to the ground. Elmer sat on his haunches, looking up at her, some gaze passing between them that could have been filled with nothing or with something that profoundly and forever breached the varmint/old lady divide.

Elmer darted away and up a tree, past the first few branches, until he found one he liked and sat there, not looking at us anymore.

"Good-bye, Elmer," Polly called up to him.

She looked at me. "Let's go home." Her eyes were bright.

Five

Soon after we set Elmer off to live in the wild, my thoughts returned to Garland. I had a brainstorm. Basic math told me that if Polly had been eighteen at the time of her lover's crime, that crime must have taken place in 1952.

Dalton began shaking his head when I described my idea, but Pete, who was drinking beer nearby, was intrigued.

"Boy, don't be such a wussy. That old lady's not gonna come over here and kick your ass because you looked up something on the Internet."

"You don't know her!" Dalton shrieked.

Eventually it was the father, half drunk, rather than the son, who fired up the computer in his office and began the hunt, taking gulps of Shiner Bock as he surfed. "Okay, well," he told me shortly. "There is one main newspaper in Bethel, the *Bethel Sun*." He fell silent, typed something, and studied the screen. "Trouble is, they're not online, and even if they were, they wouldn't have archives going back to '52. Best bet is probably the Bethel Public Library, if those hillbillies even got one." He typed something, looked at the screen, and wrote down a number on a piece of paper. "Maybe they can help you," he said, handing it to me. "Although they ain't got a lot to go on, either, some fellow named Garland committing a crime sometime that year. Needle in a haystack territory."

I couldn't call long distance from my house, because I knew Polly would get the bill and then life as I knew it would end, so I sneaked into the teachers' lounge at school and called from there.

The woman who answered the phone at Bethel Public Library had a deep southern drawl.

"Hello," I said. "My name is Willow and I'm looking for back issues of the *Bethel Sun.*"

"Well, we got a few on microfiche. I put 'em on there myself. Took me two months."

"Do they go back to 1952?" I asked.

There was a brief silence and then a burst of laughter. "Honey, the whole damn library burned down in '72, and the courthouse, too. What could possibly have happened in '52 that concerns a little girl like you? Now stop bothering me, I'm going to lunch."

"Garland!" I shrieked. "There was a man named Garland in Bethel who committed a crime!"

"Garland?" she said. "I don't know—what, Momma?"

Suddenly a much older, much harsher voice crackled down the line. "You talkin' about Garland Monroe? That son of a bitch better not come around my house, ya hear?"

"What . . . what did he do?" I stammered.

"You related?" her voice had grown even more unfriendly. "Who the hell is this?"

I hung up the phone, my mind reeling. Had my mother once loved a terrible man, and was he still out there somewhere, loving her? Was he out of prison, back in Bethel? Or had he been transferred? Or had he escaped, Alcatraz-style, and was somewhere on the loose? He could be anywhere, imprisoned or free, dead or alive. That night I huddled in my room and, by the glow of my flashlight, I wrote the following letter:

> *Dear Garland,*
>
> *My name is Willow. My mother is Pauline Havens (maiden name Pauline Perkins). I found an old letter from you (which I did not read) and thought I would say hello. I am twelve years old and I live in Texas. I hope you don't mind me writing you but I am interested in my mother's history and know that you played a part.*
>
> *Yours sincerely,*
>
> *Willow Havens*

The next day, I mailed the letter simply to Garland Monroe, Bethel, Louisiana.

And waited.

❧

That fall passed in anticipation, and then growing disenchantment as my first letter, then my second, then my third to Garland went unanswered. I had been so sure that some kind of wonderful serendipity would cause the letters to float into the right mailbox and start a correspondence that would lead to the mystery solving itself at last. But the mailbox contained only the usual bills and notices, and, one day in mid-October, a single dead frog—no doubt a gift from the twins.

That Thanksgiving our house was full. Shel came with Arielle, and Lisa brought her new family. She had met a man, fallen in love, and married him, all since last Easter. Tom was small and thin, had a neatly trimmed goatee, and a head of wavy red hair, cut above his ears. And he had a child. A boy named Otto, who was small and a bit sickly looking, with squinty eyes as though he should have worn glasses, and a constant sniffle. He was about my age, so I knew immediately my job was to entertain him.

"Do you have a cat?" he asked me.

"No. But we used to have a squirrel."

"I'm allergic to cats. They irritate my asthma. And maybe I'm allergic to squirrels, too."

"The squirrel's been gone for months."

"Animals have dander and dander sticks to stuff. So an animal can be gone but still cause allergies. One time at church camp I climbed a tree where some kind of small animal must have been because my eyes got all swelled up and I had to go home."

"Interesting." I was already tired of him.

Lisa and Tom sat at the table holding hands. Lisa's bangs were cut short, and the ends of her hair were curled neatly. I tried to imagine her as the breechclout-wearing, bully-beating wild girl my brother spoke about so fondly, but there was no trace of that girl left on Lisa's face.

"Do you drink?" Polly asked Tom hopefully. "I can make a great margarita."

"Mom," said Lisa patiently, "it's two o'clock."

"I don't mean now," Polly shot back. "I meant in a little while, when the turkey's cooked."

Tom shook his head sweetly. "I don't drink. It's against my religion."

Polly raised an eyebrow. "What religion is that?"

"Christian."

"What? I'm a Christian."

Lisa gave Tom a look and he gulped and smiled. "I'll have a Diet Coke," he said. Polly muttered something and headed toward the laundry room, where she kept the sodas. Lisa and Tom talked about their new house in St. Louis while Otto sipped a 7UP through a straw and gazed off into space.

Shel and his wife showed up an hour later. My brother sauntered in, clean shaven but shirt untucked. He was in a silly, friendly mood. He gave me a bear hug, and I smelled my father's closet. Arielle followed him in, slender and unamused.

He bounded into the kitchen and grabbed his mother, picking her up off the floor.

"Set me down, you fool," Polly said, her legs waving. The look on her face told me she had smelled the closet, too.

"I'm just glad to see you," he said, restoring her feet to the floor and then looking at the blender. "When's margarita time?"

"You don't need a margarita. I need a margarita." She glanced at Tom. "But it's too early."

Shel kissed Lisa all over her face until she gently fended him off. He extended his hand to Tom. "Welcome to the family, you poor bastard."

Tom winced and took Shel's hand.

"Shel," Lisa said, "we don't use such language in our house in front of our child."

He looked around and saw Otto. "Hey, kid." He punched the boy on the shoulder. "Good to have another man around."

"I have asthma," Otto said. "And a squirrel has been in here."

Shel stared at him a moment, then looked over at the blender. "I'm gonna have a margarita now."

"No, you're not going to have a margarita now," Arielle said in a surprisingly strong voice.

"This is a day of celebration," he said. "Celebration because the Pilgrims didn't starve and they would want me to have a margarita."

Polly glanced at me. "Why don't you kids go play outside?"

I sighed. I knew I was going to get stuck with Otto. I decided that some kind of physical activity would keep me from having to talk to him.

"Want to play catch?"

"Sure."

I led him into the garage, where I found some baseball gloves and an old ball. "Let's go out in the front yard. There are too many trees and stuff in the back."

The twins were out on the sidewalk with a sack of walnuts and their trusty hammer. Shells were everywhere. They ignored us.

"This is Otto," I told the twins.

"Hello," Otto said.

The twins stopped arguing and looked at him.

"I don't give a shit," said the boy.

Otto sucked in his breath.

"I'm going to tell your mother," I said.

"Go ahead, tattletale retard asshole," said the girl.

Otto had turned pale.

"They're Montessori kids," I said. "Let's go in the backyard."

Otto was amazed at Polly's landscaping. Pampas grass was in bloom, and pansies of different shades filled the flower garden that ran along the back of the house. "It looks like the Garden of Eden back here."

"Except the Garden of Eden had a snake and Polly would pound a snake with a hoe soon as look at it."

"What's that thing wrapped around the tree trunk?"

"It's a squirrel zapper. I don't approve." I held up the soft-ball. "Want to play now?"

"Sure."

I tossed him the ball. Otto was fairly hopeless, lunging toward my gentle lob and missing it and falling down in the grass. He wiped his nose on his sleeve and struggled to his feet.

"I wasn't ready. Wait until I'm ready."

He caught the ball this time, and was surprisingly good at throwing it back. We had a decent rally going for a few minutes, then Otto flopped down in the grass, huffing and puffing. I sat down beside him, flopping back, too, and we watched the clouds go by together while I waited for him to catch his breath.

He looked over at me.

"Would you ever want a new dad?"

The question took me by surprise.

"A new dad?"

"Yeah, you know. To replace your old one."

I pondered this. "My mom never acts like she's interested in having another husband." I thought of the letters, and almost confided in Otto but stopped myself. A boy that sniffly couldn't be trusted.

"I don't think Polly likes me," he confessed.

The neighborhood was quiet except for the sound of the kids arguing on the driveway. A breeze came in, ruffling our hair and the pansies by the house.

"She likes you fine," I said.

"She sent me a card on my birthday but it just said 'Love, Polly' on it. Not 'Love, Grandma.'"

"Polly's not technically your grandma. She wants her own blood grandchild," I explained. "My sister married your dad and you were already around, so you're not her blood. Nothing against you."

"Well," Otto said after a few moments, "I suppose I can accept that."

The conversation lagged again. After a few moments he asked, "What's it like, having a mother who's so old?"

"She's not so old," I said a bit defensively. "She can still touch her hands flat on the ground without bending her knees, and work in the garden all day and do a cartwheel."

"I didn't mean anything bad about your mom."

"I know."

"I just mean, is it strange to have a mother who's . . . older than other mothers?"

"Yes," I said. He had hit upon my favorite subject, and I found myself grateful to speak about it with someone. "I'm afraid she'll die. I mean, I know everyone dies, but she had me so late in life. One time they were passing around the microphone at church, asking if there was anyone who had a prayer request. When the microphone came my way, I grabbed it and said, 'Pray that Polly is not gonna die.' Well, Polly was so mad at me, because everyone was coming up to her after church and hugging her and asking her what was wrong. She didn't talk to me all the way home, and when we got home she grabbed a shovel from the garage and went out in the backyard and started digging. She didn't even take off her church shoes or her hose. I asked her what she was doing and she said, 'I'm digging my grave.'"

"And I begged her to stop because it was the middle of summer, and it was so hot and the ground was so hard, but she ignored me. Finally when she was about knee deep in her grave, she stopped and said, 'Tell me I'm alive!' And I said, 'You're alive you're alive you're aliiiive!'"

The last word, "alive," hung in the air as I finished the story. The grass was cool under my arms and legs.

"So she stopped digging then?" Otto asked.

"Yeah, but she had hit the sprinkler system pipe and the yard flooded. Of course, that was my fault, too."

We didn't say anything for a few moments. The odor of Thanksgiving floated in the air, broth and potpourri. I was warming to the subject of my obsession with Polly's life span. It felt good having someone to talk to, and Otto seemed like an attentive listener.

"Sometimes I still wake up at night," I continued, "and I think, what if she's passed away? And I try to go back to sleep but the thought keeps bothering me. So I get up and I go into her bedroom and I just stand there in the dark, listening to her breathe."

"I'm sorry," Otto said in a kind voice. "That must be very hard for you."

I felt a rush of good feeling for him. "Yes," I said. "It's been very hard."

"Especially since your mother is going to hell."

A wave of shock flooded through me. I must not have heard right, especially since he said it so calmly and sweetly.

"What did you say?"

He wiped his nose, still staring up at the clouds. "That she's going to hell."

A felt a knot of rage forming inside me. "And who exactly told you that?"

"My dad."

I sat up straight. "How could she go to hell when she's a Christian?" I looked down at him. "She goes to church."

He nodded. "A Methodist church. My dad says she might as well go to a nightclub."

"But she prays!"

"She also smokes and drinks margaritas and she swears and apparently she does very rude things with her toes."

"She doesn't swear! Not really! Just words like *damn* and *hell* and *ass* and *son of a bitch*. Never the 'F' word and she's only used the 'S' word once or twice and that was directed at an animal!"

Otto looked at me with contempt. "The 'D' and 'H' words are even worse than the 'F' and 'S' words. Every Christian knows that."

I could barely breathe. "She has *one* margarita a couple of times a week," I began hotly. Then I cut myself off. I knew I'd get nowhere with this line of argument. Slowly I gathered myself. "Listen," I said softly. "Can I tell you something?"

He was still lying on his back, his hands behind his head.

"Sure."

"And you'll never tell anybody? Never tell a soul?"

He looked intrigued. "I will never tell a soul."

"Polly doesn't just smoke and drink and swear. She does other things. Terrible things."

"Really?" His nose had stopped running. Scandal was an antihistamine.

I leaned down to him very close.

"She goes to church on Sunday mornings. But she goes to another church on Tuesday nights."

"Go on," he breathed.

"The Church of Satan."

His mouth fell open. "No!"

"Shhhh. Yes."

"Oh, my Lord!" He struggled to a sitting position. "I've heard horrible stories of the things people do in that church!"

"You promised you wouldn't tell."

"I won't, I won't!"

"Okay, then. She's not just a member. She is their leader. She's in charge of the rituals and ordering black bibles and everything."

His eyes suddenly went flat. He folded his arms. "I don't believe you," he said. "You're just making stuff up."

I nodded. "I thought you'd say that. But I have proof. The church gave Polly a gift last year for all her work on behalf of the Devil. I'll show you. It's inside. But we must be very quiet."

Shel and his wife were having an intense, whispered conversation, nose to nose, in the den, and didn't even notice us pass by. Shel had a glass in one hand that contained only wet, glistening ice.

I led Otto to the sewing room and closed the door.

"Well," asked Otto, "where's the proof?"

"It's on the wall." I pointed to the painting that Mr. Chant had done of Polly, which was covered in her old tablecloth. "It's a portrait of Polly, presented by the Church of Satan." With a flourish I removed the tablecloth, and there she was in all her blood-curdling splendor, strange hair, terrifying smile, unholy eyebrows, and the foreboding, bright eyes.

Otto's mouth fell open. He began to wheeze.

"I told you." I covered up the painting. "Don't ever tell a soul or she'll turn you into a crow. I think it's time for dinner."

Polly had pulled out all the stops. She had made her oyster dressing and her special green bean casserole, her Jell-O with the fruit floating in it, and her swirly rolls. The turkey itself sat like a glistening masterpiece on the dining-room table.

"Sit wherever you'd like, Otto," I said cheerfully.

His face was very pale. He sank into a chair.

Lisa poured the hot tea into the glasses of ice, making a cracking sound. Polly was still in the kitchen and Shel was doing the honors with the electric knife. He started cutting the turkey and hit bone, but just stood there with the knife making a straining sound before Lisa looked meaningfully at Tom, who took the knife and said, "I got this, buddy."

"That is one bony son of a bitch," my brother said.

Everyone sat down to eat. Otto was very quiet, as was Arielle.

"Who's going to say the blessing?" Lisa asked.

"I'll say it," Polly volunteered. She looked around the table. "I have a lot to be thankful for. All my kids under one roof, and this is my best crop of winter squash so far."

Lisa looked at Tom. I got the feeling she had wanted Tom to lead the prayer, but she said nothing and we all joined hands, except for Otto, who simply sat there, his hands gripped tightly to one another as though in prayer in the freezing cold.

"Otto," said Lisa. "Take my hand."

"NO!" Otto burst out. "Don't let Grandma pray!"

"What do you mean?"

Otto was coming undone. His face was very red. "Because she is in the CHURCH OF SATAN! She is their leader!"

"Otto!" Lisa exclaimed. "What are you talking about?"

"I'd like to know that, too," Polly said.

"Don't lie!" Otto shouted at his sort-of-grandma, a spray of spit coming out and landing close to the Jell-O. "Willow told me you're the head of the Church of Satan and she showed me the picture in the sewing room they gave you as a gift!"

Polly shot me a terrible look. But I was calm inside. I didn't care if I was going to be punished. There lived a streak of defiance in me that came up in unexpected times. There was no bargaining or reasoning with it. Otto had insulted Polly and I wasn't sorry for anything.

"Otto told me you were going to hell for smoking and drinking and swearing, Mom," I said. "So yeah, I told him about your church."

"Willow," Lisa said, and her normally gentle tone had been replaced by a much more severe one. "That is not funny at all."

Shel suddenly began to laugh.

"Shel!" Lisa said, but Shel kept on. He couldn't stop himself. Tears ran down his face.

Arielle gripped Shel's arm. "Stop it!"

He pushed his plate away and continued to laugh, letting his forehead drop to rest against the table, his shoulders shaking. Finally he caught his breath, pulled his head back up, and gazed, wet eyed and red faced, around the silent table.

"You are so badass, Willow, just like Lisa used to be before Jesus took her."

⁓

Thanksgiving was over. Lisa and Tom and Otto had gotten up and left. Shel and Arielle had at least finished their dinner, then

Arielle had taken his keys and herded him out the door. I was alone to face Polly in the empty dining room. The silence so deafening. The turkey a mound of leftovers. The Jell-O untouched. Chairs still sticking out where they had been hastily jerked away.

Polly stood with her arms crossed, studying me as I slouched at the table. My earlier defiance had deserted me.

At last she spoke.

"Who told that boy I was going to hell?"

"Tom did."

"Because?"

"You go to the wrong church and smoke and drink and flip people off with your toes."

"I see. That two-faced jackal sat there getting ready to eat my turkey and my perfect winter squash, all the time so damn sure that I'll be serving it for Satan's birthday after I kick the bucket."

Another long silence. I was afraid to look at her.

"And Lisa?" Polly asked. "Did that weird allergic kid tell you Lisa thinks I'm going to hell?"

"No, he just mentioned his father."

"Ah," she said, her voice softer, "I knew my girl wouldn't think such a thing." But then her tone changed back. "And as for you, Willow Jane Havens. Some people have different opinions about the Bible. And when your mother's particular brand of religion is disrespected, that's when it's time to turn the other cheek, as Jesus did."

I nodded, desperately hoping to be forgiven.

"You don't make a donnybrook out of Thanksgiving, although

your brother gave it a good start." She disappeared into the kitchen. She returned with her purse, rummaging through it.

"That was a very bad thing you did. Do you understand that?"

"Yes," I said.

"Your heart is good, Willow. But your mind is evil."

She handed me a dollar.

❧

I didn't see Shel again until a year and a half later, two months before my fourteenth birthday. Arielle had left him and he'd spent several months working in a bar in Tulum before he showed up tanned and bearded and thin on our doorstep at midnight on a Sunday.

He came back with his pain and his despair and his tantalizing knowledge about the secrets of Polly. He came back to live in his old room. He came back to torment me and to give me joy. He came back to make me feel companionship, and loneliness, and dread. What I did not know was that someone else was soon to arrive. Something else. A creature named the Bear.

Coming to take Polly away from me.

II

Precious Cargo

One

fter my brother's stormy separation, apparent nervous breakdown, and migration to Tulum, we'd get the occasional postcard from him, the terse handwriting on the back in direct opposition to the bright parrots and Caribbean sunsets on the front. He combined strained details of his daily life with sudden boiling rage about the woman he'd loved and lost. He always signed with simply an *X*.

January 10

Bar is called Red Dragon, after the Thomas Harris novel.
The owner's a Rastafarian.
Arielle destroyed my life.
I live above someone's garage.

X

March 8

Group of Germans didn't leave me a dime.
Saw a squirrel today and thought of you, Ma.
Guy that sells weed around the corner is teaching me
Spanish. Mi esposa es una pinche puta.

X

"Hmmm," said Polly, studying the postcard. "I don't know Mexican, but that's probably something bitter."

෨

I awoke one Monday morning in late April without knowing Shel was in the house, but sensing something was different. I dressed quickly and went into the kitchen, where Polly was boiling water for her coffee and checking on the grits. A bowl of newly beaten eggs sat by the skillet. She turned on another burner and a blue flame jumped up. She said casually, "Best to keep quiet this morning. You'll wake up your brother."

"Shel is here?" I asked. I jumped up and down in excitement. "He's back from Tulum? How long is he going to stay?"

"Hush! Your voice carries like two pans clanging together. He was drunk as a skunk when he came dragging in last night. Thank God he took a taxi from the airport. Flapped his lip about Arielle 'til three in the morning. Apparently it's all her fault. I'm sure you'll hear all about it, including talk a thirteen-year-old is not meant to hear."

"I'm almost fourteen!"

She began dicing some black olives.

"I hope he stays forever!" I said enthused.

"Be careful what you wish for." The knife made a steady, efficient rhythm on the cutting board. "A man who comes home to his mama is never a happy man. Happy men visit on Christmas and Thanksgiving and Easter. Any other time, men come home for one reason only. Cause something broke. You ever see Elmer in this yard? Hell, no. That's because Elmer is off somewhere being Elmer. Shel doesn't know how to be Shel anymore."

She poured the beaten eggs into the hot skillet and they made a hissing sound. "That's why he's under this roof, and that's nothing to celebrate."

But I had become a student of Polly's tonal inflections, and as she spoke I heard an undercurrent of satisfaction, even joy, and this tone escalated slightly as she added, "But that's a universal truth, that a boy can always come home to his mama."

~

Shel lay in his old twin bed, fast asleep. Slowly I tiptoed across the room so I could gaze down at my brother. The morning light came in through the wooden slats of the window blind and showed me a bearded, gaunt face, skin scorched red by the tropics, dark circles under the eyes. His hair was long and stringy. He was far from the Shel I'd last seen, who was clean shaven and healthy looking. It was as though he'd left his body and soul in charge of this strange haunted man who slept on the job even in his waking moments.

I sank down onto the bed. He opened his eyes. Blinked slowly. "Willow?" His voice was a faint whisper. "What are you doing in Tulum?"

"You're in Texas, Shel. Back at Polly's."

He exhaled a long, tortured breath and looked around the room. "*Back at Polly's* is a movie written by Stephen King."

"She's happy you're here. And so am I." Just to make sure he knew I meant it, I bent over and kissed the chapped skin of his cheek, which was warm and bristly under my lips. I pulled away and found his eyes dimly lit. He reached up and rested his fingertips against the side of my face. "It's good to see you, my bad-ass little sister. Never stop being a badass, even when this world repeatedly kicks you in the nuts."

He let his hand fall away and onto his chest. "Arielle left me."

I nodded. "I'm sorry," I said, although in truth I wasn't sorry at all. Despite my brother's obvious pain, I wanted to go to LA and hug his willowy estranged wife in mid–yoga pose, as though embracing a toned pretzel, because her actions had led to him coming home. I was that selfish.

He propped up on his elbows and glanced around the room. "Does that woman ever throw anything away?"

"Why did you sign all your postcards with an *X*?" I asked. "Was that a kiss?"

"No, that's my name now. I'm an *X*. A zero. A void." He rubbed his eyes. "I had to get out of Mexico. Tulum in the late spring is no place for a man's testicles. There was no A/C in the shitty attic where I lived and my nuts were sweating all night long."

I couldn't wait for school to be over so I could get home to Shel. I raced home from the bus and pushed open the front door to his screams.

"Goddammit, that hurts!"

"Don't swear at me, boy."

I threw down my books and went into the kitchen, finding Shel shirtless and Polly dabbing at an ugly burn on his chest with a cotton ball. The room reeked of Dr. Tichenor's antiseptic.

Shel gave me a disgusted look. "Our mother's trying to finish me off."

"Look, you're a damn fool to have her name tattooed on your chest and you're a damn fool for trying to burn it off. Now it's infected."

I peered closely at the mess on Shel's chest: scabbed over, ugly sores leaking yellow fluid, from which emerged the letters still left standing . . . *ielle.*

"She left me, Ma, okay? She left me for a guy in her Jazzercise class. Can you believe it?"

"I have no idea what that is," Polly said. "I know about three-legged races. A married woman can get in trouble there, too." She dipped the cotton ball and applied it. My brother's shriek rose and then dovetailed into a snort that could have passed for laughter.

"The Oakwood in Marina del Rey is the traditional place where punted-out husbands go, but I'm back in Texas, with Polly."

"Well, that is the best place for you to be," Polly rejoined.

"Because you're not in your right mind, and your right mind was never gonna win a blue ribbon anyway."

As they bantered back and forth, I detected that peculiar tone I'd noticed between mother and son through the years. Fondness, hostility, nostalgia.

"Do you plan to get a job?" Polly asked.

"What job? My advertising career is over."

"Well, you have to do something," Polly said. "You can't just sit around and feel sorry for yourself. I'm not exactly dining with the Rockefellers with my money from Walgreens."

"I guess I can bartend again," Shel said glumly.

"That's not a good idea. That's like Willow getting a job in a Snickers factory. No, I've been thinking of a good job for you, although it doesn't pay anything. You can fix the Captain's boat. It's been sitting in the backyard for years under a tarp, and if you fix it up we can go fishing." She applied a giant bandage to Shel's chest and stood back to admire her work. "That's the best I can do. Now don't go getting any bright ideas about the rest of those letters."

❧

Late that afternoon we went out into the backyard to see the Captain's old boat. I helped Shel and Polly take the tarp off and we stood looking at it.

Shel ran his hand across the brass rail.

"Still looks in pretty good shape," he remarked.

Polly shook her head. "The inside is shot to hell. Died one

day in the middle of the lake in late summer, when all that was interested were catfish, and they were sucking the bait right off, bastards. We had to get a tow back to the dock, and then your father met his maker, and that was that, and here it sits."

Shel didn't seem to be listening. He was still running his hand over the rail. His eyes watered. "The best years of my life," he murmured, "were working on this boat with Dad."

"I know, son," Polly said in a gentle voice. "Your father loved it, too."

"Okay, then," Shel said at last. "What if we pulled the boat around to the driveway? That way I could work on it under the floodlight of the garage at night."

"That is technically against deed restrictions," Polly answered. "But we'll wait 'til someone complains and then we'll wrap their house with toilet paper."

They began to laugh.

"Remember the Diesingers' house?" he asked.

"Oh, I sure do. You got talked into wrapping it with those hooligans down the block and you were the only one caught. That's because you went back in the morning like a dummy to help the Diesingers clean up!"

"I felt sorry for them. They were old."

"You watch yourself. They were in their fifties."

⌒⌒

"But why," demanded Dalton, "can't I work on the boat with you guys? I'm good with engines. I help my dad all the time."

"Shel and I need to spend time together," I explained. "I grew up without him and I want to get to know him."

"But what about me? I'm your best friend."

"Of course you are. But you'll always be here. Shel's wife might take him back, and then he'll be gone again."

The next day my brother and I began working on the boat. He would start around noon, when I was still in class, and I would rush home every day to help him. Polly worked at Walgreens until three o'clock weekdays. She would sometimes join us, but for the most part she disappeared into her chores or her garden and let us be.

Shel's tools included those that came in a six-pack. At first he drank a few beers in the afternoon, but as time wore on, and the sun lingered later in the sky, summer arriving in a bloom of blue and pink hydrangeas, he returned to the boat after dinner to work on it some more. And then drink a little more, as June bug season broke.

And he talked. Which was fine with me. I wanted to know everything—everything about him, about her, and if I bided my time and listened patiently, some summer day the story of Garland might spill from my brother out of nowhere, subtly, quietly, like the first night of active crickets.

I thought my brother was back to stay. I thought we were going to be a family and I thought all mysteries would be solved.

But the boat was the beginning, and the boat was the end.

Shel bought an old VW from an ad in the local paper with a large piece of his paltry savings.

"Need it to get around," he said.

I wasn't fooled—he needed a car to go to the store and buy beer while Polly was at work. Or gin. He liked gin, too. My father's drink. But I said nothing. I didn't understand liquor, not then. It was simply Shel's fuel for the afternoon and later, for the evening, propelling him toward tales of Arielle's betrayal and expanding his hostile view of both future and past. Liquor was the watery present in which he lived, reinventing himself in it day by day. Shel's old car radio was set to a classic rock station and boomed music at us as he worked on the boat. Foreigner, Led Zeppelin, Boston.

Once I rose above the noise and confusion
Just to get a glimpse beyond this illusion . . .

"You know what sucks, Willow? Knowing someone. Having that knowledge is like having a tattoo you can't burn off. I know which part of my leg she used to rest her hand on when we watched a movie. I know what kind of pillow she liked. I know how she slept, and at what time of night she would kick off her blanket. I know the brand of her nail polish. Where she put her rings at night when she took them off her fingers. She mispronounced 'passenger.' Always added a syllable. And 'caricature.' She didn't know where to put the stress."

So you think you can tell Heaven from Hell
Blue skies from pain . . .

"We lived in Venice, the two of us plus a rescue cat that hid under the bed, so shy we never knew the color of its throat. Arielle and I would go out to the beach in Santa Monica, we'd smoke weed and drink Clase Azul, it's the best, you know. Clean and sharp and mild. We'd lie down on the sand and listen to the voices around us mixed with the sound of the ocean. We'd stay out there until the sand cooled under us and the voices faded away, until there was only the waves . . . and Willow, that is the sound of the people in your life, leaving you one by one."

"I bet he just sits out there and drinks and flaps his lip all afternoon," Polly told me. "That's true, isn't it? That's what he does."

Polly and I were doing dishes. She still had on her Walgreens smock. She'd worked a ten-hour day to cover for another employee and had been too eager to start dinner to take it off.

"Shel says you hate him," I said, "because you're annoyed by men who fall apart. And with him, he says it's even worse, because he's your son, and maybe you think you built him wrong."

She dried her hands on a towel, then yanked the tie on her Walgreens smock and shrugged it off.

"Shel's an idiot. Don't you think I want to make him well? But I can't. When he was a boy, I could fix whatever ailed him. Give him baby aspirin or talk him down from the tree when he thought he could fly. Now he's a grown man and there's nothing I can do or say that makes any difference. How do you think that makes me feel?"

When my brother's music or his vitriol toward his estranged wife was turned up too high, Mr. Tornello would come out into his front yard, cross his arms, and glare at him and then at the small pile of crushed beer cans on the driveway.

"Who's that old bastard?" Shel asked me the first time it happened.

"Mr. Tornello. He's our neighbor. He moved in after you left home. Polly hates him."

"Of course," Shel said, giving Mr. Tornello a little wave that sent him storming back into the house without returning the gesture. "Polly hated her neighbors back in the eighties too. Feuding is in her blood."

Shel put down his beer, picked up a screwdriver, and leaned over the motor. His shirt moved up, exposing the cell phone he kept stuck in the back of his saggy jeans in case someone called about an ad job. When he moved too quickly, the phone would slide down his butt into his pants and he had to fish it out.

Something occurred to me. "Hey, Shel. If he comes over here, don't tell him you're Polly's son."

"Why not?" he asked, still fooling with the engine.

"So we can make something up."

He twisted around to look at me. "You're kind of diabolical, Willow. I like that."

Shel also soon got a glimpse of Mrs. Burrell and the twins, as she herded them into the car one day and pulled away.

"What's her story?" Shel asked.

"Husband's never there. Twins are evil. She and Polly don't get along, either. Her grass bullies Polly's grass."

Shel snickered. "That's a new one. Someday I'm gonna write a coffee-table book called *The Feuds of Polly*, and Bully Grass will be on page one."

My goal was to get Shel to talk about his history, further and further back, way past Los Angeles and Tulum and the woman who'd done him wrong, back into his teen years and his boyhood and eventually to that day in the closet and the letters he found with his then heathen sister. But Shel was stuck on the broken seventies LP that was Arielle and her betrayal, and as the days of summer grew hotter, his hair grew longer and his shirt rode up as he labored on the engine and his back sweated and his cell phone sank so far into his pants only the top of it was visible. "Maybe you should try Internet dating," I told Shel one night at dinner. "A girl from my class has an uncle who got divorced and then met someone that way."

"What's his ad gonna say?" Polly asked. "Drunk, hates women, no job, lives with mother?"

My fourteenth birthday came in mid-June. Shel helped Polly tie some balloons to the boat and squeeze a card table onto the deck, which they festooned with a plastic table cover from Walgreens that had different-colored ducks all over it. They made me sit in the swivel seat of honor and sang "Happy Birthday," Shel trying out his companionable tenor, and my mother going off-key quickly but soldiering on. Polly then handed me a small box. My heart began to sink. I hoped it wasn't another watch. I hated watches. They reminded me of time, which reminded me of death.

Sure enough, it was a Seiko.

"Do you like it?" she asked.

"I love it," I lied, and let her put it on my wrist.

Shel also handed me a small box, so exquisitely wrapped that I was sure Shel could not have done it himself.

"You got me something?" I asked, touched.

"Of course I did. You're my little sister." He was drinking from a glass of plain Coca-Cola. That was already present enough. Slowly I pulled the ribbon and fiddled with the clear tape on the wrapper.

"Daylight's burning," Polly remarked.

"Hold your horses, Ma," Shel said. "She wants to save the paper."

Finally I extracted a small jewelry box. I opened it and gasped. Inside was a gold chain and a circular pendant that had the likeness of Sitting Bull's face engraved on it.

I held it to the light. "Oh, my God, Shel!" I exclaimed. "It's beautiful."

"Ah, yeah, well," Shel said. "I noticed the Indian poster on your wall and thought you'd like it."

"I just can't believe," Polly remarked, "that you stopped talking long enough to learn anything about her."

Shel took a morose sip of his drink. "Thanks, Ma."

Dalton and I had a birthday ritual going as far back as I could remember, so after our broken boat celebration I headed over to his house for my traditional cupcake. Dalton had shot up two inches over the school year. His face had thinned. And he looked strangely well tended for a Saturday. He had on his best chino pants and a clean T-shirt. His hair was cut and freshly washed. Also—shoes.

"Going somewhere?" I asked him when he answered the door.

"Nah," he said, looking embarrassed.

"Look what I got!" I said. "This stupid watch, and this really cool Sitting Bull necklace."

"Nice. Come out to the back."

"Where is everyone?" I asked as we walked through the empty house.

"Dad and his girlfriend are at the movies."

The goose came running toward me as soon as we hit the backyard.

"It's her birthday!" Dalton snapped, waving his arms, and the goose retreated.

A small table with two chairs was set up in the middle of his yard among the milling pets. A cupcake sat on top with a candle sticking out of it.

"You remembered!" I said.

"Of course I—STOP IT!"

It was too late. One of the poodles had risen up on his hind legs and knocked the cupcake down, and now every animal, goose and dog and chicken, was swooping in to take their share. A great pecking and snarling and squabbling commenced as we stood watching.

"I'm sorry," Dalton said.

"That's okay. I think they left me some icing."

He handed me a little box.

I looked at it. "What is this?"

"Nothing."

I opened the box. Inside was a little charm bracelet. Purple glass beads and a silver heart.

"Dalton," I said, "you didn't have to give me anything."

His ears moved. "It's nothing compared to the other stuff you got."

"No," I insisted. "I love it." I put it on my other wrist and fastened the clasp. "I like it so much more than a stupid watch, I promise."

He put his hands in his pockets and kicked at a weed. "So guess what?" he said. "I'm leaving for the whole summer."

"What?" I blinked. "Why?"

"My dad got a job in Jackson, Mississippi, running the bull at a nightclub. Says the money's really good."

"Oh." My heart sank a little. I had been neglecting him since Shel had returned, and now he was leaving. The thought of summer without Dalton seemed much worse than the ruined cupcake. "What are you going to do with the animals?"

"Take 'em all with us, like Noah's ark."

"You're coming back though, right?"

"Yes, of course I'm coming back. You know, Willow . . . I'm fourteen, too. We're both fourteen now."

He said it in a meaningful way, like *fourteen* was a code for something profound and mysterious. He held out his hand and I thought we were going to shake on this being fourteen business, but then his hand closed around mine and he held it. He leaned toward me slowly. Time froze in the confusion of the moment. Just before our lips touched I pulled away.

"Willow," he said, but it was too late. I was running for the back gate. I threw it open and ran all the way home. I did not understand this new Dalton, and if fourteen was all about moments like this, then fourteen was going to be quite a year. It made no sense to me. Dalton was my friend. How could he be something else? I didn't want him to be something else. It was too sudden a change, like going to the garden and finding orange pumpkins, when they weren't due until fall.

And yet I kept replaying the moment his lips had moved so close to mine. What if they had connected? What would have changed? Or would nothing really have changed?

By the time I went back to his house two days later to try and make sense of it all, I found the place locked and dark. The backyard still full of cars but empty of wildlife. Everyone was gone.

Two

The end of June approached. Too early for sunflowers. Too late for hydrangeas. Bountiful crops of okra, eggplant, cucumbers, and summer squash. Twins and aphids lying low. And a hard rain, and a bank of clouds that came in and lingered and spoke of fishing possibilities.

Polly was getting restless.

"Why isn't the boat ready yet?" she demanded.

"Motors are tricky. You try fixing a motor," Shel replied.

And yet, one day soon after, the boat was fixed. Shel had been working all afternoon, in rare concentration. I sat cross-legged on the driveway, reading a book about Secretariat, the horse with the incredible stride that never gave up. Suddenly I heard the motor roaring. I dropped the book and leaped to my feet.

"You did it!" I shouted.

Shel looked quite pleased with himself. He waved his wrench in the air like a trophy. "What do you think of your brother now?" he crowed.

Of course, he made me fetch Polly out of the house, where she'd been cooking her okra and tomato dish.

"Well, I'll be," she marveled, listening to the motor hum. "Never thought I'd hear that sound again. Time to go fishing! And tomorrow happens to be my day off. Good job, boy. Let's eat. Rice is getting sticky."

She went back in the house. Shel looked after her. He dropped his wrench in the grass.

"Well, that's that, I guess," he said.

Polly wiped her brow. She wore an eggshell blue hat with an enormous brim and the ribbons of the hat dangled untied, moving in a wind from the south. We had caught nothing for hours, and Shel had spent his time maneuvering the boat in response to Polly's barked instructions on where she wanted to cast.

It was still hot but, according to the position of the sun, well after six. Shel hadn't brought any beer and was clearly bored and done with this day. He looked over at Polly, whose line was bent double and whose expression remained neutral, meaning she had hung up her line.

"Cut yourself loose and let's go home," Shel said.

It had been a lovely afternoon, lounging there in my shorts and T-shirt, Shel bare-chested, in cutoffs. I didn't care that we hadn't caught anything. But clearly Polly was feeling defeated.

Shel twisted the key in the ignition. Nothing happened. He tried again. The engine whined.

"What's wrong?" Polly asked.

"Sounds like the carburetor flooded."

"I thought you fixed the boat!"

"Yes, Mom," he said evenly, "I did fix the boat, but obviously it broke again. I'm sorry I couldn't fix it forever."

"Well, could you fix it 'til we're back on the dock?"

Shel sighed. "You're welcome. You're welcome for me spending half the summer on our driveway trying to get this boat ready for you. But nothing is good enough for you, is it?"

"No," she said. "I have these crazy dreams of a boat that runs when you turn the damn key."

"Fine. I'll call the marina and get a tow."

"Sure, save us all."

The sun sank low on the horizon, leaving a streak of yellow over the flat, gray water of the lake.

Polly went to work securing her poles, smoothing out the lines and then keeping them in place with her bread-bag ties, as Shel held the phone to his ear.

"It's just ringing and ringing," he announced.

"They closed at six," I mentioned.

Shel stuffed his phone into his pocket. "Let me try to get the boat going again."

He set to work, the engine wheezing, and Shel swearing as Polly rolled her eyes. Finally she stood up and took off her sandals and hat.

Shel glanced at her. "Where do you think you're going?"

"I'm tired of waiting while you monkey around. I'm gonna swim for it."

"No, Mom, you are not going to swim for it. The dock is half a mile away and you are seventy-two years old."

"And a seventy-two-year-old woman couldn't possibly swim or do anything of any use to anyone, is that what you're saying?"

Shel sighed. "Not now, Ma, just be quiet for five seconds so I can fix this—"

Splash.

"Goddamn it." Shel tossed his phone on the deck, kicked off his flip-flops, and went in after her.

I dove in, too, hitting the water that was the perfect temperature as it closed over my head and I heard the underwater sound of space and the brief panic of my body before I bobbed to the surface. Like my brother and mother, I was a good swimmer, and I took off after them as we all raced each other. Shel and I drew close to Polly and her determined stroke, half freestyle, half dog paddle, and then we slowed down, instinctively letting her lead, letting her win, and the sun went down and we swam in darkness, stars overhead. Polly and Shel would lift their heads to snipe back and forth at one another, and I wished that dock was a million miles away and we could keep swimming together in the lake of recalcitrant fish and warm water, on and on and on.

Shel had been hoping for a reconciliation with Arielle but it wasn't meant to be. Lawyers were involved now—at least, she had a lawyer.

"How am I supposed to afford a lawyer?" he asked. "Those LA assholes, fleecing you for whatever they can get. Making a profit off broken love. A profit, Willow."

It was a surprise to us when Shel came back from the hardware store one day in a jovial mood.

"You'll never guess who I ran into," Shel said.

"Who?" Polly asked.

"Phoenix Calhoun."

"That weird kid who lived on our block?"

"He wasn't weird. He was different. And he's not a kid anymore. He's a grown man."

"You're still boys, far as I'm concerned. He was nutty as a pinecone. Remember when he adopted that bear from the woods?"

"Ma, that was from a movie."

"Oh, okay." She nodded. "But he ate rocks. I remember that clearly."

"He swallowed one small pebble, Ma. On a dare. He just moved back from Michigan. He's divorced, too. Works as a programmer."

"A programmer?" Polly asked. "Is that computer stuff?"

"Yes. Computer stuff."

"Ah," she said. "Perfect for a weirdo like him."

But Polly confided to me later as we stood side by side at the sink, rinsing and stacking, that she was glad to hear Phoenix was back in town. "He was a dear boy. Struggled in school and his parents weren't worth a hoot, his shoes weren't fit to wear to a dogfight, and the only decent haircuts he ever got were ones that I gave him, 'cept for that time he jerked and he got a real short one. But he might be good for Shel. Calm him down a little."

I shook the water off a trio of spoons and put them in the dishwasher. "But what if they just get together and talk about how much they hate their ex-wives?"

Polly considered this briefly and then shook her head. "That Calhoun boy couldn't hate a soul on this earth. Besides, do you think he'd get in a word edgewise with your brother?"

Phoenix made his first appearance that Saturday. He and Shel had decided to make a day trip to the beach in Galveston, and I had begged both Shel and Polly for permission to go with them. Shel caved fairly soon but Polly was harder to convince.

"Please, Mom," I begged. "Please let me go!"

"Who's driving?" Polly demanded.

"Phoenix," Shel answered. "And he doesn't drink. He's never had a drink in his life."

"I can't believe that, him being a friend of yours," she said severely.

"Well, it's true."

Polly sighed. "I suppose you can go," she told me. She pointed at Shel. "But remember, no shenanigans."

Phoenix showed up midmorning as instructed. Mr. Chant had come over with a box of strawberries for Polly and was bending her ear about his new sprinkler system when I heard the rattle of a car and threw open the front door to find Phoenix rising up out of an old brass-colored Chevrolet. He was a looming figure at well over six feet, square shouldered and bald as a cantaloupe.

The twins were playing on their driveway.

"Hello, kids!" Phoenix called.

The girl looked up at him. "You're a big ugly dumbass."

"Yeah," said the boy. "Fuck you."

"You are so cute!" Phoenix picked up the boy and held him up in the air. "I once had a little brother just like you but he grew up a long time ago."

"PUT ME DOWN, ASSHOLE!" the boy screamed.

"PUT HIM FUCKING DOWN!" his sister screamed.

Phoenix set the boy down. "Sure, little guy!"

"I'm going to tell my mommy, you dick!" the boy screamed, and ran into the house.

I studied Phoenix as he walked toward me. A little dog jumped out of the car and tried to follow him, yapping at him. He scooped up the dog and carried him, flailing, back to the car, where he rolled up the window on the passenger door and put him inside.

"I'll just be gone for a minute, Gravity!" he assured him.

Gravity's muffled howls came floating over the lawn as the little dog threw himself against the windows with frantic thumps. Phoenix strolled up to me.

"Hi, you must be Willow!" he said. "Shel told me about you." He held out his big hand shyly and I took it. His eyes were very kind and his bald head perfectly shaped. He wore an old pair of jeans, a faded Hawaiian shirt, and Nikes.

"You look like your beautiful mother!" he exclaimed. "It's such a miracle one of her old eggs and the Captain's old sperm made you! It's from God. Do you believe in God?"

I stared at him. He stared back at me in amazement. "You know what's funny?" he asked. "Your mother always hated squirrels, and you kind of look like a squirrel! Like, the same eyes and mouth! Can I call you Little Squirrel?"

I thought about this. Polly would absolutely despise that nickname. "Sure," I said.

Gravity's yelps drifted from the crack in the window, high and desperate.

"It's okay, Gravity!" Phoenix called back. He turned to me. "Gravity is an amazing sniffer dog. He once lived in a nursing home but he could sniff cancer on the old folks and it started making them nervous, so they dumped him in a shelter and that's where I got him. He's got the nose of a bloodhound, that's for sure. You got cancer, boom, he knows it." He looked at me with sudden concern. "You don't have cancer, Little Squirrel."

"That's good," I managed. "Come in." He followed me into the foyer.

"I'm in your old house!" he announced. "I haven't been here since I was seventeen!" He looked into the pier glass mirror in the foyer, studying his face. "Hello, seventeen-year-old Phoenix," he murmured. "Here we are again."

I didn't want to disturb him, so I waited patiently until he and his younger self finished their reunion. Mr. Chant's voice drifted out of the kitchen. ". . . So the idiot I got to help me screwed up the watering zones, Miss Polly, and that explains the depressing condition of my crape myrtle. . . ."

When we finally entered the kitchen, Polly was staring at Mr.

Chant with her arms crossed and a bored expression on her face. Shel looked tortured.

"Miss Polly!" cried Phoenix fervently, rushing up to take both her hands in his. "It has been so many, many years."

"Well, hello, Phoenix," Polly said, somewhat stiffly; she put her arms around him. Her head came up as far as his sternum. He hugged her fervently as Mr. Chant watched them, the look on his face suggesting that, in his mind, he was inserting a crowbar between them and wrenching them apart.

"Don't break my ribs," Polly warned Phoenix. "I'm an old lady."

"You are still so beautiful," he murmured as she broke free. "I can tell you now that you were my first love at the age of twelve, Miss Polly. You were my ideal, and I told my wife that if she only lived halfway up to your standards, she'd make me a happy man. She divorced me last year."

Polly lifted her chin to study him. "You haven't changed a bit, Phoenix Calhoun, 'cept your hair has skedaddled. You're still just as goofy as hell."

Phoenix smiled and blushed. "Yes, I am totally bald now. Did you get my Christmas cards? I sent you a handmade card every year."

"Yes, I did."

"You never wrote back."

"No, I didn't. I meant to, but you know I'd start thinking about it again in the spring, when it was too late, then I'd think well, damn it, next Christmas for sure."

"No worries," he assured her. "That's perfectly perfect. One

Christmas Eve, years ago, when my folks were still alive and I was home visiting, I cleaned your rain gutters and strung up Christmas lights."

"Where was I?"

"Church."

Polly looked bemused. "That was you?"

"Yes. I figured you might want your house to look festive, because I got word your husband had croaked."

"I'm Bob Chant," Mr. Chant suddenly interjected. The little man thrust a hairless arm out to shake Phoenix's hand, pumping it hard.

"Nice to meet you," Phoenix said, and turned back to my mother. "I still remember your amazing pecan pies, Miss Polly. Do you still make them?"

"Hell, no," she said with a sniff. "Damn squirrels stripped my pecan tree because my tree-hugging daughter keeps turning off the squirrel zapper."

"I will murder every squirrel in the world for you," Phoenix vowed. "I will go jihad on their ass."

Mr. Chant wasted no time throwing his hat in the ring. "I would NEVER harm one of God's creatures," he said sternly. "But I would trap them all and release them at the edge of town. Every last one!"

Polly seemed unmoved by the efforts of her admirers. "More varmints will just come and take their places."

Shel stood up and stretched. "You ready, Phoenix?"

"Absolutely!" Phoenix declared.

Polly fixed Phoenix with a steely glare. "I understand you are driving?"

"Yes, ma'am, I'm driving. Yes, all the way."

"And you will stay sober?"

"Oh, yes, ma'am, I have never had a drink in my life and never will. I've been through a very sad divorce and never took a sip of alcohol, although I did a lot of running in the woods."

Polly knitted her eyebrows while she considered the statement.

"And you will not be discussing things that a fourteen-year-old girl should not hear?"

"Oh, no. We would never."

Polly waved a hand at me. "Because my daughter is precious cargo, do you understand?"

"Yes, yes!" Phoenix echoed. "Little Squirrel is precious cargo!"

Shel rolled his eyes. "Jesus, let's go."

◌◌

We tore down I-45 as my brother sat shotgun and I held Gravity on my lap. He had eaten the seats of Phoenix's car, and white towels now covered the places where the leather was gone. I could feel the metal parts of the car underneath my haunches. I tried to put on the seat belt, but it had been nearly bitten in half.

Shel wasn't talking. He was busy drinking one Corona after another (we'd stopped by the 7-Eleven, of course) as though catching up with some internal beer clock. When he finally paused for breath, Shel and Phoenix started reminiscing. Phoenix alternately laughed at Shel's stories with his boyish giggle and tried unsuccessfully to shush his swear words.

"Ah, don't you worry 'bout old Willow," Shel said, drinking from his bottle. "She's heard everything by now."

"I'm precious cargo," I told my brother.

"Ha!" he said, and took another swig.

Phoenix glanced at me in the rearview mirror. "Your mom was like a second mother to me," he said. "She helped me with my homework and cut my hair. And she'd always give me good advice, things my mother wouldn't say, like 'Phoenix, don't go barefoot in winter. And stop sleeping on the roof.' And she made the crows leave me alone."

"The crows?" I asked.

"There were two of 'em. I think they were mates. They used to attack me on the way to the bus stop. One day your mother ran out and started swishing at them with her broom. They never bothered me after that. Your mother is a hero."

"You've always put that old lady on a pedestal," Shel said dismissively. "Try living with her."

"Oh, that would be wonderful!"

Houston passed us on either side of the freeway. Buildings crowded each other, skyscrapers against tire stores, the freeway cool and clean, summer traffic, white smoke trailing out of tall towers and billboards advertising DUI attorneys.

Phoenix and Shel had moved on to the high school section of memory lane and were trading stories back and forth. The fabric on the ceiling of Phoenix's car had somehow come loose, and draped his bald head as he drove. When Gravity wasn't sleeping on my lap he sat, wide awake, staring adoringly at his master, his whole body quivering as though the back of Phoenix's neck was a solid lamb treat. Occasionally he would let fly a long, slow whine and Phoenix would call cheerfully, "Good boy!"

For a good hour, Gravity's pining need for his master in every tendon was the only wistfulness in the car. Arielle was gone, vanished, back in California doing some yoga pose with her new lover, chased away from Texas like a flea by a dog's scraping paw. I had my brother again—albeit a brother who was drinking beer so fast we had to stop twice for a pee break before we'd even reached the 610 South Loop. I sat back, the A/C faulty but the conversation new and electric, Phoenix to Shel and Shel to Phoenix, luxuriating in the space and time of the eighties, back when they were teenaged boys doing boy stuff, ogling girls, flexing their muscles, and riding skateboards in empty pools. This was the brother I had been denied and who was now back with me, elbow resting on the open window, hair blowing back.

Phoenix kept trying to include me in the conversation but I was content to listen.

"Remember when your guinea pig died?" Shel asked Phoenix. "And Lisa tried to raise it from the dead?"

"Oh, yes!" Phoenix cried. "Just croaked all of a sudden. Lisa made me pray over it and I was afraid of your sister so I did. Every day for a month."

"Wait," I said from the back seat, "every day for a month?"

"Yeah," said Phoenix. "I kept Lionel in an empty Popsicle

box in the freezer so he would be all fresh and ready to go once he came back to life. Lionel was still in there when I went away to college. And I'll never forget your mother's words of wisdom. . . ." His voice dropped, turned reverent: "'All that praying wasted on a dead varmint that couldn't even shake hands or fetch or do Jack crap.'"

We had hit the southern part of Houston, the part that fades into long stretches of pastureland on the way to Galveston, when Arielle came back. I'm not sure exactly what evoked her. But Shel turned to Phoenix and said, "How was your divorce?"

"Good!" Phoenix answered. "Surprisingly friendly."

Shel snorted. "Wish I could say the same for mine."

And so it began. I slumped in the back seat, sorry I had come. I saw Phoenix's eyes shift in the mirror toward me, confused and helpless. His childhood with his friend had been banished to the trunk and now he was being treated to Shel's series of discontinuous snapshots of his betrayal and ruin. Phoenix and I were trapped and we remained that way as we rocketed down the freeway and hit the scattered palms and the beaches of Galveston.

Shel did not buy more beer at our final 7-Eleven pit stop and this briefly cheered me before I realized he had a bottle of Old Tom in his backpack, which he pulled out when we had set up our chairs on the beach. It was a quiet day so far, a few families scattered around and two young guys wearing lifeguard shirts played Hacky Sack next to their wooden stand. Shel began to drink, a baseball cap pulled down over his eyes, his shoes kicked off, bare feet in the sand. He had turned our beach day moody and dark, but Phoenix regained his look of boyish enthusiasm when he took down his bodyboard from the roof of his car. "Ever ride one of these?" he asked.

"No," I said.

"Want me to show you? Shel, can I show her?"

Shel held out his hands in a gesture of weary indifference and stared out at the waves. Phoenix kept his shirt and jeans on as I headed into the water in my new blue swimsuit.

"Where's your suit?" I asked him.

"Ah," he said. "Jeans are fine for everything."

"But won't you get waterlogged and drown?"

"Irrelevant."

We got chest deep, Gravity barking from the shore, and Phoenix showed me how to catch the small waves that came at leisurely intervals, and for an hour I forgot about Shel and just followed Phoenix's patient voice as he taught me how to balance my body. "Excellent, excellent," he kept saying. As we slogged out of the water, dripping, he said, "I was lying, back at your house."

"Lying?" I asked.

"About murdering the squirrels. I was just trying to please your mother. They are cute little critters." As we made our way toward the ecstatic dancing of a hysterically relieved Gravity, I had a question for Phoenix, one that had been on my mind ever since Shel had first mentioned him.

"Phoenix," I said, "you work with computers?"

"Oh, yes," he said. Gravity leaped into his arms, licking the water drops that ran off his bald head. "That's how I make my living. I design and code Web sites."

"Do you know how to find things on the Internet?" I asked.

"Things?"

"Like people?"

"Sure. I can find anything if you give me enough time."

"I need to find a man named Garland Monroe. All I know is he committed a crime in 1952 in Bethel, Louisiana, and he went to Breezeway Prison for it in 1953."

We reached our chairs and got our towels. My brother barely glanced at us. He was drinking, his lids half closed.

Phoenix set Gravity down and tapped the side of his head. "Garland Monroe. 1952, Bethel, Louisiana. Breezeway Prison, 1953. I will hunt him down for you, Little Squirrel. Everyone is on the Internet, even if they don't know it."

Despite my brother's drunken stupor, Phoenix's confidence about finding Garland had brightened my mood. "That would be so great," I said. "It's very important to me."

"If it's important to you, it's important to me." Phoenix looked down the beach. "I'm gonna do some sprints. I'm training for the Houston Marathon."

"Sure," said Shel, waving a sleepy hand at him, and Phoenix took off running with Gravity in hot pursuit. I put on some suntan lotion and sank down in the chair next to Shel.

A wiry, unkempt guy ambled up to us. He wore a bandanna and board shorts and a long T-shirt that said SURFTOWN on it.

"Hey, I'm Denny. Got a light?" he asked.

"Nah, man," Shel said. "Don't smoke."

"That's okay. Mind if I sit down?"

The guy looked creepy to me, but Shel said, "Sure. This is Willow."

"Hey," I said, looking away and crossing my arms.

Shel handed him his bottle and Denny took a quick drink.

"How's the water?" Denny asked me.

"Fine," I said flatly.

My brother and his new friend hit it off right away. Denny, apparently, had a wife who had treated him terribly, too. "I came home one day," he told Shel, "and the bitch had taken everything. I mean, everything. All the way down to a *Men's Health* fitness calendar I'd thumbtacked on the wall. She took the thumbtack, too. She wanted me to suffer, man."

My good mood faded quickly as they went on about their rival Queens of All Bitches, tormentors of their souls, passing the bottle back and forth, each trying to outdo the other's stories, neither one listening. The day didn't matter, the sun didn't matter, the view didn't matter. All that mattered was they had been wronged.

I sat very still, arms still crossed, as I heard both the ugly tone and the slur deepen in my brother's voice. I felt something on my bare leg and looked down. It was Denny's hand. Just flung there casually, his fingers curled a bit, resting halfway between my knee and my thigh.

I looked at Shel, but Shel, drunk and sloppy now, wasn't paying any attention to me. I jumped up, grabbed the board, and headed out to the waves, looking for Phoenix and finding him far down the beach, a furry dot of loyalty chasing his big frame.

I waded out alone with the board into the sea, my only sanctuary from the ruins of this day. The waves were quiet now, just little bumps. I put the board down and lay on top of it, my hands hanging into the water, my body bobbing, the sun cooler, behind a cloud. I was alone. Maybe it was best to expect that I would remain that way, alone, despite all my struggles and endeavors to be part of something bigger. Part of Polly, part of the Captain, part of Lisa, part of Shel, part of the blue, stringy, threaded sphere that held them all to one another. The sun came out and hid again, came out and hid again, and by that rhythm I was just about to doze off when suddenly there was a voice in my ear.

"Hey, kid."

My eyes flew open and there was Denny, waist deep in the calm water, holding on to my board.

"Hey, better watch yourself," he said in my face, smiling. "You're drifting out to sea. Don't want to float away, do you?"

He placed his hand on my back. "Just gonna guide you to shore now," he said. "Just gonna keep you safe."

I was frozen. Literally unable to move or speak. The hairs on my neck were stiff with prescience and my brain was trying to turn its engines on so it could think and react. My heart pounded. Breath lost somewhere. He had stopped tugging on my board and now stood still, bracing his body, one hand holding the board, the other beginning its slide down my back as a scream rose in me and went no further, his hand continuing smoothly under the elastic band of my bikini bottom . . . the word NO trying so hard to escape me. . . .

A sudden rush of water rolled me off the board and I fell away, dropped down into the boil of cold water, the undersea world taking me, flooding my senses, everything dark until I came alive, kicking my feet, moving my arms, finding the sun flat on the water and moving for it, surfacing to find the board floating away and Phoenix standing in the water still as a statue, holding Denny's legs as Denny's submerged head and upper body fought and thrashed under the water.

The look on Phoenix's face was neutral. Gravity yapped hysterically from shore. The lifeguards ran down the beach toward us.

"Phoenix," I said, "let's go, let's go," but Phoenix was in another world, some state of deep relaxation or simply the absence of any urge to stop drowning this man.

The lifeguards reached him, tackled him, grabbed his arms, and tried to pry Denny away, but Phoenix held firm, his muscles hard and angled in the sunlight. Finally they managed to drag Phoenix's limp doll away from him. Denny coughed and sputtered as one of the lifeguards pounded him on the back.

"Let's go, Phoenix!" I urged him.

I grabbed hold of his shoulders and rode piggyback as he floundered back to shore, abandoning our board. We ran for our chairs, where Shel was passed out, his chin on his chest. Phoenix grabbed my brother, I grabbed the chairs, and we ran to the car and stuffed ourselves inside. Gravity jumped in the back seat with me, and Phoenix floored it out of the parking lot. No one said a word. Phoenix had a sunburn on the back of his neck. Gravity's hysteria had worn the little dog out. Shel's head rested against the window.

Shel mumbled, "I used to be a fun drunk, but I graduated."

∾

I tried not to break into tears as we left the palm trees and oil refineries of Galveston and headed home, Phoenix ashen-faced in the rearview mirror as we hit I-45 and headed north. Shel was passed out, his head against the window.

"I'm sorry, Little Squirrel," Phoenix kept saying. "I have failed your mother. You are precious cargo."

"I'm okay," I kept assuring him. But I was not.

Shel had woken up by the time we reached our house, slightly more sober, but Phoenix still had to help him out of the car, and in the process, Gravity got loose and ran toward Polly, who stood with her arms folded, glaring at Shel.

"Grab him!" Phoenix pleaded, and I darted forward and managed to corral the tiny, writhing, yipping creature, lifting him up and putting him back in the car.

"Got a little burned out there," Shel said.

"I'm terribly sorry," Phoenix told my mother, his face a deep red, his posture full of shame. "I'm so embarrassed. I should have kept a closer eye on him."

"Willow," Polly snapped. "Are you all right?"

"Yes," I managed, fresh tears falling.

"Then why are you crying?"

I wouldn't answer her. My brother had failed me utterly, but I was no snitch.

Phoenix was trying to help Shel walk, but he broke free and staggered a few steps on his own.

"I'm fine!" he slurred.

Polly glared at him with utter disgust, then looked at Phoenix. "What happened?"

"A guy on the beach came after your daughter, so I drowned him a little," Phoenix said.

"A guy? What guy?"

"Nothing happened, Mom," I said miserably. "Phoenix protected me."

Shel looked confused. "What guy?"

"Get in the house," Polly told him, her voice cold.

"Nothing happened," I said. "Let's not talk about it."

"This is my fault, Miss Polly," Phoenix said. "I will never forgive myself." He turned around and went back to his car, head bowed, as we herded Shel through the front door.

"Phoenix," I called, but he didn't look up.

"Let him go," Polly said grimly. "We've got other business."

Once we were inside, Shel briefly nudged a wall with his shoulder and then headed for his room.

"No," Polly said. "Both of you go in the den."

This we did, although navigating the pivot seemed to give Shel some trouble. We sat there in silence, Shel at one end of the couch, myself at the other, my eyes straight ahead, arms crossed. Polly rustled around in the kitchen. Shel closed his eyes. I thought he was asleep until he said, "When I do math problems in my head, the room stops spinning."

Finally Polly entered the room, carrying a mug of coffee and a Snickers bar. She handed me the Snickers bar. "Here it is, nice and cold. It won't make up for having Shelton for a brother, but it's a start."

She handed the coffee mug to Shel. "Drink this. You'll need it."

Something was strange about Polly. Something about her voice and her stance now, back straight, shoulders squared, facing us, the look in her eyes that went beyond rage and disappointment.

"Ma," Shel whined. "It's so late."

"Shut up," I said. "Mom, what's the matter?"

She seemed a bit nervous, uncertain, and this terrified me. "Mom!" I insisted.

She heaved a deep sigh and crossed her arms. "I was going to wait until tomorrow to tell you both this. But now seems like as good a time as any, now that your brother has turned a simple trip to the beach into a God only knows."

"Tell us what?" I demanded. "Tell us what? Mom!"

"They need to run more tests," she answered at last. "But the doctors found something."

Shel's eyes were lidded. The significance of the remark seemed to pass him over, but the shock of those terrible words hit me full force. I jumped to my feet.

"What do you mean?"

"Now calm down," she said. But I was an expert on reading my mother's body language and intonations and I couldn't help hearing the slight waver in her voice. She pulled one hand off its death grip on her elbow to reach out and stroke my hair. "It's okay, baby. Nothing's for certain yet."

"Don't say any more." Tears were falling, horror washing over me. "Don't say it, don't say it."

"Listen, listen, stop . . ." Her voice was so gentle and kind that it terrified me. "We don't know anything for sure. I went to the regular doctor and he sent me to some fancy doctor, some know-it-all; they put me through the X-ray machine and something's in me so here we are."

"The Bear." I said the words and they hurt me and I held my stomach as though something clawed me there.

"No, not necessarily, honey."

I looked back at Shel and his eyes were no longer lidded. He sat up straight and stared at Polly. "Mom," he whispered.

"So they're gonna do what they call a biopsy and that will tell us everything," Polly continued calmly.

"No, Mom," I said. "No, no, no, no."

"It's *all right*, Willow."

"Then stop talking so nice!"

Shel rose unsteadily to his feet and reached for his mother.

She backed away from him and held up a hand.

"Shelton." Her voice was cold. "You never take another drink under this roof, or you pack your bags. I won't have two Bears in this house."

Three

Polly let me sleep in her bed that night, a king-size four-poster she and the Captain used to share. But I couldn't sleep. I stared at the ceiling, devastated. In my mind the worst-case scenario loped along like a runaway spaniel, leash trailing, enjoying its freedom and eluding all pursuers. I had already seen her on her deathbed, attended her funeral, grown up without her, desolate, alone.

"Please wait until they do the test before you get the headstone," she snapped, but it was a kinder retort, a gentler one, and that hurt me more.

Shel appeared before dawn in the kitchen, where I was already up and pacing. He moved slowly. He had on his jeans from the night before. His chest was bare. His sunburn made the wreckage of the Arielle tattoo stand out on his chest like a taunt. He turned on the light over the stove, and even its faint glow seemed to hurt his eyes. He slumped down at the table.

"I'm so sorry, Willow."

"It's okay," I said. It was. We had bigger Bear to fry.

"I can't believe it," he said.

I folded my arms. "Remember your promise."

He raised his head and blinked.

"Promise?"

"You promised to stop drinking."

He let out his breath, and I imagined the last precious molecules of his beloved liquor moving out of his mouth and floundering around the kitchen like birds kicked too soon from the nest. "I think I remember saying that now."

"Well, you have to if you're going to stay."

Shel shook his head. "Listen, Willow, this is a bad time. I am hungover as hell and I just got some potentially terrible news about Mom." He noticed the three bottles of beer and a half bottle of gin I had lined up on the counter.

"All the liquor," I said. "Pour it out."

He gave me a long-suffering look. "You sound different. Like you hate me."

"I don't hate you. I have other things to hate. But Mom doesn't need to be upset anymore and you have to do this for her."

"All right, all right!" His voice had a sharpness to it that I put down to whatever headache he'd built for himself out of sand and sun and betrayal and booze and stupidity.

It was still dark outside. The stream of gin pouring into the garden sounded like a twin peeing. The floodlight illuminated Shel's sad face.

"This is hard for me," he said.

"Okay," I said, my voice neutral. I was in no mood for Shel or his frailties. My mind was back inside the house, with my mother.

He started on the beer. It foamed on the ground. In the distance, I could see a bottle cap of pink light slowly taking shape. It would be a new day, soon.

"Maybe it's nothing," I told Shel. "Maybe there's no Bear at all."

"If not," he said grimly, "what a waste of good Modelo."

Shel and I had made breakfast for Polly by the time she wandered into the kitchen in her nightgown, rubbing her eyes.

"What's this all about?" she exclaimed.

"Can't we make you breakfast?" Shel asked, setting down a plate of scrambled eggs and toast in front of her while I poured her orange juice.

"You kids are spoiling me," Polly said. "But I will have just a couple of ice cubes in that juice."

"Shel poured all his liquor out, Mom," I said. "It's all floating in the garden."

Polly's fork hovered above her plate. She and my brother exchanged a quick, guarded glance. He put the saltshaker on the table and I saw his hand tremble slightly. She looked down at her eggs and began to eat and said not a word, and I imagined that giant foamy stain in the garden, the sun rising on it, the stain growing smaller and smaller until there was nothing left but green things.

Shel insisted on taking Polly to work that day. "I can drive, dummy," she protested, clearly thrilled by both the sobriety and the attention but trying to hide it.

"I'm thinking about the people coming the other way," Shel answered. "You drive like a bat out of hell."

Her biopsy was in three days. There was nothing to do but wait.

⟡

We all sat facing the doctor. He had thinning black hair and wore glasses and had a way of stroking his thumb with his index finger. His office was windowless. He had a portrait of his family on his desk—his wife's hair was blond and feathered, eighties style. She looked too young for him. His boys were smiling like they didn't mean it.

The doctor turned his computer screen to face us. He tapped a dark mass on the X-ray image with the tip of a pen. "The tumor is not large," he said. "But it is malignant."

His tone and manner annoyed me. So calm and clinical that I could not tell whether it was bad news or good news. So practical. I rested my fingertips on Polly's arm. She didn't move. She looked at the doctor.

"So what?" she said. "What does that mean?"

"I'd like to try to shrink this with radiation," he said. "We've had good results with your kind of cancer."

Your kind of cancer. I thought of the garden. I thought of the stain, drying in the sun.

"So what are her chances?" Shel asked.

The doctor turned the computer back around. "For what?" he asked.

"To *live*, you idiot!" Shel snapped.

The doctor's eyes didn't change.

"Sorry about him," Polly said. "He stopped drinking three days ago."

I looked at Shel's hands. They trembled slightly on his knees. He looked sickly, as though he'd been poisoned by a virgin daiquiri.

Finally the doctor answered, "If your mother responds to the radiation, that's a very good sign."

And so it began. Shel drove Polly to her radiation treatments while I rode in the back seat, refusing to miss a single session. She seemed fine afterward, if a little tired. She had stopped smoking, abruptly and without announcement. The smell of her favorite cigarettes, Virginia Slims, was no longer on her breath when she came back from the garden or kissed me good night. She no longer chomped on wintergreen candy to hide the odor, or flicked the butts into an old flowerpot she emptied every season. I should have been thrilled, but I was not. Her lit cigarette, rising and falling in an arc to her lips, had been a steady pendulum for fourteen years, and now that pendulum was still. What other habits would soon fall away? Singing in the garden, swearing, breathing?

Dalton, sad and unkissed, was still gone for the summer, and Phoenix had vanished, no doubt out of sheer consternation over his part in the Great Beach Disaster, which paled in comparison to this new one. And so when Polly went to work, as she still insisted on doing, Shel and I were left alone. Together we worked on the boat, soberly, efficiently, wires connecting where they should, no music, no Arielle. Now it was just talk of Polly filling that boat.

"I can't lose that old lady," he whispered to me one day, eyes red. "You understand, don't you?"

"I understand." I said this with a lump in my throat that hurt me when I spoke or swallowed or breathed or said my mother's name.

Polly had made Shel and me promise to tell no one—not even our sister.

"I told you for the last time, we are not letting Lisa get wind of this unless you want her and her sniffly boy and her two-faced jackal husband and Jesus all piled up in the house with us, because you know Lisa would make a beeline over here just as soon as she heard." She could not keep the pride out of her voice at the statement. The idea that Lisa would come running at news of her illness evidently pleased her. "Would you like that, Willow, entertaining Otto and playing 'Für Elise' over and over and watching me as Lisa makes me choke down that lemon balm tea she thinks solves everything? Would you?"

"No," I admitted. "But it's not right, her not knowing. It's not right, all the secrets you keep." I had decided that I would tell Lisa myself, should things get worse.

Had I not been consumed with worry over Polly, I would have been able to turn my full attention to the marvel that was my emerging brother: his true self, his genuine thoughtfulness, the way he had stepped in and taken charge of the family as that summer passed, becoming its captain, guiding the ship. He got a job writing some copy for a friend's chicken restaurant chain, which brought in enough money to pay some bills and buy groceries.

"See?" he said with pride. "I can still be a shill for corporate America."

He didn't want Polly to work at Walgreens anymore. "Quit your job. I can work for this family. I can hunt around for more advertising work, and if worst comes to worst, I can go help out Old Red."

"Old Red, the mechanic?" Polly said, then started to laugh. She laughed so hard she turned crimson and began to cough.

Shelton scowled. "Nice, Ma," he said. "Die in a fit of evil."

This was the best time in my life. This was the absolute worst time in my life. I had a sober and complex brother. I had entered his life at last and the three of us were a family. A family with a Bear for an unwelcome pet.

Because Polly wouldn't leave Walgreens, neither would my brother and I. We prowled the aisles, read all the birthday cards out loud, and pawed through the magazines while Polly sighed from the counter and the assistant manager made noises low in his throat.

"Please leave," Polly begged.

"We'll leave if you leave, old lady," Shel growled.

But she didn't. She worked right up until the day in late August when we went to receive the new biopsy results from the doctor. We all sat in the waiting area, Polly between my brother and me, calmly reading a *Redbook* magazine while I folded my arms and shivered.

"Don't look so gloomy," Polly told me, glancing my way.

"She'll be fine," Shel added. "We'll take her fishing again when this is over. And I'll rig the boat to break down so she can laugh in my face."

Finally we were ushered in to see the doctor. He didn't even let us take our seats.

"Looks good," he said simply.

"You're kidding," Shel gasped.

Polly blinked at him as a surge of joy rose up inside me and I jumped a few inches off the ground, suddenly ten again.

"We got lucky," he affirmed, and then finally waved us into the chairs and began going through the results. The upshot: The Bear, merely a cub, claws soft, teeth sharp but not savage, was gone. Gone completely. Chased out by a cloud of radiation. And Polly was Polly, the sickness stripped away, the mother intact, alive, going forward.

We took the back way down the old farm road, rolling our windows down, cows ignoring the pounding of an extended Doors song as Shel and I sang along with it.

"Turn off that music," Polly growled. "That boy sounds high on drugs."

When we got home, I had to get on my bicycle and pedal down two streets. I had to throw it down in the overgrown grass of the house with the green roof and the neglected shingles. I had to open the gate to the backyard, march straight in, goose coming at me, wings wide, neck stretching out, but I didn't care, I was immune to the beaks of the world, now that the claws were gone, and there was Dalton, coming out from under the hood where he'd been working, his hands black, even taller than I remembered him, his hair uncombed, stains on his jeans, shock on his face as I grabbed him and gave him the kiss he had wanted when the summer first began.

⁊

Dinner was jubilant. Fried chicken, with okra and eggplant from the garden, and mashed potatoes. Polly was alive, stripped of the Bear and filled with sass. She was mine, and so was Shel, and so was Dalton. I had more people than I'd ever had before, more than I'd dared to dream.

I woke up in the middle of the night and had to rouse myself to go and stand at Polly's door, to listen to her breathing and to convince myself that this was all real, that the news was good.

On the way back to my room, I stopped by Shel's room. I peered into the doorway and found his bed unmade but empty. After wandering the rest of the house and still not finding him, I opened the front door and looked out into the driveway to see if his car was there. It was. And so was Shel, sitting in the swivel chair on the deck of the boat.

I padded out, my pajama bottoms flapping, bare feet in the cool dark grass, to find my brother drinking out of a glass. I could smell the liquor before my eyes adjusted enough to see the bottle by his feet. He looked at me, heavy lidded. "Ah, Willow," he murmured. "You should be asleep." His voice was sweet, slurred, content. My heart dropped. I thought I'd never have to see him like this again. Shock and disappointment moved through me. That sudden, bracing loneliness. He was my brother and yet not my brother. We were there together and yet we weren't. I could no longer share the joy of the news. He had corrupted it by celebrating it this way, by doing something Polly feared and hated and could not control, here on the evening of her victory.

"Come here, baby sister," Shel encouraged.

"You're drunk," I said, and the hurt in my voice must have registered, because the glass that was rising to his lips went down to rest against his thigh.

"Not very. Come on, don't worry about this. I just woke up and couldn't sleep, came out here, one thing led to another, such is life."

"I'm going back to bed." My good mood was gone. The spell was broken.

"Willow," Shel's voice was pleading, gentle. "Don't go. Come sit with me. Please. Just like we used to."

The tone in his voice was so companionable it made me hesitate despite myself. "Stop drinking. Stop drinking and I will."

"Look." He threw back his head and drained his glass. "I'm done. No more." He set the glass down with great ceremony. "Come on up here. I was just thinking about Mickey. You never knew Mickey, but he was the craziest dog. Long body and short legs, he ran like a Slinky with feet. The Captain loved that dog. . . ."

He'd talked about Mickey before. But there was another story coming up, about the man I never knew, the dog I never knew, told by the brother I thought I knew, and I could not resist. I climbed on the boat and sat down cross-legged, listening as he spoke from his swivel chair, on a motionless boat in a waterless sea made of neighborhood and asphalt, putting my anger at his weakness aside for the moment, as I had done so many times that summer.

Shel did not notice it when I picked up the bottle and took a drink from it, the liquor hitting my throat with a shock, hot and sharp, a warning contained in the stark, bitter taste of it. I don't know why I did it. I suppose I had been wondering all summer what it would feel like. And now that the relief of my mother's recovery had been celebrated, I had been surprised, waking up that night, to find my fears about her weren't over. I didn't want to be afraid anymore. And Shel's gulps of his bottle or his can of beer seemed to spread a certain kind of peaceful courage across his face. I wanted that peace, that courage.

For the next hour, I stole sips from the bottle. And sure enough, I felt calmer, more centered. The stars overhead seemed to promise something, a higher vision that made sense of the world, and the part of the circle that was death.

Even the night air seemed perfect for eternity. Maybe eternity wasn't so lonely after all. My brother was off in a nostalgic land of boyish shenanigans and long-ago memories of an older woman he dated in high school, a woman with long, thick hair and swinging hips, to Polly's consternation.

"Her name was Lidia. But Polly called her Yolanda. Refused to learn her real name. "

That name, Yolanda, seemed funny to me all of a sudden. I giggled and found that I couldn't stop.

"What are you laughing about?"

"Yolanda," I gasped, laughing harder now.

"It's not that funny."

"Yes it is."

My voice was slurred—there was very little liquor left in the bottle, a fact Shel discovered when he picked it up and held it to the light.

"Oh, Jesus Christ, Willow, what have you done? You drank it, didn't you?"

"A little."

"Shit, you're gonna get me in such trouble!" His voice went high in his panic, and the sound of it made me laugh some more, my sides hurting, the stars swirling overhead. Like the one-eyed cat, my perspective seemed narrowed; I had to turn my head to sweep the sky and find the moon, which was fuzzy and spiraling into the cosmos.

Shel struggled out of his chair. "You've got to go to bed. Jesus Christ, what have I done?" He took me by the shoulders, helping me off the boat, and set me down on the driveway, but my legs didn't work and I collapsed, cool cement under my hands, head spinning.

"Get up, Willow, come on, get up!"

Shel was trying to pick me up, but I turned and vomited on the driveway, then rolled on my back and shut my eyes tight against the swirling stars.

The front door opened, and I heard Polly's voice. "What the hell is going on here?"

I looked up and saw her there in her nightgown and slippers, her arms crossed and expression severe.

"I didn't know, Ma! I swear I didn't know it. I would have

stopped her!" Shel cried, and then Polly was leaning down to me. "My baby . . ."

I sank into darkness to a noise that sounded like an argument taking place in an aquarium, anger encased in bubbles that rose as I sank down to the bottom of it all.

⁂

I awoke to light. Not morning light. It was the wrong color, the wrong shape, as it flooded my room and danced across the walls and over my books. Something about the light, so merry but unnatural, gave me a dreadful feeling.

I was in my bed with a wet cloth draped over my forehead, which slid off as I sat up. A rubber trash can was next to the bed, reeking of vomit.

The way the light bobbed and weaved was wrong. Ominous. My head was pounding and my stomach felt empty, floating unmoored inside me like a runaway jellyfish that couldn't get back home. I got up off the bed and looked out my window.

The boat was on fire. Flames were crawling on it, red and orange, smoke pouring off it under the floodlight. Shel, shirtless, in his underwear, was battling the flames with the garden hose. Polly, in her nightgown, watched him. I rushed from the room, dizzy and stumbling, through the house and the open front door. Neighbors had gathered on the street; sirens wailed in the distance.

Shel was screaming, "Why? Why?"

Mr. Tornello grimly inched across his lawn, holding a bucket of water, as Mrs. Tornello cried in a high, plaintive voice: "Be careful, honey!" From her place on her lawn, Mrs. Burrell shrieked, "Get inside! Do you hear me? Get inside!" presumably at the twins, who lingered somewhere in the darkness. Mr. Chant appeared with his own bucket and went up on his ineffectual tiptoes to throw it on the blaze, which ruffled like a skirt and then regained its full strength.

But Polly was curiously silent. Arms folded. Studying the flames. And then I saw the can of gasoline at her feet.

Shel's face was red and sweaty from the heat. "Get back in the house, Willow!" he screamed.

It was then that Polly finally spoke.

"Let her watch."

Four

The firemen were gone. The neighbors gone. The police gone. The general excited hubbub that delights in a sudden blaze on a quiet night was gone.

Shel was gone.

Vanished sometime during the night, leaving his clothes, his cell phone, and his laptop. The smoking husk of the Captain's boat sat under the blackened floodlight. A large plume of smoke damage was splayed across the garage door, and the shingles of the roof were singed.

Polly drank her coffee calmly. She looked like she hadn't slept all night and there was a weary stillness about her, an absence of fighting spirit. The police had issued her a citation and almost taken her to jail.

"It was my fault, Mom," I explained tearfully, for the third or fourth time. "Shel didn't know I was drinking."

She just shook her head. "I've lost my son," she murmured. "Don't know how it happened, don't know when. Don't know what I did wrong. But he's gone, and you're here, Willow, and I had to protect you. Don't you understand?"

The fact that Polly was asking for my understanding should have tipped me off that she was in a rare fragile state, and possibly astonished at her own act of retribution. But I was merciless in my rage.

"You set the only thing he loved on fire. You destroyed it. You destroyed him!"

"Oh, no, I didn't!" she snapped. "He destroyed himself!" Her voice cracked and her eyes got dangerously bright, so bright she had to rise and stare out the kitchen window, which framed part of a peaceful street. It was Saturday, nearly September. Nothing in the look on her face was an invitation to speak again, and so I went to my room.

Polly scraped up the money to have the boat dragged away, and Mr. Chant hauled himself up a ladder to paint over the damage to the garage door. The blackened shingles stayed, though, which served as a grim reminder of that night. Polly was fined an additional five hundred dollars by the Homeowners' Association board.

The twins, of course, enjoyed the scandal, taunting me when they saw me in the yard, yelling, "Your mommy is a firebug!"

"Maybe she'll come and burn down your brat school so you won't get away with all your bullshit!" I screamed back, using a rare curse word that sent them scurrying for their gate.

"Shel will be back," Polly said. "He wouldn't go off without his clothes or computer or his phone." But Shel did not come back. Polly had to work double shifts at Walgreens to pay off her fine, but she always called to check on me and always asked, "Did anyone call?"

Meaning Shel.

At first my answer—*no*—was always brief and angry. I still blamed her for driving my brother away, and the burned marshmallow she had made of my plans for a reunited family. But, as the days passed and then the weeks passed, and her voice grew sadder, I felt sorry for her.

"Well, he may have called but, you know, I was at school."

Polly solved that possibility by procuring an answering machine at a garage sale, so that for a mere ten dollars her heart could be broken, day after day, by a lit red "0" in the box that designated the number of calls, except for the off chance that Mr. Chant had checked in on her, or Mr. Tornello was mad, or Mrs. Burrell was mad, or any of the other neighbors were mad in simmering feuds that had once delighted her. She haunted the mailbox, waiting for something, anything. "What if he's sick somewhere? And what is he eating? He left his credit cards here at home."

Her friend, the sheriff, was sympathetic, but helpless. "Sorry, Polly," he said. "He's a grown man. There's nothing the police can do about it, besides filing a missing person report."

Polly did just that, but no one seemed interested, and after several weeks the police stopped returning her calls.

She had always suffered from insomnia, and now it came back full force. She wandered around the house at night, restless.

The pecans fell. The squirrels grew thick coats. The cat on

the fence retreated inside. Polly sighed more often. Her okra suffered and so did her vegetable soup.

Still, I had someone to turn to in this time of sorrow and regret.

I had my boyfriend, Dalton.

We sat on his bed up in his room, face-to-face, holding hands, entwining fingers, as we spoke about Polly: Bear-free, son-free, victorious, and bereft. That kiss that I had finally returned after a full summer of keeping it to myself had led to others. Many others. Now he fascinated me. The color of his eyes and the expressions of his face. The ears that still moved, but more subtly, as though adolescence had restrained them. The sound of his voice and the way he approximated his father's grammar. All these things I loved about him and though I was not yet ready to say *I love you*, I was close. So close I would have been there already were I not so worried about my mother. She did not yet know about Dalton and me, and the fact that this woman who could seemingly hear a spider mite creeping toward her cucumbers from inside her kitchen could not hear the change in my voice when I spoke his name, alarmed me. In desperation, I searched through Shel's things for Phoenix's number, and Dalton helped me look for him in the labyrinth of the Internet, but Shel's friend had vanished in a spiral of shame after that day at the beach, and was nowhere to be found.

"I don't know what else you can do about your brother," Dalton told me.

"I feel like it's my fault."

"No, it's not. I didn't know him but it sounds like he and

your mother were going to have a big blowup, one way or another."

"That's true. But they loved each other."

"My father says love is like a sand castle you build too close to
the water."

"I'm not sure what that means."

Dalton shrugged. "He's kind of been in a bad mood since his
last girlfriend left him."

One day, the answer floated down to me in church. I happened to be sitting next to Melissa Gathers, a girl my age I had
never liked and never would. Before the service began, she was
yammering to her friend about how she was going to spend
Christmas in Tulum. Polly was up and about, chatting to some
choir people, her back turned to me. I leaned, uninvited, into
the conversation.

"Tulum?" I said.

Melissa turned and stared at me. "Yes, Tulum. What about it?"

"Can you do me a favor?" I asked, barging ahead before she
could answer. "Could you mail a postcard for me when you're
down there?"

"All I have to do is mail it?" she asked.

"Yes, just drop it in the mailbox. It will be stamped and everything."

And that is why, in early January, Polly came back from the
mailbox lighter than air, clutching in her hand a postcard with
bright red summer flowers on the front, postmarked Tulum and
bearing no message at all, simply signed with one shaky letter.

X.

"Look!" she said, shoving the postcard at me. "Shel's back in Mexico. He wrote us, see? He's thinking about us."

The obvious relief on her face broke my heart. I took the postcard from her hands and pretended to study it. "Looks like it's from him, all right."

She took the card back and studied it again. "Yes," she said at last. "At least we know that."

Five

The subject of Garland was still in the back of my mind. The mystery and the intrigue. The trail went hot again one day when Polly was at work and I had just gotten off the school bus and was checking the mail. I still had my schoolbag slung over one shoulder. I shuffled the mail in my hand: an electric bill, an AARP bulletin that was sure to annoy Polly, and then . . . an envelope addressed to me, in unfamiliar handwriting. There was no return address.

I tore the envelope open and read the letter.

GARLAND MONROE
1334 OLD FARM ROAD
TAYLOR LAKE, LOUISIANA 85466

In prison for MURDER from 1953–1961! No other details found. Be careful Little Squirrel! You are precious cargo!

Your friend

Phoenix Calhoun

Murder. The word filled me with a tantalizing dread. Polly had been in love with a murderer. But who had been murdered, and why? And what was Polly's role in the whole thing? I went into the house, threw down my schoolbag, and read the note again.

I decided not to consult Dalton, who would have counseled against any correspondence.

Instead I got out the stationery that Aunt Rhea had sent for my last birthday and immediately rewrote the same letter I'd written two years before—the one that said that I was Willow Havens, daughter of Polly, and I wanted to say hello. I felt brave and defiant and very attuned to the romantic undercurrent of the universe, moving beyond the years, beyond misunderstanding, beyond crimes like murder. Still in the early stages of infatuation, I believed myself to be the agent of Fate who would finally reunite my mother and her true love, now that she had beaten the Bear and was ready for companionship. It was not that I dismissed my father, the Captain, or didn't want to understand and celebrate my father's role in Polly's life. I just wanted her to be happy, and if this mysterious person had once meant so much to her, maybe he could cure her loneliness. I'd read about the butterfly effect in school, how something as simple as the beating of wings in one part of the world could lead to great cataclysms centuries later, and I wanted my wings to be the ones that led to Polly and Garland's epic reunion.

I hiked down the street and mailed the letter from an unfamiliar mailbox, lest Polly discover it and rain her wrath down upon me. And I waited.

"You shouldn't have done that," Dalton said when I finally told him. "You should have left well enough alone."

"I don't like well enough," I replied. "It doesn't do you much good when you're seventy-two."

"What if he comes to your house and murders you both? Then what?"

"He's old now. Old men don't murder people. They look at birds."

I waited for weeks with no response. Then one day, a lovely Saturday early in the spring, came a knock on the door. There stood a deliveryman, holding a vase containing a dozen roses.

"Delivery for Pauline," he announced.

My heart jumped. I took the vase and carried it into the kitchen, where Polly was working on a crossword puzzle.

"Oh, my," she said. "What beautiful roses!"

"They're for you," I said. I put the vase on the table and watched her face as she opened and read the card. Her expression was guarded, careful.

"Who are they from?" I asked cautiously.

"An old friend. No one you need to know about." She quickly put the card away and went back to her crossword puzzle. But later that day I saw her adding aspirin to the water that held the rose stems—her favorite trick for preserving the blooms. Surely she would not nurture something that wasn't important to her. And yet, she said nothing.

∽

Spring arrived early, and with it the planting of tomatoes, green beans, and squash, the tilling of the soil, urging the garden back into fertility, beating back the new spring varmints. I enjoyed keeping the secret of Dalton away from my mother, the thrill of holding his hand covertly as we watched television, the love notes and the ever-changing nicknames for each other. If Polly kept her secrets from me, I could keep mine from her. Tit for tat. In my mind, I made a worthy and crafty adversary.

Until the day I was helping Polly pull weeds in the garden and she remarked, "Lots of work to do around the house and the yard. Gutters need cleaning and poor old Mr. Chant threw his back out. Seems to me your boyfriend should be making himself useful."

I dropped a handful of pulled weeds. "My boyfriend?" I asked, incredulous.

"That Dalton boy," she said simply.

"Mom!" I gasped. "How did you know?"

She cackled derisively. "You think I was born yesterday, Willow? The way you two snicker and bat your eyes at each other, the way you smile like the cat that ate the canary when you say his name? The way he stares at you, his ears moving like a choo-choo train? Also, he's combing his hair and tucking in his shirt."

I was so astonished I couldn't speak.

"I don't mind him, actually. Even though his daddy cares nothing about maintaining a decent house or yard, it's hardly the fault of the son. Besides, I believe it's always best to start out with someone who's already afraid of me. I'm getting too old to have to put the fear of God into some new boy every few months, so hold on to him. And call him and tell him to get down here and help me clean our rain gutters."

"She knows?" Dalton asked.

"And she thinks you're a good choice," I said, struggling against my own disappointment. I had wanted my first love to double as my first act of defiance, so her approval ruined every-thing. "She needs help with the rain gutters," I added.

"Rain gutters?"

"All clogged up with pine straw. We'll hold the ladder for you."

"Is this a test?"

"I think so."

"Oh, my God, what if I fail?"

"You'll do fine. Nothing to throw up a Snickers bar over."

His voice sounded cross. "That was three years ago."

Dalton hiked over the following afternoon after Polly got back from Walgreens. We spent the next hour holding the lad-der while he raked the pine straw away from the gutters and into the grass. When he got down from the ladder he was scratching himself viciously. Small red dots had appeared all over his arms and face.

"Ah," said Polly, "you must be allergic to no-see-ums. Terrible little varmints. I'll fetch the witch hazel."

But the witch hazel didn't help. Dalton's dots puffed up and his dad, Pete, had to come and pick him up before dinner and take him to an after-hours clinic for an antihistamine shot.

"Never happened before," Pete told Polly, calm about the matter. "Then again, I never made him clean our rain gutters."

"I bet you didn't," Polly said.

But that next weekend she told me I could ask Dalton to the movies, and that she would go along as our chaperone. Dalton was dressed in a button-down shirt and a pair of nice jeans. His shoes squeaked on the way into the theater. He sat in the middle between Polly and me, with his arm next to mine.

A few minutes into the movie, Polly whispered to me, "Who picked this movie? Is it supposed to be a comedy?"

Halfway through the movie she fell asleep, her head nodding forward, and Dalton leaned toward me, closer, closer, his skin pale in the movie light and his lips coming in for a long, sweet kiss, bought and paid for by the cleaning of the rain gutters and the tendency of the body's epidermal layer to swell in response to attack.

"I'm awake," Polly announced as Dalton jerked away from me. "Watch the damn movie."

⟋⟍

Polly wasn't finished with Dalton. She needed him to help her wheelbarrow a pile of mulch she'd ordered from the local nursery into the backyard to spread on her flower beds. Fortunately for him, our rotting fence was beyond repair and falling down on all sides, and she needed to order a new one rather than put him to work on it. The lowest price she could find was twelve hundred dollars.

"Highway robbery!" she exclaimed. We shared a common fence with all three of our neighbors, and Polly expected them to contribute. The Simmonses, a bland family who lived directly behind her, quickly capitulated when Polly asked them if they would share the cost of replacing the back fence. "They're good, boring people," Polly said in praise, but my theory was that they were simply afraid of her.

Next up were her enemies on the left and right, the Burrells and the Tornellos.

"They're never going to pony up for that fence," I said.

"Why shouldn't they? The fence on the left side rotted because the Burrells kept their firewood piled against it. And that old obese cat riding the fence for ten years on the other side didn't do it any good, either. I shouldn't have to pay for it all while they get a brand new fence."

One day, Polly announced: "I have a plan."

"What is it?" I asked.

"The Kill Them with Kindness Plan."

"Well, that sounds okay."

"Jesus says in the Bible to make friends with your enemies and turn the other cheek and really try the nice way first to get them to go in on a fence."

"I don't remember that particular verse," I said.

"Well, maybe you should stop daydreaming about that Dalton boy in church, sassy brat."

Polly quickly warmed to her own idea, thumbing through her old Rolodex of recipes. "Not much to offer vegetable-wise this early in the spring," she said. "But I make a helluva crawfish étouffée. Let's see . . . I have some squash with bell peppers I canned. And a few green onions have already come up . . . some strawberries, too . . . I'll make my special strawberry pie to keep those Montosaurus brats happy. . . ."

"You're going to invite the twins?" I asked, flabbergasted. "You hate the twins."

She kept flipping through her Rolodex. "To every thing there is a season, and a time for being nice to brats under heaven and what have you. You're in charge of the invitations."

"Me? Leave me out of it," I replied. But of course I had no choice, and was soon hard at work at the kitchen table, gluing brightly colored pieces of paper together and coming up with a short, catchy phrase that did not have the word "fence" in it:

AN EVENING AT POLLY'S

Polly's dear neighbors on the left and the right are invited to come over for . . .
A home-cooked meal on Saturday March 3, at 7:30 in the evening.
Dress is casual! No need to bring anything!

"That's perfect," Polly said after she scanned it briefly. "Not too short, not too long. But inviting. And 'An Evening at Polly's' sounds fancy."

"But, Mom, why would they come?" I asked. "They . . . hate you."

"Do you know what an honor it is to get a home-cooked meal from Polly Havens? Why, when the Captain was alive, folks would come from miles around. And, God knows, Darcie Burrell can't cook worth a damn. You should have tried the eggplant Parmesan she tried to hoist on me at the church bake sale. No wonder her children turned to Satan. He probably showed up as an angel of light and promised them a decent meal."

I shook my head slowly. "No one's going to come to your dinner. They think you're a crazy firebug who almost burned down their houses and they're not gonna help pay for a new fence. You are just kidding yourself."

"That's why I'm putting you in charge of going over there with the invitations. Get them to accept or don't come home at all."

"Me? Why me?"

"Because you are more diplomatic than I am. I guess you got that from your father. Also, you're a liar. Make up a good reason why they should come."

"But I can't lie on command!" I argued. "I only lie to get out of trouble or to amuse myself and it's totally not fair. . . ."

Polly was gravitating toward her purse. She handed me a five-dollar bill. "I can't believe I'm forced to hand you money to help your poor old mother. You are going to make a great highway robber one day with your cold heart and your love of the almighty dollar. Now get on out of here and get the job done."

Five dollars wasn't chicken scratch.

"I need to think about it some," I said. "Come up with a plan."

"That's the spirit, you lying dog," she said, brightening. "Want a Snickers bar for fuel? Here, take two. I need that fence."

⁓

The boy twin, Jared, answered the door. He was nine years old now, and had gained a little weight.

He looked at me blankly.

"Hi, Jared," I said. "Is your mom home?"

"Hi, Jared," he said, in a high girlish voice—what I assumed was an imitation of my own. "Ith your mom home?" He'd added a deliberate lisp. I felt the hair rise on the back of my neck.

"Jared, please, let me talk to your mom. It's very important," I said, trying to keep my voice calm and steady.

"Jared, pleath let me—" Mrs. Burrell suddenly came into frame in a whiff of jasmine-scented cologne. She had on a floral dress and a beaded necklace that seemed too tight around her throat.

"Well, hello, Willow," she said. "What brings you over? Is everything okay at your house?" *Okay* was apparently the new word for "Is anything on fire at your house?"

"We're fine," I said, then darted my eyes to the left and shifted on my feet.

She studied me. "Are you really fine?" she asked, and it was almost possible to like Mrs. Burrell at this moment, but I fought the urge. I had work to do.

"I'm doing well," I said pointedly. "But I'm not sure about my mother."

"Really? What's wrong?"

"Well, she's just having little spells. She calls them 'dizzy spells' but I'm not sure. She kind of gazes off into space and says funny things and then later she doesn't even remember."

"Come in," said Mrs. Burrell. "Tell me all about it."

I could imagine she was adding Polly to the prayer list at church this very moment. Soon I was sitting on her couch, drinking a glass of her lemonade, which was far too sweet but good enough for me, feeding the lie gently.

"You know my mother is very proud," I said.

Mrs. Burrell nodded vigorously. "*Extremely* proud," she said, in a tone that made me lift my head and give her the evil eye.

"Tell me more about her symptoms," she prodded.

"Sometimes she talks to people who aren't there. She'll say, 'What?' and then turn around and look at me and say, 'Did you hear that?'"

Mrs. Burrell leaned closer in. "I've never told a soul this," she said, "but do you remember last fall after the big storm, when the limbs were down?"

I nodded.

"Well, early the next morning I saw her standing out in the front yard and talking up the tree. She was saying, 'Elmer, is that you? Are you okay, honey? Did you survive the storm?'"

I let out a small gasp.

"What?" she asked.

"Elmer is her dead husband. The father I never met."

"Oh, dear," she said. "I didn't know."

We sat in silence for a few moments, the ice in my lemonade

glass swirling around and the twins arguing from a distant room. There was a muffled thump, and the boy screamed, "Mom, she hit me!"

"Not now!" Mrs. Burrell screamed back, and then turned to me. "I don't want you to take this the wrong way," she said, her eyebrows knitted with Christian worry, "but your mother has done her share of swearing and being unneighborly in the past. This brain tumor may just be a wake-up call."

"Brain tumor?" I gasped. "Do you really think that's what it is?" I handed her the invitation. "Polly wants you to come to dinner. And bring Mr. Burrell and the kids."

"She wants me to bring the children?"

"Yes, absolutely."

She let out her breath. "I'm not really sure this is a good idea. Putting so much pressure on your mom, this dinner party."

"Oh, no," I said. "It's exactly what she needs."

❧

Mr. Tornello was dressed, if you could call it that, in a long shirt, boxer shorts, and a pair of mules. He had a couple of days of whiskers and looked newly awakened, although it was five o'clock in the afternoon.

"Apologize?" he asked, incredulous. "Your mother wants to apologize?"

"Yes," I said. "She's had a change of heart about a lot of things ever since the fire. And she did mention that your act of bravery helped save our house." (After spilling his bucket of water, Mr. Tornello had dragged his garden hose over and soaked down the smoke after the firemen were done.)

"I don't believe you. Now go on. I've got television to watch."

Mrs. Tornello, wearing a long pink gown, drifted up behind him holding a *TV Guide*.

"What's happening?" she asked in her sweet, flimsy voice.

He yanked his head to her. "The old bitch next door wants to have us for dinner."

"Excuse me," I said. "I would rather you not call my mother that word."

"She's right, Ron," said Mrs. Tornello, hitting him softly on the arm with the *TV Guide* with the force of a butterfly's wing. "That is a terrible word to call someone who is inviting us to dinner."

"I just don't believe she's sorry for anything," he said. "She's been a damn terror for the past twelve years."

"She's had a change of heart," I repeated.

"Well," he said, "I'm glad she at least got that drunk off her driveway."

His wife rolled her eyes and sighed. "You are terrible," she said, and drifted away.

I handed Mr. Tornello the invitation. "She's making crawfish étouffée and strawberry pie."

He read the invitation, snorting gently through his nose. "I'm gonna have to think about this. But I've got to admit, I haven't had a good meal in years. My wife's not exactly magic in the kitchen."

❧

I had my reservations. It wasn't that my mother wasn't a master chef, or that I thought my neighbors couldn't, perhaps, be bribed on matters of shared fences. It was simply that I could not imagine Polly sitting down at the table and dining with the people she'd hated for so long.

"I don't think this is such a good idea," I told her.

"How do you think I've survived all these years? I adapted. And if grizzlies can grow extra fur in the winter, I can be nice to the neighbors."

"Just have a couple of margaritas before they come over," I suggested.

Polly spent all afternoon that Saturday whipping up her specialties. I was in charge of measuring and chopping. Although I did not share in Polly's belief her scheme would work, I was looking forward to the fireworks that would be sure to follow when Polly combined her favorite recipes with her dreaded enemies. The strawberries were washed and stems removed for the pie, the dough rolled and pinched. She'd bought two pounds of crawfish at the local fish market, and the "fancy" kind of rice at the store. It was good to see Polly at her best, even though her best was prickly with guile. I have to admit I was in a near jolly mood myself as I set the table and we waited for the guests.

Mrs. Burrell and the twins were the first to arrive. Mrs. Burrell looked lovely in a blue knit dress, her hair pulled back. The twins rushed past my mother and me to immediately begin banging on the piano as Polly growled softly.

"Jared! Madison! Stop it now!" Mrs. Burrell ordered. She peeled them off the piano and hustled them to the table.

Mr. Tornello arrived next, alone, wearing a white button-down shirt his frail wife had probably almost died ironing, and a pair of decent corduroys. He'd shaved, and slicked back his hair with some kind of pomade that smelled musky.

"Where's the missus?" Polly asked.

"She had a dizzy spell. She sends her regrets." He'd never been inside Polly's house before and looked around, the expression on his face like the ones in thrillers when the detective enters a warehouse. He sighed when he saw the children at the table.

"Hey, kids," he said without enthusiasm.

They stared at him.

"And hello, Darcie." She went to kiss his cheek and he waved her away.

I poured the iced tea, Polly served the salad, and the dinner began.

"Aren't we going to have a prayer?" Mrs. Burrell asked.

Polly stared at her a moment. "We usually pray only on special occasions," she said, "but of course we can pray tonight, yes, why not?"

"When it comes to Jesus, every meal is a special occasion," Mrs. Burrell said. She looked at Mr. Tornello. "Would you like to lead us in prayer, Ron?"

"Hell, no," he said gruffly. "I don't pray. Don't believe in it. Now, Delores, she'll pray 'til the cows come home, but not me, no, sir."

The others at the table stared at the atheist in their midst.

"You're going to hell," Madison declared.

"Now that's not polite at all," Mrs. Burrell said.

"You don't talk back to your elders, little girl," Mr. Tornello growled. "I raised my children to respect adults and I see that practice has fallen by the wayside."

The fence in Polly's eyes began to collapse. She hastened to smooth things over.

"Different strokes for different folks," she said briskly. "I'll say a quick prayer and Mr. Tornello doesn't have to pray with us."

Mr. Tornello rolled his eyes, Polly bowed her head, and the rest of us followed. At the age of fourteen, I was still quietly agnostic, but I desperately wanted the evening to go well, so I went along with the prayer, clasping my hands together.

"Dear Lord," she began, "thank you for giving me these wonderful neighbors through the years, and bless us as we, as neighbors, sit down to share the many blessings that . . ."

A low trumpet sound started from the other end of the table and sustained itself for several seconds, cutting Polly's prayer off in midsentence as her eyes flew open and her head rose. She stared at Jared, who put his hand over his mouth and snickered as his sister laughed out loud.

"He has a weak sphincter," Mrs. Burrell explained. "Jared, please apologize to Miss Polly."

"Sorry, Miss Polly," he said with a smile.

My mother's brows were twitching furiously. She looked like a cat was licking her face too hard.

"*Amen*," she said severely, and we began to eat.

During the salad course, Polly seemed to have calmed somewhat, talking with Mrs. Burrell about the recipe while the twins dueled with their salad knives and Mr. Tornello demonstrated his odd habit of stirring the fork around his plate before taking a bite. He removed the croutons from the salad and then remarked as Polly watched him, "These croutons are stale."

Polly glanced at me and I shot a glance back that said: *The fence the fence the fence.*

"It's going well," I said encouragingly, as we went to bring in the next course.

"I hate everyone in that room," she said.

"I know, Mom, and you're doing a great job of hiding it."

"Those brats are so impertinent. And that old goat was staring at my salad like it was going to kill him."

"We've only got the dinner and the dessert and then you're home free."

She started dishing up the crawfish étouffée. It smelled of bay leaves and conciliation. "Lord, give me strength," she said.

Polly tried to make nice again during the second course, politely asking the children how their classes were going.

The boy and the girl shrugged in unison, Polly's least favorite gesture on earth. Mrs. Burrell jumped in eagerly. "Oh, they're so modest!" she shrieked. "They both got green ribbons for the poem they wrote together! They're naturals, just like their father."

The twins looked bored. They had barely eaten their salad

and hadn't touched their crawfish. Mr. Tornello was stirring the rice and sauce around on his plate.

Polly simply stared at Mrs. Burrell and I marveled at my mother's complete refusal to acknowledge social cues. But the fence outside was not getting any younger. It was buckling under the moonlight as we spoke, the bright eyes of varmints peeking through the cracks, bully grass sending over its shooters. . . .

"LET'S HEAR IT!" I said heartily, as my mother nearly jumped. "The poem, I mean."

"Come on, kids," Mrs. Burrell urged. "Tell them your sweet poem."

"No," the boy said.

"Tell us the poem and you'll get candy corn for dessert!"

Polly bristled. She had her special strawberry pie sitting in the refrigerator, something no store-bought candy could measure up to, but she held her tongue.

The twins stared at each other, candy in their pupils. And they began.

> *Old cat, old cat sitting on the fence*
> *You have one eye . . .*

"That's my cat!" Mr. Tornello exclaimed. "That's Marty!" He seemed oddly thrilled that a poem had been written about his zero-personality cat.

> *Sometimes you sigh*
> *And you are bald in places*

And we make funny faces.
You are going to die.

Mrs. Burrell began clapping. Mystified, Polly and I joined in the applause, which petered out quickly.

"Well," Mr. Tornello huffed, "that was pretty good until you killed him."

Polly had an odd glint in her eye, a glint of suddenly found opportunity, and I soon discovered the context.

"Speaking of the fence . . ." She leaned forward, ready to make her pitch. "As you know, our common fence has seen better days. It's rickety and rotten and there's that hole on your side, Darcie, that is propped up with that plywood slab for going on two years."

Mr. Tornello was staring hungrily at the twins' plates. Madison moved her plate over to him and he ducked his head and began inhaling more crawfish.

"Marty almost fell off in the wind yesterday," he mumbled. "Fence was moving like a snake."

"It's funny you brought up the fence," Mrs. Burrell said. "My husband and I were looking over our closing papers because we were thinking of refinancing. And we were taking a look at the plat map . . ."

Polly's eyes darkened.

". . . and you know something? The fence is wrong."

"What do you mean, wrong?" Polly snapped.

Mr. Tornello had graduated over to the boy twin's plate and was burrowing into it as though his frail wife had not cooked him a meal in fifteen years and he'd been subsisting on cat food. His ravenous eating did nothing to break the sudden tension in the air.

"According to the map," Mrs. Burrell continued, "our property line extends three feet further into what was assumed to be your backyard. So when we get a new fence, we'll be taking that property back, of course."

Polly put her fork down. I saw her eyes and tried to nudge her with my foot but found her shin rigid and unresponsive. She was processing this information and I could almost hear the machinery turning inside her. "The plat map is wrong," Polly said. "I know the county surveyor personally and he assured me when we bought this house decades ago."

"Plat maps don't lie," Mrs. Burrell said sweetly. "Of course, that means your dogwood tree will have to be cut down, but the good thing is that we'll finally have room for the playhouse the kids have been wanting."

"Your kids need a jail, not a playhouse! You will not take down my dogwood tree!" Polly shrieked, abandoning all attempts of diplomacy. "It's been in our family for decades! I cut switches from that tree for my children!"

"She's right," I said.

"Well," Mrs. Burrell said, "I don't believe in corporal punishment."

"If you did," Polly shot back, "maybe your kids wouldn't be such brats."

Mr. Tornello looked thoughtful. "Maybe our fence line isn't right either," he mentioned.

"You shut up, Tornello!" Polly ordered, then turned on Mrs.

Burrell again. "I had to jimmy-rig that plywood over the gap in the fence years ago because your twins were sneaking in and peeing in my garden."

The kids exchanged looks, their eyes very wide. Mr. Tornello finished his food and now had three empty plates down at his side of the table.

Mrs. Burrell reached for her purse. "Listen, I am terribly sorry to hear of your brain tumor," she told Polly, "but I will not listen to such insane stories about my children."

"They peed in my garden and my daughter SHOT THEM IN THE ASS!" Polly trumpeted.

"That was you?" gasped the boy as his sister looked stricken.

"Damn straight she did!" Polly crowed at Mrs. Burrell. "And she'll shoot you in the ass if you touch my fence and that goes for you, too, Tornello!"

Mrs. Burrell, purse clutched in hand, seemed suddenly frozen to her seat, her eyes giant and her mouth open as if in a silent scream.

The boy glared at me. "That hurt," he said. "You little bitch."

Mr. Tornello stood up. "I will not stand for this fighting and swearing. This has been a terrible dinner party and I'm sorry I came!"

"Sure!" Polly shot back. "Now that you ate all the food like a starving coyote!"

Mr. Tornello shot her a single, glowering stare and lurched out of the kitchen, down the hallway toward the den.

"Wrong way!" I called after him but he paid me no mind.

"You are a sad, sad woman," Mrs. Burrell told my mother, as

Mr. Tornello floundered around the den, confused. "And we are going to put up our fence where it belongs and there is nothing you can do to stop us!"

"Oh, I'll stop you all right," Polly said. "With a court order or with buckshot, matters not to me. Like my daughter says, I've got a brain tumor the size of a baseball and I might as well die in prison."

I heard the door into the backyard open. "Wrong door, Mr. Tornello!"

"Oh, he'll find his way out," Polly said. She fixed Mrs. Burrell with a withering glare. "You can leave, too."

"I knew I shouldn't have even tried to be friends with you. My husband always said to just stay away from you, but no, I tried to do right by the Bible and—"

An unearthly scream came from the backyard.

Polly's eyes flew open wide. "Ron!" she gasped. She bolted from the room, the rest of us hot on her heels as we rushed through the den and into the backyard, where we found Mr. Tornello next to the pecan tree, laid out on his back.

"Oh, my God," I breathed. "The squirrel zapper!"

"Ron!" Polly shouted. Mr. Tornello was suddenly without anger, without crankiness. Polly knelt next to her old enemy. She looked up at me, eyes meeting mine.

"Call an ambulance!"

❦

And so there it was. The end of the worst dinner ever, with my mother traumatized, Mrs. Burrell horrified, and unkillable Mr.

Tornello dead in the grass under the passive eye of his cat on the fence, who did not move or seem alarmed. There was nothing the paramedics could do. They put down their paddles and threw a sheet over our deceased neighbor and hauled him away. The cops didn't really know what kind of charges to bring against my mother, if any.

"I'm sorry, I'm sorry," Polly kept saying. "I had noticed my daughter turned the strength on the zapper way down, but the squirrels were climbing the pecan tree to get to the bird feeder and so I turned it way up. But I never, never wished this upon my neighbor. We weren't the best of friends, but we were friendly. He'd just eaten three plates of my crawfish étouffée."

The twins were making a scene, dancing and pantomiming electric shock and then falling in the grass, so the policemen ordered the Burrells to go home. One of the cops went over to break the news to Mrs. Tornello.

"Oh, the poor woman!" my mother cried. "Who will take care of her now?"

"You probably should, Mom," I said.

She glared at me. "Mind your own business, Willow. And make these officers some coffee."

Mr. Tornello had died of a heart attack, the coroner said. The squirrel zapper hadn't electrocuted him. It had merely startled him, and that was enough. Suddenly my mother was without her nemesis of so many years. Oddly, I think she missed him. Somehow his absence altered the plane of her existence so that the forces so steady from her left and her right were lopsided, just a cool breeze instead of a steady storm front and the promise of thunder.

"I know this sounds crazy," she told me in a weak moment, her nicotine level low in her blood, her margarita level high, "but I kind of liked the old bastard."

Mrs. Burrell never took back her three feet of property and no one helped pay for a new fence and the old fence continued to rot. Polly took down the squirrel zapper and buried it as an act of atonement and also obedience to the police, who had told her to get rid of it for the safety of the neighborhood.

"You won, squirrel varmints," Polly whispered over the grave of her contraption, putting an invisible cigarette to her lips before she realized she no longer smoked. "Come and get it. The yard is yours."

And yet the squirrels were largely absent that spring. It was almost as if they'd witnessed the squirrel zapper take down a two-hundred-pound man and decided that the bounties of Polly's yard were not worth the risk.

The gardening still had to be done. Polly gathered her strength and threw herself into the spring planting, and I helped her after school. "A garden is God's way of saying life goes on, so get over it," Polly told me grimly. "No matter what happens, you've got to keep the garden going."

Meanwhile, the oddest thing was happening next door: Mrs. Tornello was coming alive. She'd sweetly, passively, accepted Polly's repeated apologies, the flowers and fruit and pies and covered dishes, and the ride to the funeral, where she'd sat between my mother and me in a lavender suit and a hat with a fake flower, hands folded on her lap while the minister went on about how wonderful her dead husband was. But as the weeks passed, she seemed to strengthen. Now I often saw her giant old Buick ease out of the garage and glide off to places unknown. Even more intriguing: A red Cadillac began appearing on her driveway, sometimes overnight.

"I think she has a gentleman caller," Polly said in awe, gazing out the window. She swiveled her head around. "Willow, I'll give you five dollars to watch that car all night and see who comes out."

"But, Mom, I have school tomorrow."

"Oh, big whoop," she snorted. "I used to stay up all night helping my dad nurse sick cows and would score a hundred on the spelling test the next day."

I took her money and made my report in the morning. "It's an old man," I said. "Nice-looking, actually. Wears suspenders. Great posture."

"Well, I'll be damned," Polly said. "Wonder if she always had him on the side, just waiting to move in like a wolf once the husband was out of the picture. Anyway . . ." She took a sip of coffee. "None of my business."

Early one morning in May, I found Mr. Tornello's old cat dead in the grass on our side of the fence.

"Ah, hell," said Polly, when I called her to the scene. "Poor old cat finally keeled over. Surprised it didn't take that old fence down with him. Well, the least we can do is bury him. Go on over and ask Mrs. Tornello if she wants you to dig the grave in her backyard."

"Why me?" I demanded.

"What, grave digging's too good for you? I'll give you a couple of bucks."

I wasn't crazy about the idea of telling poor Mrs. Tornello that our yard was hosting another dead family member, but I slogged over and rang the bell. Mrs. Tornello answered and I stepped back, amazed. Gone was the stooped, frail old lady, vaguely friendly, vaguely sweet. She was decked out in a snow-white dress and wearing silver bangles. Her white hair was in a new fancy sweep, and she wore pink lipstick and a string of pearls. She had a purse on her arm, as though she were going somewhere.

"Hello, dear!" she cried with more animation than I had ever seen. "How are you?"

"I'm fine," I said, "but I'm sorry to tell you your cat is not."

She blinked. "My cat?"

"You know," I said. "Marty. He died." My words came out quickly so I could get it over with. "We found him on our side of the fence. He looked very peaceful."

"Ah," she said.

A man in a natty suit came up behind her—the same one I'd spied coming out of her house. He had a pleasant face and a short, neatly trimmed goatee.

"What's the matter, Delores?" he asked.

She turned to him. "The cat's dead."

"My mother wants to know if you want him buried in your yard, or ours," I said.

"Oh," she answered, "your yard is fine."

❧

I cried over Marty's grave. Polly wanted to know why, but I couldn't answer her. Still, my tears unsettled her enough that

she made me my favorite pecan pie that night, with another favorite for dinner: boiled artichokes and Hamburger Helper.
But I could not be consoled.

"Dear God," Polly said, as tears began to roll down my cheeks
even as I nibbled at my pie. "It was just a cat, and had even less
personality than most."

"I'm fine," I said, "I'm fine," and went to my room to cry some
more. Marty, dead in the grass, reminded me of something I'd repeatedly pushed from my mind: the sight of Marty's owner, Mr.
Tornello, also dead in the grass. His eyes wide open, pupils frozen,
eyelashes still. An old man's skin full of nothing. Three meals
somewhere in his belly. All the cantankerousness snatched by
something no one could see. All the years, the memories, aches
and pains, threats passed over the fence. All gone. An old man and
then a shell. A cat and then a shadow. Living things and then something of the same consistency as the contents of my mother's pile
of mulch.

Was death that easy? And when would it take her away from
me?

III

The Bear

One

I was fifteen years old now. And overnight, it seemed, I had outgrown my mother. She was like an outfit that was too tight across the chest. Too short in the legs, showing the bare skin of my ankle. I no longer belonged to her. I belonged to myself, to the world outside the boundary of the garden and the yard. I was impatient, impertinent, distracted. Consumed with the things I didn't have and what we could not afford.

I hated wearing secondhand clothes, and being left with the ancient boom box that had once belonged to my brother. I could not drive myself, could not work and earn my own money. Even so, I found jobs where I could: babysitting, yard work. I even folded clothes for a woman from my mother's church, and kept the money in a drawer. Stacks of twenties and tens and ones, and the smaller promises of quarters and dimes and pennies.

Someday I'd get away.

Just leave, like Shel and Lisa.

Just leave her.

I rolled my eyes, shrugged my shoulders, slammed the door. I was moody and unkind.

"The better the child, the worse the teenager," Polly said. "And you were a glorious child."

"*Was* a child!" I shot back. "I'm not a child anymore!"

"And you know everything and your poor old mother is stupid. Went through it with Shel, went through it with Lisa, although she had Jesus as a backup and didn't play fair. And I suppose I'll live through it with you."

"It must be a terrible thing," I said, "living with me."

"Ah, sarcasm. Been through that, too." She said it as though sarcasm was a very hard winter and she'd sat on the porch watching satsumas burst. "Go ahead, I figured I was gonna lose you when the teenage years hit. But you'll come back to me. Children always do."

"Shel didn't," I said, and didn't even flinch at the look on her face.

"Don't you sass me," she said quietly, and left the room.

I bought a shirt (too tight, Polly said) with some of my earnings and wore it twice a week. I started putting on lipstick and mascara in the bathroom at school. Stuffing my bra. I tried cigarettes in the parking lot, was late for class, and no longer loved my teachers.

Dalton had grown two more inches and broadened across the shoulders. He was really becoming a man now. Polly took a look at his new muscles and put him to work. He mowed our lawn, trimmed the bushes, kept the rain gutters clean, changed the oil in Polly's ancient car, and planted a redbud sapling, dug it back out, and planted it somewhere else when Polly changed her mind.

"You can't kill him, Mom," I said crossly. "So stop trying."

"Just trying to get some work out of your paramours," she shot back. "Lord only knows you're not the helpful sort."

Dalton and I wrote e-mails back and forth, walked together to classes. Made out in the parking lot and in the back of the old cars in Dalton's backyard, listening to Tom Waits and John Prine. We had deep conversations and big plans. We added to the animals in Dalton's backyard sanctuary: two more rescue dogs, a three-legged raccoon pup his dad had discovered by the side of the road, a neighbor's castaway tortoise, and a cat that showed up one day, emaciated and scruffy, and fattened up to get into raucous, hissing, honking fights with the goose. Dalton's dad went through two more girlfriends, but Dalton and I were intently committed. It was our world, so perfect, and it was a new one. I wasn't borrowing music, I wasn't playing old games. I wasn't growing up inside the blown glass of someone else's story. We were new and we were alive and if I had one foot left in Polly's world, it was only because she clung to an ankle.

I had friends now. Samantha and Ava. They lived in newer, better neighborhoods. Wore Lucky 7 jeans and stylish wedges. Owned cell phones. Had older brothers and sisters who drove nice cars, and had other nice cars waiting for them when they turned fifteen and could procure a charade of a learner's permit. They were both on the student council, and had that crisp, tailored look that high-achieving girls in my school preferred. I was glad to be their friend, although they constantly harped about my clothes.

"Here," said Samantha one day at the mall, holding a skirt up to me. "You would look so cute in this!"

"Try it on," Ava urged.

"I can't," I said.

"You can't afford it?" Samantha asked.

I didn't know what to say so I said nothing. My friends ended up buying me the skirt.

"It's too short," Polly said, eyeing it.

"I can't take it back. It was a present and I don't have the receipt."

"Well, that solves that, then. Give me that skirt. I'll put it up in the closet for when you turn eighteen and you can be as trampy as you please."

"Mom!" I wailed. "Don't do that! I have to wear it to school or they'll think I don't like it!"

"Tell them your mama doesn't want you to have a baby yet."

"You are so UNFAIR," I said bitterly, fully committed to my new habit of enunciating certain key words in a complaint. "You have no idea what it's like to be POOR when your best friends are RICH."

"You're right, sassy girl," Polly said. "It's pretty easy to be rich and I've just been lazy about it."

I stormed off to my room to sulk, crossing my arms and sitting on the bed, my spine erect and stuffed with the hard gristle of injustice, as the blender whirred from the kitchen.

"Of course," I thought bitterly. "She can afford her margarita mix, THAT'S FOR SURE."

Later that night I heard Polly on the phone with Lisa. "It's not right," she complained. "Mothers are still supposed to be young when their kids become teenagers. It's like coming down with the flu, only the flu is made of hate. How will I survive this?"

She was silent for a few minutes before bursting out: "Jesus isn't gonna help me with a teenager, Lisa. He was good with lepers and whores and blind people, but he can't cure the smart-ass years and you know it."

Ava and Samantha were up on the latest music, Beyoncé and Fergie and Avril Lavigne. Their mothers were young and slim, talked about Pilates and spin class, and had high young voices, easy laughs, and Fendi purses. Their houses looked like mansions and they had Mexican crews to come in and clean them. They went out to eat at restaurants I had never heard of, and on the occasions I went with them, they always insisted on paying.

"Why don't you ever have your friends over here?" Polly asked. "You could play that old Parcheesi game Shel and Lisa used to love so much. Or Twister."

"NO ONE plays Parcheesi and Twister anymore. Unless they live in a cabin in the woods somewhere."

"I suppose inviting them to go fishing would be out of the question."

"Yes," I answered, rolling my eyes. "DEFINITELY out of the question."

The new potatoes had come in and she was tackling the eyes

with the fervor she always had in early spring, when the crop was new. "Well, how about asking them to dinner over here," she went on, pointedly ignoring my tone. "I have some of that vegetable soup I could heat up, or if they're in a fancy mood, I could make chicken à l'orange . . . used to make that back when your dad had important people over for dinner . . . I also have some fresh asparagus. . . ."

"No, Mom," I said, gentler now. "That's not a good idea."

"Don't you go sassing off and tell me I killed a man at the last dinner," she said in a warning tone.

I said nothing.

"What is it?" she asked. "Is it the house? The house embarrasses you?"

"It's old," I said at last.

"Well, yes, of course it's old. We've been in this house for decades. A house is like a human—it can't help getting older. But it's cute, isn't it? In a quaint sort of way?"

There was a subtle pleading tone in her voice that I didn't hear often and picked up on immediately. "Yes," I said, mustering kindness. "It's cute."

"And I keep it very clean. Probably much cleaner than those other mothers do."

"Well, they have help."

"I see."

I turned to leave.

"It's not just the house," she said. "It's me, isn't it?"

I stopped, turned back.

"Don't be ridiculous. There's nothing wrong with you."

"I'm old. And I'm country. And that embarrasses you."

"Of course not!" I said, so hotly that I confirmed it was true.

"Ah, Willow," she said, her voice defeated. "You used to be so proud of me. All those lies you'd make up. What I wouldn't give to hear one more lie."

ᶜ⌒ᵔ

The Bear came back so stealthily that I was not even aware he was living in our house. For one thing, Polly was suddenly as sneaky as a teenager. Keeping to herself. Whispering on the phone. "Don't touch the mail," she warned me. "That's private stuff. I'll get it." At first I wondered if she and Garland had gotten together at last. But then, once a week she began returning hours late from work, her smock stuffed in a bag, and on those nights she would never eat dinner.

"I'm working late," she said. "Trying to make some extra money. You've gotten expensive." I was a liar and knew a liar when I saw one.

"What do you think she could be doing?" I wondered to Dalton by my open locker.

"Maybe she really is working late," he said.

"No, something is wrong," I said. "I can feel it."

I needed to follow her, and for that I needed someone with a car. And then I remembered that one day, rummaging back through the things my brother had left behind, I found something I'd missed the first time. A phone number.

Late that night, after Polly had gone to bed, I made a call.

"Hello?" The sound of Phoenix's voice evoked a brief, aching memory of my lost brother.

"Phoenix," I said. "It's Willow Havens."

"Little Squirrel! I'm so glad to hear your voice. How are you?"

"I'm fine," I said. "Why did you just disappear? Where have you been?"

There was a short pause. Phoenix said, "I've been right here the whole time. I figured your mother didn't want me around after that day at the beach. And I felt responsible for your brother getting so drunk."

"Well," I said. "He's gone now."

"Gone? Where?"

"I have no idea. Listen, Phoenix, never mind all that. I have a favor to ask you. Can you—"

"Yes."

"—follow my mother around and see what she's up to?"

"How fun!" he exclaimed.

"Good. Pick me up Friday. That's the day she's always late."

"Absolutely, Little Squirrel."

Phoenix looked the same, but Gravity had put on a little weight and his fur had grayed a bit, but he was no less hysterical. He yipped and yapped from the back seat as Phoenix guided his car through the traffic. The seat belt was still too gnawed to put around my body.

We pulled into the Walgreens parking lot and waited. At exactly 3:07, Polly ambled out the door in her blue Walgreens smock and her brogans, clutching her brown purse. I watched the face she wore when she wasn't with me—a bit blank, devoid of her spitfire personality, and weary.

"There she is, Phoenix," I said, pointing. "How does she look to you?"

"Beautiful," he breathed.

"No, I mean, does she seem different at all?"

He stared as she got into her car. "Even younger."

We waited until she pulled out and then followed her. "See?" I said. "She's not going north. She's going south. Why is she going south?"

"Are you sure you want to know?" asked Phoenix.

"What do you mean? Of course I want to know!"

"You never know about secrets," Phoenix said. "Sometimes they can bite you in the ass. My father was a secret beekeeper. Don't know why he kept that from my mother. No one knew until after he was dead and my mother disturbed the hive. They had to rush her to the hospital and give her epinephrine."

I was barely listening. I was watching the top of Polly's head as she drove down the street, hands at ten and two. When had her head disappeared so far down below the headrest?

The traffic in her lane slowed, and like a rifle shot she pulled the old Chevy into the next lane.

"Jeez," Phoenix said. "Your mother drives like a bat out of hell."

"Don't lose her!"

Phoenix tailed Polly through town, keeping up with her strange darting and dashing. "It's like chasing around a tadpole!" he exclaimed, but I stared straight ahead, hands clenched, in a darker mood. Especially when we reached the west area of town, and the medical buildings began appearing.

Polly slowed and turned into a parking lot of a giant building with a sign: **Sloane Halford Patient Parking.**

"Oh, my God," I breathed. "Not here."

"Now don't get all upset. There could be another explanation. Maybe she volunteers here now."

"The Bear is back," I whispered.

"What is this bear? I don't understand. Hold on to Gravity. If he gets in the building he'll go berserk sniffing all the cancer people." He opened the door and got out quickly, leaving me in the car with the suddenly frantic creature. Both of us were watching our masters walk into that building, both of us were quivering and whining, hearts beating fast, because neither one of us understood the universe, and its notions of separation and time. We both lived in a black-and-white world where nothing existed between complete security and utter desolation.

Phoenix disappeared into the building and returned minutes later and slid into the car with a grunt.

"Well?" I asked.

"She lost me. Old lady's quick as a rabbit. Darted down a hallway and I went to follow and she disappeared."

"She's always been quick. Although she seems slower lately."

"Well, not slow enough."

There was nothing to do but wait.

Gravity went back to licking Phoenix, graduating to his neck and then his collarbone, as Phoenix attempted to entertain me with his theory that black holes in the universe might actually be explained by the action of multiverses and then moved on to the quantum idea that there were many identical universes out there at this moment, endlessly replicating, in which a man and a girl and a dog waited in a car outside a medical building where an old lady was possibly getting treatment. Then he went on to discuss gravity, which Gravity thought meant not the force but the dog, and barked each time he heard his name.

The sun went down and left us in darkness. The lamps came on in the parking lot. Finally I saw Polly emerge from the building, clutching her purse and slowly making her way to the car.

"There she is!" I exclaimed.

"Stay cool, don't blow your cover," Phoenix advised, but it was too late. I had hurled myself out of the car and run through the parking lot, Gravity escaping with me and hot on my heels. Polly looked stricken, freezing in place as I came barreling up to her and threw myself upon her in a frantic embrace.

"Mom!" I shouted. "Mom! Mom!"

"Dear God. What in the hell are you doing here?"

Gravity rushed up, yipping, darting around me to jump up on my mother. Suddenly he flopped to the ground on his belly, cowering and whining.

"And what is wrong with this damn dog?"

❧

Later that night, I slumped on the couch, soaked in tears. Polly regarded me stoically. Phoenix was gone and so was his dog.

"Why didn't you tell me?" I asked again.

"Why? Because I knew you would act like this, getting all hysterical. And for God's sake don't go scurrying over to tell Mrs. Burrell. The last thing I need is Psalms in my ear and some damn poem the Montosaurus kids write about how I'm gonna kick the bucket. God knows what they'd rhyme that with, but I can imagine."

"When were you going to tell me, never?"

"Correct. I'll be good as new in a couple of months and you would never have known had you not got the Calhoun boy to sneak around and follow me to the hospital."

I shook my head, more tears falling. "It's my fault," I said. "I should have nagged you more about the cigarettes. You would have quit sooner than you did."

Polly snorted. "Sure, because I always listen to what you say and follow your orders carefully, just like you follow mine. Now suck it up. Watch some TV."

"You can't die. Not when I'm a terrible teenager. You have to wait until I outgrow it."

"Oh, my baby," she said gently. "You got a runt's constitution when it comes to making your way in the world, and I suppose that's my fault. But you've got nothing to worry about, hear me?" She pushed herself to her feet and approached me, leaning down to embrace me.

"It came back," I whispered.

Two

The world as I knew it—the same world I'd been try-ing to leave—fell apart. I wanted to go back in time, to when I was younger and so was Polly. When the Bear was hidden or unborn or simply in the code of her cells, its own desires muted by her ferocious energy and iron constitu-tion.

Her hair fell out in tufts. I'd come home and find them sit-ting on the backs of couches, sills, balanced delicately on the napkin holder, caught in the machinery inside the toaster, or simply floating through the air like tiny, faintly orange fairies, too weary to grant any wishes. I gathered up the hair and kept it, as though she'd need it someday. Finally she took to wearing a scarf. And she slept. Once she fell asleep at the table at high noon, her face as peaceful as a girl's.

I saw the Bear all over our house.

The way her slippers, usually positioned nightly by her bed-room door, were now simply dropped, toes pointing in different directions. The calendar, on which she wrote huge and tiny things almost every day, contained rows of empty squares. The uncooked chicken spoiled, as did the deli tuna salad. And the freezer in the garage emptied, because it was easier to thaw something than to cook. The utensils, once so carefully arranged in the drawers with the little spoons cupped inside the little spoons, big spoons to big spoons—was a tangled world of anything goes, of bone-tired slaphazardry. The steak knives pointed any which way, a bottle opener thrown in somewhere, anywhere. *What did it matter?* said the drawer. *I'm so tired,* said the shelves of the refrigerator. *Is it not yet night? The day is so long,* said the keys of the piano, dusty and still.

The milk in the refrigerator would go bad now. Polly had been such a guardian against spoiled milk, her delicate nose perched above the open carton, eyebrows making diagnostics, lips suspicious, mind doing math about sell-by dates. Now the milk was sour, and I imagined that sour milk was the scent of the Bear inside her body, rampaging through her bloodstream, drinking her nutrients.

Most disturbing of all, her garden was growing wild. With no mother to tend it, it was putting out the wrong fruits, making the wrong friends. Unpicked cucumbers hung on the vines, bully grass invaded, green beans were too tough to snap. Weeds that were supposed to be pulled and banished were taking root, spreading wildly. And the varmints were getting bolder. And if the garden stood up in its crib and howled for her, its voice was lost to the wind.

Perhaps it was my fault. My abandonment of her. My embarrassment over her. The way I'd drifted from her just wide enough for the Bear to insert his terrible paw. If I had been watching her, she would still be well.

"That, uh, sounds a little crazy," Dalton told me, his hand in mine. "You can't cause cancer by being a teenager." He was trying so hard, but his attempts at consolation were beginning to annoy me. The things that I loved about him, his gentleness, his awkwardness, the way he searched for words, simply did not work on my anxiety and fear. The Bear, terrible and relentless, needed a real man to confront him. A man named Chet or Doug or Brink. With rough knuckles and a studded belt and a leather jacket. As the Bear grew more possessive, so did Dalton. He wanted time for us, more phone time, more hallway and movie and parking lot time. He wanted to kiss me harder, let his hands wander, plan our future, but I was not available to him, I was starring in a weepy matinee about a girl whose mother was dying.

I was no longer interested in Ava and Samantha. I found them suddenly shallow and dull. Always talking about clothes and boys, as girls in healthy families are allowed to do. Completely absorbed in their own world, safe enough to be obnoxious and unloving and uncaring and not pay the price.

We were at the lunch table together. Samantha and Ava were going on and on about a party they were planning. I was staring off into space, thinking about terrible things.

"WILLOW!"

"What?" I snapped, jerking my head around.

"What are you bringing to the party?" Samantha said.

"Nothing. I can't come. My mom needs me."

"But," Samantha said, "the party's on Saturday night. Your mom's chemo is on Fridays, right?"

"Right," I said, hearing my own voice turn cold. I couldn't stand the casual way she said *chemo*, like it was nothing. Just a word. "She has *chemotherapy* on Fridays and she's exhausted all day Saturday. Can't even go to work. So, no, I won't be going."

"Not even for a little while?" asked Ava.

"Maybe I don't give a shit about your party," I said evenly.

"What?" Ava gasped. "How can you say that?"

"Because," I answered, my words icy now, rage strangling me, "it is not give-a-shitable. It means nothing to me, and nothing in the grand scheme of things. It is just a stupid party."

"Well," said Samantha, "aren't you a little bitch."

"And your mother is thirty-eight years old, so fuck you."

∽

Polly still insisted on working at Walgreens, although she began to take weekends off to sleep after her treatments.

"You shouldn't be working at all," I said.

"Where's the money gonna come from, then?"

"I can get more babysitting jobs. And Lisa and Tom can help us."

We were at the kitchen table and she was a third of the way through a crossword puzzle with a fine felt marker. The blanks would have been filled by now before the Bear came back to live with us. Agitated by my suggestion, she tapped the pen against the newspaper, little black dots appearing on the page and bleeding into the fiber of the paper. We had been going back and forth again about whether to tell Lisa about the Bear. I was pro and Polly very con.

"I'm going to send that Bear packing, just like the first time, so why trouble her?"

I shook my head. "You keep too many secrets."

"Well, one more won't hurt."

I could no longer sleep at night, so alert for any sound: footsteps, breathing, a pulse. Some kind of aural diagnostics on my mother that the house would offer in the dead of night, if only I would listen. And how selfish could I be, sleeping, dreaming, when this information was being offered? I got up, listened at her door, took her slippers, one pointing toward the bed, one pointing toward the wall, and straightened them perfectly. And sometimes I crept closer, into her bedroom, right over her, to her face in moonlight, the sweeps of light coming in and showing patches of her scalp through her thin hair, and a vein that ran down the side of her nose, and her closed lids, and the expression she had when she was at rest and fooling no one. And I got so close that I felt the warmth of her, lingered there, watching her, my stomach killing me, some Bear cub inside me stirring, perhaps, turning in its sleep, realizing now was not the time, maybe in sixty years. But if I was destined to be eaten by some future Bear, I wanted it to come and get me now. In the darkness of her bedroom I imagined the two Bears, the adult and the cub, could carry my mother and me like two salmon in their mouths as they slunk into the stars.

Despite Polly's remonstrations I no longer paid attention in class. Now I felt so weary that darkening in the multiple-choice questions with a pencil seemed too tiring and so I left them blank. I had thought, all these years, that these collected learnings would lever me into adulthood armed for something important. But now, the lessons had decomposed into the ramblings of middle-aged women who were there to make a living and drill into me things that may or may not mean anything at all. School had become like church to me, and I was not a believer.

One morning I went into the kitchen and there was Polly, in her Walgreens uniform, the morning light coming in and darting through the stained glass prism, throwing tiny, cold rectangles of color against the muted background of her new wig, which was the color of Elmer. It turned her into something more ordinary. She looked like a cashier at a Walgreens store who was wasting away from a mysterious disease and who found making change from a dollar exhausting.

"Well?" Polly said. "What do you think?"

I didn't answer.

"I had to do something. My manager suggested it. He tried to say it nicely, but the long and short of it was that an old woman with two hairs left wasn't appropriate for a cashier so close to the beauty products. Of course, his prominent gut and canker nose do wonders for the men's products. Now come on, tell me how it looks, really."

"It's nice," I managed.

She looked at me and sighed, frustrated. "Then why are you crying?"

"I'm not crying," I wiped my face on my sleeve. It was just the thought of that hair never again changing color, never subjected to her crazy concoctions of vinegar and lemon juice and various cheap dyes mixed together and kilned into something hellish under the hair dryer. It was just a wig, just a color.

"It could be anyone's wig," I said, my voice breaking.

"What does that mean?"

"You aren't just anyone."

"Of course not. I'm your mother. Come here, come here." Her arms reached out, beckoning me. Bruises on them from the needles, age spots from time. I knelt so I could press my ear against her sternum, bones hard like the machinery of Phoenix's car seat. I embraced her and the Bear inside her and the hunger inside it. I felt her heart beating as her fingers stroked my hair. Out of the corner of my eye I saw her biscuit, barely gnawed.

"I promise you, baby," she whispered. "I'm still mean."

෴

Polly wanted to drive herself to her treatments, but Phoenix wouldn't hear of it. "You could get in an accident, Miss Polly. I couldn't live with that," he said adoringly. Phoenix became a one-man car service.

"It's your fault," Polly said, "unleashing that weird Calhoun boy and his rat dog on me. Why did you ever call him? Now I can't get rid of him."

"First of all, he's not a boy. He's a grown man. And I think it's sweet, how devoted he is to you. He's right. You shouldn't be driving. You weren't the greatest driver in the world even before the Bear ever darkened our door."

"Listen, sassy girl. I might be in a weakened state, but one time my daddy found a dead rattlesnake and that rattlesnake came back to life and bit him in the kneecap, and I will bite you, too."

"Good," I said. "I want you to bite me."

"You're a strange girl and I love you."

She was saying *I love you* a whole lot more and it disturbed me. *I love you* was something said in movies by weak people who lay on cots as heart monitors beeped slowly.

"Just be nice to Phoenix. I think it's very convenient we have him here to drive you."

Gravity went along with us. To keep the little creature from whining and crawling on his belly when he sniffed my mother, Phoenix had rigged up a muzzle with oil of lavender rubbed on the inside to keep the Bear scent away.

"A dog that neurotic should be put to sleep," Polly remarked.

"Mom," I said, "Phoenix can hear you."

"Oh, yes, I heard her," Phoenix said, watching the road. "You're absolutely right, Miss Polly."

Nothing my mother said, or anyone said, seemed to bother Phoenix. He did not appear to live in the past or in the future, but in such a precise fraction of now that you could not pare the now down any thinner and still contain him. Like a dog, he lived completely in the present, those easy moments made up of comfortable slices: the length of a dropped treat, the distance between an open mouth and a thrown Frisbee, those moments between the circling and the lying down.

Even when a black Corvette cut him off and the driver shot him the bird, Phoenix remained implacable. "You never know what's going on in a man's mind," Phoenix said. "Maybe someone stole his stereo. Or maybe it's the birthday of someone dead. Or maybe he's sick and he's just lost faith in his chiropractor's tea."

"Still," Polly said, her hand out the window and her middle finger in the air, "might as well say howdy."

"Do you remember ever being really upset?" I asked him once while we were sitting in the waiting room while Polly was down the hall getting her treatments.

He thought a long time, his hands folded, his big frame crammed in a plastic chair and his feet stretched out in front of him. A tiny monitor mounted on an upper corner of the waiting room played an episode of *Judge Judy* and several people stared at the monitor dully. Through the passing weeks, the people had become familiar. Some of them looked hopeful, some afraid, some tired, but mostly they seemed bored. Chemo was a sluggish rescuer, slow as molasses, like an army moving in to save a group of settlers from marauding Indians an inch at a time.

"Yes," he said. "I get upset. Like the time my mother set my father on fire."

"She did what?"

"Well, he was dead. What do you call that?"

"Cremation?"

"Yes, cremation. I thought Dad was gonna get a funeral and I was going to see him asleep with his eyes closed, and it was just a shock to me when my mother brought home his ashes."

"She didn't ask you?"

"No. She got it at a discount. I forgave her, of course. Just wasn't ready to see him turned to dust."

"I don't want to see my mother turned to dust, either! I'm not ready!" The other people looked up at me.

"Don't worry, you don't have to be. She'll be fine."

"I'm afraid I won't be able to follow her where she goes," I said. "Because I don't believe in God."

"Well, she drinks and swears, right? Maybe you can follow her to the other place."

"Phoenix!" I was annoyed now. "That is a terrible thing to say."

Phoenix's brow was smooth and untroubled. "I'm just giving you options, Little Squirrel."

An old woman with a gauzy dress and a headful of gray curls leaned over. "You have to pray," she said. She had a single hair caught in her argyle sweater, one that had been there the week before, and the week before that, and I had so longed to reach over and pull it out.

"I do pray," I said. "But I'm not sure I believe in God enough for him to hear me or to care, and I'm afraid maybe I'm just riling him up by asking him for a favor because he knows I don't totally believe."

"You have to pray for yourself first," the old lady explained. "Then once you are saved, you can pray for your mother."

"Little Squirrel, don't engage," Phoenix murmured, to no avail.

"Well then, how do I know when I'm saved?" I asked the lady.

"If you aren't sure, then you're not saved." The old lady went back to watching the TV.

I clutched my stomach and stared at the place in the wall where there should have been a window, but wasn't.

"Don't worry about that old bat," Phoenix whispered loudly. "In a parallel universe where the trees are still the same and dogs still lift their leg to pee but notions of right and wrong have been slightly altered, I would have punched her in the face."

The old lady glared at him.

"I think she heard you," I said.

Phoenix offered her a shy smile and she hardened her glare.

He turned back to me. "One time my dad said something in too loud of a whisper, and my mother cut him right across the snout with a straight razor. He had the scar for the rest of his life."

∽

I pulled the books from my locker and closed it as I finished talking, putting the lock on and spinning it hard. Dalton was still standing there. His shirt was buttoned wrong, making a bump in the cloth. His jeans were faded at the knees. His eyes watered.

"Look," he said. "Come on."

"I'm sorry," I said again.

"I know you're upset, you know, because of your mom. . . ."

"It's just not a good time for me." I had never broken up with someone before, and I could not find the words that would make him accept it and go away. So I kept trying.

"It's not you," I said. "You're great."

"Then why?"

How could I explain that the things he did were not enough and the things he said were not enough and if I hadn't been reaching for him I could have guarded her better?

"I told you. This is not a good time in my life."

"Well, we can deal with that together, can't we?" There was a certain heartbroken quality to his nervousness now, a pre-emptive grief. A vein beat in his long neck. His eyelashes fluttered.

"I have to go," I said.

"Wait."

I turned and walked away quickly.

"Willow!" he called behind me. "Willow!" I walked faster. I hated hearing that high tone in his voice, the one that meant all is lost. We had plans. We had rescued pets and engaged in deep conversations. We had solved the world. We had listened to Tom Waits in the backs of broken cars. We had grown up together. We were meant for each other. He was precious to me, vital, and somehow this all meant that, to save my mother, I had to give him up.

∽

The years had been good to Ms. Jordane. She had gotten a job as a counselor in my high school, right down the road from my old elementary school where she had once been a gym coach. She had a bigger office, with bone-colored walls, matching felted wing chairs, and a butcher-block desk. Her hair was cut into a near pixie, and parted on the side. She had a wedding ring on her finger. The cheerful, tomboyish gym teacher of my elementary school years was long gone.

She was now called Mrs. Spencer. Somewhere young, bouncy, happy, free Ms. Jordane lay dead, a clipboard in her hands and a whistle around her throat, and this new creature, less human, less real, and therefore far less comforting, had taken her place. I slumped in one of the wing chairs, my hands knitted together. I had somehow kept my failing grades from my mother, but my teachers were apparently rat finks and had kicked the problem upstairs. If I could go back in time to the younger version of the woman before me, who was thirty pounds heavier, and filled with a boy's heartiness, she would have found me crying on the playground, asked what was wrong, got me in a headlock that steadied my place in the world, then told me everything was going to be okay as she jogged back toward the bleachers, her whistle bouncing against her chest. But this new Mrs. Spencer was here to gather information and check off boxes.

I was not inclined to speak, but if I did I would have said: *This is what life does to you. It takes you any way it can. Sometimes it hits you with a truck. Sometimes it promotes you, but always, life is there to take away the parts that are just you and replace them with something common to a crowd.* But I just crossed my arms and thought about my mother, wondering what she was ringing up, wondering if she felt dizzy or if her wig was on straight.

"You've been skipping class." Mrs. Spencer looked down at her notes. "And your grades have really slipped. Your teachers are concerned about you."

I wondered if she remembered me from gym class. I wondered if she ever ran a fingertip along her face and felt the stump of the single hair growing back and thought, for just a moment, of letting it live. I wondered if she was ever walking through the parking lot, briefcase in hand, when a stray Frisbee flew over her head and if she forgot herself and rose in the air to catch it.

"Well?" she said.

"Well, what?"

"What do you have to say about that?"

"My grades aren't that bad." My voice was sullen, defensive.

"Is anything going on . . . in school? At home?"

She'd like that. She'd like to hear the story of sick Polly. It would connect the dots so cleanly and evenly. Sick mother equals sad daughter and Mrs. Spencer could ledger out the problem mathematically and solve it with some kind of structured empathy she'd learned in a book. I looked out her window. The promotion had earned her a piece of empty sky with an old cloud hanging there as though it were in the contract.

"Willow?"

"I think I'm pregnant." I watched her eyes open wide, her mouth fall. She hadn't expected this and she made a noticeable effort to smooth over her reaction. Her shoulders straightened.

She tapped her pen, leaving marks across a piece of paper that had my name at the top.

"Why do you . . . Are you sure?"

"Pretty sure, yeah." I folded my arms and gazed at her bookcase, which was full of titles about family systems and communications and accelerated learning.

"Who is the boy that you . . . the father?" she asked, clearly flustered.

I sighed, shifting in my chair, glanced out the window one more time. "I'm not sure. I mean, it could have been a lot of guys."

Her eyes widened again before her learning found her and shored her up. "Everything will be fine. We'll work this out together. Does your mother know?"

I shook my head.

❧

I knew Polly was going to be angry about the bad grades and I was right. I had rushed in the door to confess preemptively before Mrs. Spencer got on the horn. I had convinced the counselor that calling, rather than holding a conference, would be the best course of action. Polly would never have forgiven me if she had not only been dragged back onto the school grounds, but in such a diminished capacity, trembly hands and an ill-fitting wig, without her fire or her falcon but with a Bear inside her.

Polly had made herself a cup of Anger Tea, now that Anger

Margaritas didn't sit well in her stomach. Her Walgreens uniform was off but she had not switched her wig to the scarf she used when she wasn't working. I looked at the wig and then away.

"You're not to be moping around wallowing in self-pity and letting your grades go to hell, Willow. You are not allowed to do that."

"I'm sorry, Mom," I said. "I just didn't feel like studying."

"And I don't feel like putting on a damn Walgreens smock and selling five-dollar wine to a drunk first thing in the morning. Why don't I just quit? Why don't we both just quit together and sit in the yard all day and be dumb and poor?"

"Sorry," I said miserably.

"And now, apparently, fancy Ms. Master's Degree is on the case. Did you tell her you can't keep up your grades because your poor old mother has one foot in the grave so that she'd feel sorry for you? And does she feel sorry for me now?"

"No."

The whole idea of Mrs. Spencer's pity seemed to outrage her. She took a sip of her tea, her eyebrows going up. "You didn't tell her about the Bear?"

"I knew that would make you mad."

The phone rang. "That's probably her," I said.

Polly took another sip of tea and set it down determinedly. "I don't need any more problems."

"I know."

She went to answer the phone and I retreated to the living room and then moved in again to listen in the doorway.

"Yes, yes," Polly was saying. "I agree, it is not like Willow at all to let her grades slip and she has just got a talking to, and I can assure you . . . what circumstances?"

A steep pause, the silence a hiker makes while dropping from a cliff of medium height. "What?" Polly turned, saw me standing there, and shot me a look. "I see," she said into the phone. "Doesn't know who the father is. Ms. Jordane, or Spencer, or whatever you call yourself now, I can assure you that my daughter was pulling your leg. Have you looked at her? Does she seem like the type that would hop in the sack with multiple suitors? She was seeing some neighbor boy and I doubt he'd know where to put anything if you drew him a picture. Yes, maybe you did need to honor her truth but that was not *the* truth. Joke's on you. Yes, I agree it's not funny, but she really has been under considerable stress lately. Family problems. No, I don't want to discuss it with you. It's personal. Do you know what personal means? I peed a little last time I coughed, will that do as personal information for now? Yes, I will have a talk with her about lying. And I promise you her grades will improve from this day forward." The old authority was back in her voice. Her back had straightened. She said good-bye and put the receiver down. Suddenly she was old again. Sick. She sighed heavily and made her way slowly to the kitchen table, where she slumped down into a chair.

"Why in the hell did you tell that woman you were pregnant?" she demanded.

"I knew you'd get mad at me if I told her you were sick."

"How about telling her you're depressed? That's popular these days."

"I was trying to make you laugh."

"Laugh?" she said. "Laugh?"

"Yes."

"Willow . . ." she began, and stopped, her voice trailing off. And then, to my astonishment, she did start to laugh. It was a ragged, thin laugh—her old cigarette habit and the Bear had pawed it back and forth—but it came out in waves, growing. Her shoulders shook. Her eyes watered. The laugh seemed to take over her body, pouring out of it, a statement against wigs and chemicals. "I mean, my God, Willow, you don't know who the father is? Who would say that? You are just too much, Willow, you are just so wicked. . . . If Shel, if Shel could be here . . ." The laughter changed, strangled on itself, and tears poured down her face. Her body shook and I could not tell what was happening, if I should laugh along or embrace her. That was the problem, I did not know what to do, but she seemed lost in some moment, so I tore off a paper towel and handed it to her and glided from the room, her sobbing laughter following me.

Three

Summertime. School was out. Dalton stubbornly kept showing up to cut Polly's grass, moving the mower back and forth, careful around the pampas grass, as I watched out the window but would not come outside.

I wouldn't see him. I couldn't.

Polly had been in chemotherapy for months. And now we sat in the doctor's office. It was the same doctor as before, with the same expression and the same family portrait on his desk. Nothing had changed. "Willow?" said the doctor. "Did you understand what I just said?"

"The chemotherapy is not working," I repeated in a flat voice.

Polly sat next to me, a scarf over her head, her purse in her lap. She had reached over to take my hand and I had closed two of my fingers around hers but not the others. Enough to comfort but not to surrender. This news would not leave us clutching each other. It did not deserve such a gesture. Time passed. A few seconds, then more. Time kept passing and passing no matter what we did. It had slid inside my training bra and made my breasts grow. It had killed the eggplant crop and given birth to the peppers. It was, at this very moment, under my mother's scarf, pulling up hairs like garden weeds. Time was worse than the Bear. At least the Bear forgets to kill things sometimes.

"So," the doctor said, "about the operation . . ."

"Don't like the thought of it," Polly murmured.

"You'll be in very good hands. You've got one of the best surgeons in Texas."

"That's not a lot of praise. Texas is a pretty dumb state."

My stomach held all the pain from my body. My hands were numb, my arms and face. Inhaling hurt, so I breathed shallow.

"So," Polly said, "no more chemotherapy?"

He shook his head. "No. No more."

"Well, goody. Because that stuff was awful and wasn't doing a damn thing anyway." I could tell she was trying to will the strength back in her voice, put the falcon on her shoulder again, be the hero, be the rock. A tear slid down my face out of nowhere and I quickly wiped it away.

"Go home and rest," said the doctor. "Get ready for the operation."

"And what if the operation doesn't work?" asked Polly.

He spread his hands. "Then our choices are more limited."

"I don't like that doctor," I said as I led my mother to the waiting room. "Always so calm about everything."

"What do you expect him to do?" Polly asked. "Cry and beat his fists on the wall and scream 'All is lost?'"

Phoenix stood up as we entered the waiting room, a question on his face and the answer flying back at him from ours.

"Oh," he said.

"We're operating," Polly said. "Gonna cut the Bear right out of me."

"Good," said Phoenix, nodding. "Carpet bomb his ass."

"No, we already tried to carpet bomb his ass. It didn't work."

"Right," he said, nodding. "Right, right." He seemed to be trying to gauge the hope involved in this procedure, looking from my mother's eyes to mine. We walked out into the summer light, the air warm and the clouds fluffy. My mother walked briskly, as though to prove her vitality. I slouched along, hands in my pockets.

Gravity began going nuts from the car when he saw Phoenix.

"Can't you shut that stupid dog up?" I barked.

"Pay no mind to her," Polly told Phoenix. "She's mad because our doctor's not a big fluffy rabbit."

Phoenix let Gravity lick him until the creature sedated himself, then put on his lavender-scented muzzle so he wouldn't sniff the Bear on my mother, and whine, and we all piled into the car. "This has been the worst day ever," I said, tears brimming.

"Now come on," Polly turned to say to me. "The operation might work and then everything will be fine."

"Sure it will," Phoenix murmured. "Everything will be perfectly perfect."

"Then why didn't the doctor give us more hope?" I demanded. "He just stared with his arms folded like it didn't matter to him either way."

"The doctor's not the one to decide whether I live or die," Polly said. "That's up to Jesus. Drive, boy."

We moved into the traffic and Phoenix put on the radio.

"Don't get on the freeway," Polly ordered. "Take the farm road."

The road was narrow and shadowed by loblolly pines that grew wild by the sides of the fences. The ditches were filled with flowering thistle. The wind moved through the elderberry bushes, setting free their blooms and splashing them across the windshield.

"Floor it," Polly said.

"Really, Miss Polly?"

She jerked an index finger forward in a silent command, Phoenix put his foot on the gas, and Gravity pressed back against me as we shot down the road, the wind whistling through the open windows and the antenna swaying as though to the beat of a song. Phoenix jammed his finger on a button and Tchaikovsky filled the car, moving through our clothes and our ears and out the windows. Angry Tchaikovsky, raging at the sky, moved into my body where my stomach was still clenched and filled it with a quivering bass.

I could not let her go. I could not be me without her.

There was no me. There was no me.

The wind whipped my hair, but could do nothing with bald Phoenix, and all it could do to my mother was rustle her scarf.

∾

To Polly's great annoyance, I told Lisa.

"Wonderful," Polly said. "Here they all come." She was holding her crossword puzzle pen like a cigarette and sipping at a margarita now that the smell of it no longer made her nauseous.

"You can't just keep secrets from your children," I said. "It's not right."

"They don't need to come rushing down to Texas. I feel pretty good, all things considered."

"The doctor said you were gonna feel better when you stopped chemotherapy. That doesn't mean anything."

Lisa made a big fuss over Polly and tried to keep her from doing any of her housework. She also brought over her concoctions and teas and potions and ointments that she tried to foist upon our mother. "Oh, come on," Polly said. "I'm not even gonna try that stuff. When chemicals can't hurt that Bear, you think he's gonna be scared of some bee balm and otter tongue?"

"There's no otter tongue in these products," Lisa said testily. "All natural ingredients, no paraffin, no fillers."

"If you'll stop talking, I will choke it down," Polly said, rolling her eyes over to give me an aggrieved glare. Tom was his usual overly friendly self, and Otto was a teenager now, still asthmatic but more sullen and removed.

"I know your mother isn't in the Church of Satan," he told me when we were alone. "That was a lie."

"You're right. I lied."

"It wasn't funny." Otto and I were outside in the front yard. Otto was showing me his remote-controlled plane. It came dangerously close to the azalea hedge in the front garden and then gained altitude.

"I thought it was pretty funny," I said.

"Lies are never funny. And they make Jesus very sad."

"Well, Jesus sounds easily depressed."

The plane moved over and buzzed the mailbox.

"See that?" said Otto. "See what I did?"

"Yes, I saw."

Otto glanced over to the neighbor's yard. "Do those terrible kids still live there?"

"Yes, but they've outgrown killing things on the driveway. They're in private school now."

"So, what's up with Grandma?" he asked.

I stiffened. It sounded so weird for him to call my mother "Grandma." Completely against the order of things. He hadn't done anything to deserve sneaking into the bloodline like that. Like a carnival ride he was too short for.

"The chemotherapy didn't work and so now they're gonna try an operation."

"My dad said an operation is risky at Grandma's age."

"What does your dad know?" I said crossly. I turned around and started walking toward the front door.

"Willow," Otto said. I turned around. He was still busy with his controls, following his airplane's travel. He didn't take his eyes off it when he said, "I'm sorry about when I told you Grandma was going to hell. I was twelve. I thought I knew everything."

Four

Tom had to fly Otto home for summer school, but Lisa stayed for the operation. We sat on either side of Phoenix in the waiting room. Dalton had mailed me a tiny glass angel (*To watch over your mother*, the note said), and though I had not thanked him for his gift, I now held it in my hand. Lisa had dark circles under her eyes. She hadn't slept. I knew this, because when I hadn't slept, I'd walked past her room and heard her weeping. She treated Phoenix with a warm affection that startled me. They exchanged memories of Polly: He reminded her of how Polly had sat him down one day long ago and taught him basic table manners.

"Spoon to the right of the knife," he said now. "I never forgot that. Mostly because she rapped my knuckles."

"She liked you," Lisa said. Her careful eyeliner was gone; her hair was uncombed.

"She gave me gloves for Christmas one time," Phoenix added. "When I grew up my hands got bigger and it got harder to put on the gloves, but I didn't want to give them up, because they were from her."

"Can we all pray?" Lisa asked.

"Of course," Phoenix said. "Let's pray to the universe."

Lisa suddenly rabbit-punched him in the ribs.

"Ow," said Phoenix. "That hurt. I remember when you used to punch me hard like that before you found Jesus."

"*Speaking of,*" Lisa said.

"Okay, sure," Phoenix said agreeably. "Let's pray to Jesus."

We held hands. Phoenix's hand was big and warm. Lisa's prayer started out strong and then weakened when she said the word "mother," declining from there into tears. Phoenix picked it up from there.

"And watch over us and be our friend and make sure everyone is all right. Thank you, Jesus," Phoenix said.

"Amen," we said.

And waited.

The nurses came and got us and let Lisa and me visit Polly before they wheeled her away into surgery. They had given her something that looked like a shower cap and a light-blue gown to wear. She seemed small on the bed. The anesthetic had taken effect and she was connected to a monitor that checked on her with beeps and lights and numbers. *Too much math,* she would have said if she were not in some twilight world where speech was not outright banned, but discouraged.

"Mom," I said, leaning over, "can you hear me?" I had fought my terror for days. The doctor had warned me that this was a major operation on an elderly person, describing it so clinically that I, for a moment, forgot he was talking about my mother, and now she was minutes from being wheeled away from me and perhaps not coming back. No one could give me odds I was happy with, and I could not stand to look directly at the heart monitor that was so calmly registering what was most precious in the world as though it were just another rhythm on a typical workday.

Her hand felt neutral, neither warm nor cold.

"Mom," I said.

Her eyelids fluttered.

"It's Willow. Lisa's here, too."

"I'm here, Mom." Lisa's voice broke.

"My girls," she mumbled. "And where's my boy? Where is Shel?"

Lisa and I exchanged glances. "He's outside," Lisa said.

A nurse came in with two orderlies. "It's time to take your mother to the O.R., honey," she said to me, so kindly that I burst into tears.

"You'll be fine, Mom," I assured her, feeling my lips tremble and trying to control them.

"Of course she will," said the nurse.

"I don't . . . ," Polly murmured.

They were fiddling with her monitors.

"Don't what?" I asked.

"She can't talk, honey," the nurse said.

". . . want to be alone," Polly finished.

"You're not alone!" I insisted.

"Honey, you're gonna have to get out of the way," the nurse said.

I whirled on the nurse. "She's not alone! Tell her she's not alone!"

"She can't hear you."

The nurse's calm voice enraged me.

"Yes, she can! What do you know?" Tears streaked my face.

"Yeah," said Lisa, her voice rough and angry and pre-Christian. "What do you know?"

My sister and I leaned down to Polly and spoke as one.

"*You are not alone!*"

✒

When the doctor came into the waiting room, his face was neutral as always, and it stayed that way as he told us that the operation had taken longer than they had anticipated, and—my heart stopped, Lisa gripped my hand—the Bear had been wounded but not chased away; the Bear was not to be chased away. It was very present and alive. Unbowed and growing.

"Oh no," Lisa whispered.

"I'm sorry," he said. Something flickered across his face. Something helpless and regretful, and that hurt me worse than all of his stoicism. It meant complete and utter defeat. It meant that he was small and could not control the world.

The recovery room was dark except for at the light from a small table lamp next to Polly's bed. Her roommate, a Latina woman, was asleep.

Polly looked cheerful and her hand was warm. I was not sure whether the doctor had been in to see her yet and I couldn't tell by the look on her face. The surgical cap was gone and her scarf was back on. "That's what I want to see when I wake up," she said. "My beautiful girls."

We said nothing. We were dazed. She was alive, but for how long?

She squeezed each of our hands. "See, I came through it just fine."

I took a breath. "Did you talk to the doctor?"

"Yes. But you know me. I don't put too much stock in what doctors say. They say the Bear got away from them when they were chasing it around my old bones with a knife. Maybe it ducked in some dark hallway, or behind a plant. That Bear is crafty. Got to hand it to the old varmint."

We wouldn't leave her. We slept in the hospital room in two chairs by her bed. I'd wake up in the middle of the night and find Lisa staring out the window, a disappointed look on her face, as though she had just questioned the actions of her chosen God. Then, I'd look at my mother, who slept peacefully. Clocks were alive, counting the seconds, always moving forward, undoing things, that slow pulling of the shoelace that would murder the bow. Time would take our mother away from us, tune her sleep down to an empty space.

Phoenix had slept in his car in the parking lot all night so Gravity would not feel alone in the universe. I imagined him leaning back on his ravaged seat, eyes closed, starlight coming in through the windshield, the dog in his arms, peaceful at last next to his master's heartbeat and the gentle slowness of his breathing, slowing down time and its craven gait. Gravity enjoyed a dog's belief that his master was with him now and therefore that meant he would be there forever. These arms holding him would never be stolen by the light of dawn.

Polly came home five days later, moving slowly but claiming to feel fine, just fine, and looking it, too. Margaritas tasted good and so did coffee. And the smells that had driven her from the kitchen—mustard, cinnamon, rosemary, plain milk—were tolerable again. The doctor had warned me that how she felt would not, for a time, be an indicator of how she *actually* was. Chemotherapy had sickened her, but the Bear, growing now in its absence, was remarkably companionable. Her apparent health was a lie, and yet it gave me hope as her eyes brightened, as the tiny scab of her IV wound blackened and fell off her arm, as her hands steadied. She could wring the sheets again, and started putting them on the clothesline instead of in the dryer. New growth of tiny hairs showed on her scalp when she took off her scarf. It seemed cruel to me, nature making her new like that as though dressing her up for an audience with the Reaper.

She finally made Lisa pack her bags. "Go on now, baby," she said. "You've got a man and a boy to take care of in St. Louis."

I didn't want her to go. I knew her now. The things that made us sisters were now so clear. But my mother was right. Lisa had another family waiting for her. We said our tearful good-byes at the airport.

"I really don't want to leave," Lisa confessed, sniffling.

"Ah, now you go on," Polly said. "You can't stay here forever."

Lisa reluctantly got on the plane, and my mother and I were alone again.

The two of us tackled the garden, now a mass of unharvested, rotting vegetables, old cucumbers, tomato vines collapsed on each other, tangled weeds, various blights, invasive grasses, and the manure of varmints that roved by night. We did the best we could, working side by side, Polly's vigor both real and, I suspected, supplemented by her need to show me comfort by way of stubborn vitality. *I'm not going anywhere, baby,* said the motion of her hands as she yanked out weeds by the roots and threw them into a pile.

I'd forgotten much of my garden knowledge during the time I'd been away in teenager land.

"No, dummy," Polly said, "that's mint," as I pulled the long green shoot from the ground.

How I loved the sound of that deprecating nickname, *dummy*. Dying mothers don't use that name. Dying mothers say *angel* and *sweetheart,* and so I pulled some more mint so she could punch me in the arm.

"Did a goat kick you in the head, girl? Or are you just stubborn? Leave that damn mint alone, I need it for my tea."

I could almost believe that the Bear had been a terrible dream and that all was well, until Elmer came home. Polly had left the sliding door to the backyard open to catch the night breeze as we watched old reruns of *Dr. Quinn, Medicine Woman*. Elmer crept in, scampered across the carpet, and ended up on the foot of Polly's recliner, sitting on his haunches between her slippered feet. Only one squirrel could be so tame and so fearless.

"Elmer, my boy!" She held out her hand to the creature. "Come here, my sweet baby."

"Get out of here, Elmer!" I screamed. "Get out, get out!" I was filled with a shaking rage at the sight of him. I wanted to throw him across the room.

Elmer trembled and stared but held his ground.

"What on earth is the matter with you, girl?" Polly asked in wonderment.

"Why is he here?" I demanded. "Why is he back now?" I hated him for what it meant for a wild creature to return home to the mother who raised him. I was not much on religion, and superstition was the only form of worship available to me.

Elmer moved up into Polly's lap and she stroked the center of his tiny head. "There, there, Elmer," she soothed. "Don't let the crazy girl scare you."

I stormed to my room and slammed the door. I hated nature, I hated the ways of the world, I hated time and God—if God were of a sufficient heft and mass to feel my hatred. I needed a miracle and so I did the only thing left to me. I went to my desk, carefully tore a piece of paper from a spiral binder, and began a note:

> *Dear Garland,*
>
> *It's Willow again. I know who you are. I know you sent my mother roses. I'm writing to tell you that my mother is very ill. The doctors have given up. Maybe you know of some way to help. If you do, please answer.*
>
> *Yours sincerely,*
>
> *Willow Havens*

Phoenix could not pass up the opportunity to be essential, and so he had taken it upon himself to shop for groceries, clean the gutters, fix the A/C, and at least attempt to cart my mother around wherever she needed to go. Dalton still showed up, still mowed while looking in my direction, there behind the window. Mr. Chant still came by, scones in hand, but was cheated out of the hard work by his bad back. He could only glare with envy as Phoenix hammered something back into place up on the roof.

"That weird Calhoun boy is underfoot constantly, thanks to you," Polly complained.

"Why do you keep calling him a boy? He's a man."

"You kids all stay kids to me."

"He loves us, Mom."

"Well, he needs to spend more time at his home and less at ours."

I was determined, for the most part, to live in the world of the now, where Polly was fine and the garden was tended and the familiar squirrel who now wandered the perimeter un-zapped was just another squirrel. I was in my room one day, brooding, when I heard three sharp raps on my door.

"What?" I said sullenly.

"Hey, Gloomy," called Polly's muffled voice. "Letter for you."

An envelope appeared under the door. I jumped up from my bed and snatched up the envelope. Across the front was my own name in a scrawl of a black felt pen. No return address. I tore

open the envelope and out fell two things: a newspaper clipping and a note that read:

> *I can help your mother*
> *337-555-4592*
>
> *Junior Quade*

Five

$\mathcal{P}$olly went back to her old job at Walgreens, so she was at work while Phoenix and I studied the newspaper clipping from the *Bethel Sun* in the kitchen. The news story was entitled:

SMALL TOWN HEALER THE SUBJECT
OF SCORN AND ADORATION

In the photo, a small, wiry man with slicked-back hair stood holding a Bible in his left hand and resting his right hand on the head of a man on his knees. Even in black-and-white, the kinetic energy of the photo shot through me like a bolt of lightning.

The caption read: *Junior Quade heals Darvin Jones of heart congestion and diverticulitis.*

"Those are biggies," Phoenix remarked.

"Says he's also healed people from gout, asthma, blindness,

pneumonia, and demons," I said. "And he grew a man's foot back."

"Allegedly," Phoenix said.

"And he raised someone up from the dead . . ." Now I read word for word: ". . . 'but detractors at the scene of the tractor accident say the man was merely stunned.' What do you think, Phoenix?"

"Well, I don't know, Little Squirrel. There are people who say the placebo effect is so great that the body is tricked into mounting its own defense. And there are people who say that miracles are possible. And then there are people who say that it's all a bunch of rat shit, unfortunately. But then again, this may be a sign from the universe that in some way might lead to your mother's recovery. Who knows?"

"Do you think Junior Quade is Garland's son?" I asked. "Different last name."

"Maybe," he said. "You should call him."

"You're right."

"Can I listen on the other phone?"

"No. You'll just make me nervous."

Phoenix looked disappointed but retreated to the living room with Gravity as I went to the wall phone and referred to the letter for Junior Quade's number. My hands trembled as I punched the buttons. I heard ringing.

"It's ringing!" I shouted into the den.

"That's encouraging!" Phoenix shouted back.

It rang and rang. I waited patiently for ten rings and then gave up. Just as I was replacing the receiver I heard a click and a man's voice.

"Hay-low?"

"Hello?" I said.

"Who's thaar?" The southern accent was so thick I could barely understand it.

"Willow," I said. "Willow Havens."

A long pause. "Willow, are you a buh-lee-var?"

"A . . . a believer? In what?" I stammered, confused.

"In the Bible. In the Lord and the Lord's Son, Jesus the Christ." His voice was rapid fire. "Because I must tell you, I sense disbelief, and if that be true, I can't help you none with your poor ma."

"I believe in certain—"

"Liar!"

Another voice came on the line: "Don't call Little Squirrel a liar! She's been through a lot!"

"Who the Hay-ull is that?" Junior Quade demanded.

"Phoenix," I said, "get off the phone."

"Listen, little girl," Junior Quade said, "I cain't help them who don't believe. So work on your belief. That's my advice."

The receiver clicked and we heard a dial tone. "Phoenix!" I shouted, hanging up the phone. "You scared him off!"

"I'm sorry, LS," Phoenix said as he and Gravity came into the kitchen. "I was just trying to protect you."

"Well, now what am I gonna do?"

"Just forget him," Phoenix said. "He sounds like some kind of nut."

"But what if he actually can heal people and he could have healed my mother?" I said. "I've got to try."

"Try, how?"

"Just like he said. I'm going to work on my belief."

～

It turned out that for a country boy, Junior Quade had quite a Web presence. He had his own site full of testimonials and videos, as well as a YouTube channel filled with healings and several press conferences and footage of tent revivals in which he appeared with a snake around his neck. I saw people go up to him in wheelchairs and then he'd grab their foreheads and pray and they'd get up and walk. Old people with canes would throw them away and young children with oxygen masks would rip them off to ecstatic cheers.

One thing was for certain—Junior Quade put on a great show. I was on the fence as to whether the show was real or not. A skeptic's Web site had done a special report on Junior Quade and asserted that no independent study existed to confirm that he had ever healed anyone. And yet, could all those fervent people giving their testimony be lying or mistaken? One man had even posted his kidney scans, before and after. After looked pretty good, I had to say.

Of course, I told Polly none of this. That night after she had gone to bed, I sneaked into the kitchen and rang Junior Quade again.

"Hay-low?"

I spoke quickly, before he could hang up. "While it's true I'm not a believer, at least not totally, my mother, Polly—Pauline— Havens, is a devout Christian. And maybe when I witness the miracle of her healing, I will also become a devout Christian, so there's that."

A long pause. "If your mama was such a God-fearing woman, you'd have thought she wouldn't have done what she done to my daddy all those years ago. But that ain't for me to judge, I reckon."

"Are you Garland's son?" I asked.

"Garland's son? Hay-ull no. That man is my worst enemy in the world. Next worst enemy would have to be your ma."

"Then why do you want to help her?"

"Because Garland came over and asked me hisself, and Jesus has called me to put aside my earthly prejudices and do his will. And if this is his will, then *so be it*. If you weren't such a heathen, you might understand."

My mind was racing with so much information to absorb.

"What did Garland and my mother do?"

"Well, that ain't for me to tell you. That's between you and your Jezebel ma."

"Jezebel?" I said, prepared to get my hackles up, but I calmed myself. "Can you come to Texas?"

"Hay-ull, no. You got to come down here to Bethel to receive the blessing. What, you think the springwater from that place in France traipses over to you, too? No, you got to come to the miracle. The miracle ain't gonna come to you."

"My mother doesn't ever want to come to Bethel again, that's the problem."

"Way-ull, she caused a lot of trouble down here for sure. And I ain't 'speshly happy to see her. But that's the only way it's gonna work so you and me ain't got no choice."

"Can you guarantee that my mother—"

"Okay, I'm insulted as Hay-ull now. You can't ask for a guarantee like I'm a lawn mower repairman. I can't tell you that your ma's gonna start up in three or four pulls. Might take fifteen. Or maybe the engine's busted for good. Some things God wills and some things he does not. I'm gonna hang up now."

"No! No! Don't hang up!" I shouted. "We're coming! I'll get her there somehow. What's your address?"

"My address is 1405 You Got to Be Kidding. I am Junior Quade. Ever-body in town knows exactly who I am and where I am at any given moment. Just pull up and ask the first person. Now be there at one P.M. next week, on Friday. I'll wait for you at the church."

"But—"

Dial tone.

I went to bed with great resolve that night. I was going to find the miracle needed to heal my mother, and all I had to do was get her to return to a town she swore she'd never set foot in again and let a preacher who was likely crazy as a bedbug lay his hands upon her.

"Absolutely not," Polly said. "Of all the dumb ideas you've ever had, this is absolutely the dumbest." She was carving the eyes out of red potatoes, her hands so quick and efficient you would have thought she was in the prime of health.

"But, Mom," I pleaded, "it's our only hope."

"Stop it," she said. "You are giving me a headache. Now go outside and play. Make a friend."

"I don't play!" I said. "I am sixteen years old! And I don't have time for friends. I am too busy trying to *save my mother's life*!"

"Oh, Willow," she sighed. "How 'bout starting with the potatoes, if you want to help?"

Next I enlisted Lisa, who was surprisingly open to the trip, especially after I mentioned that Junior Quade was a fervent Jesus Fan and Man of God. Lisa then got on the horn with Polly and made her case for half an hour as Polly rolled her eyes and pointed her finger at me and said mean, silent things with her lips.

"Don't ever sic Lisa on me again," Polly said when she finally got off the phone. "That is playing dirty and you know it."

"You owe this to me," I said.

"I don't owe you crap, kid. My life is mine."

"No, it isn't! It's mine, too! And it's not just your decision!"

I kept up the nagging, the crying, the yelling. I enlisted the ever-willing Phoenix, who made a calm and deferential argument until Polly literally chased him out of the yard.

"See?" she replied when she came back, triumphant and barely breathing, into the house. "Could I have chased that idiot around if I were at death's door?"

But I had quickly seized upon what I perceived as a last chance against the Bear that was silently colonizing my mother room by room, until he owned the whole mansion of her, the foundation, and the garden.

I didn't have much time.

I called her boss at Walgreens. I called the ministers at church. I called Mrs. Burrell, who came over and rang our doorbell seven times while Polly hid in the back bedroom. She yelled at me, she threatened me, but I did not relent. This was war and I was going to win. I had to win.

❦

"What are you doing?" Polly asked. It was Saturday now. I had six days to get her to Bethel, and Phoenix, my constant ally, had mysteriously left town.

"I'll be back in a couple of days, LS," he'd said. "Got some business. No worries."

We were in early August now, the arc of summer steepening, the grass outside stiff and dry. I had my backpack on. Inside my backpack were two changes of clothing, five cans of Spam, my flip-flops, underwear, two washcloths, a toothbrush, a bar of soap, and a roll of toilet paper.

She was sitting at the table, sipping her coffee. The crossword puzzle was nearly done. She still had on her pink robe, and her pink scarf matched it. Her eyes were very green this morning. The light dancing.

"I'm running away," I said.

"Don't be ridiculous."

"I'm not gonna stay here and watch you die. You can't make me do it."

"You're bluffing."

"You'll see. You think this is a joke but it's not. I asked you for one thing, one thing, and you won't do it for me!"

She shook her head. "Come on, baby." Her voice gentle now. "I know this is a terrible time for you, and you don't have your brother or your sister around. And for some reason, you ran off that Dalton boy. I know it's hard, but we have to accept that there's nothing left to be done. And enjoy each moment. Now, please, don't give me trouble."

"You're giving *me* trouble," I shot back. I went into the garage. I punched the door opener and as the door rose and re-vealed a blue sky clear of clouds, I wheeled my bicycle out into the driveway.

"Willow," Polly said behind me, "that's enough. You get back here." There was the old authority in her voice, a tone that would have stopped me in my tracks a year ago. But a lot can change in a year.

I got on the bike and began to pedal.

"Willow," she said. She began to walk very fast, trying to catch up to me. I pedaled harder and she broke into a run, in her robe and her pink scarf and slippers for the whole neighborhood to see, running with all her strength, her breath coming out in gasps, but I pumped the pedals harder and harder until I could not hear her breathing anymore. Just before I turned the corner, I heard her call my name, this time, exhausted, breathless, plain-tive: *Willow.*

I didn't know where to go, so I took the path most obvious, down the street, to the right and to the right again, then three houses on the left, where Dalton lived. Once I arrived, I didn't know what to do there, so I laid my bicycle down in the grass and sat on the curb by the mailbox. Weeds flowered and bloomed in the cracks on the empty driveway.

An hour passed. I hugged my knees, exhausted and without a plan. Pete's old Chevrolet pulled up, and Pete and a woman with long, brassy red hair and a sundress got out.

"Hey," he called to me, "what you doing, girl?"

"Nothing."

"Okay," he said agreeably. "Suit yourself." He jerked a thumb toward the woman. "That's Aubrey. She's new."

The woman waved. They went into the house and I reached over and gave the back wheel of my bicycle a spin, watching it move around and around. Before it slowed to a stop, I heard the front door open behind me. Footsteps came toward me. Dalton sat down next to me. Grease was streaked on his jeans. He smelled sweaty, with an undertone of the lime deodorant he favored. The leather bracelet I'd given him still hung on his wrist. His face was sunburned. He needed a haircut.

"Hi," he said. His voice was husky and uncertain.

"Hi."

He looked out into the neighbor's yard across the street.

"A preacher in Louisiana thinks he can save her," I said. "But she won't go."

"It would be worth a try," he said at last.

"She's stubborn."

From behind the fence, one of the poodles barked, a high yipping sound, then was quiet.

"What did I do wrong?" Dalton asked. "Just tell me what it was and I'll fix it."

I hugged my knees. "You didn't do anything. I just can't be with you right now. I have to think about her."

"I can help you think of her."

"No, you can't. No one can."

He shifted, touched my arm.

"I'll be here," he said.

I jerked my arm away. "Don't say that, because I know what you mean. You mean after she's dead, you'll be here."

I got to my feet and retrieved my bike. He looked up at me.

"I don't know what to say to you. Everything I say is wrong. I love you, Willow." He dropped his head and began to cry into the crook of his arm, and I wanted to let go of my bike and run to him, embrace him and tell him I loved him, too, but I thought parts of me would stick to him. Parts I needed for my mother. I began to cry, too, as I pedaled away.

I had nowhere to go and so I went back home. Defeated. There was nothing I could really hold against her. Nothing I could use to threaten her. She knew I wouldn't run away. Knew I couldn't leave her.

The house was empty and quiet. I called her name and no one answered. I checked her room and then went into the backyard, where I found her inspecting the garden and, astonishingly, smoking.

"Mom!" I said, shocked at the cigarette in her hand.

She turned and took a puff. "There was one left in the pack. Wasn't going to let it go to waste. After all, what harm would it do if this crazy preacher is going to heal me?" She took another puff. "And honestly, what harm would it do if he doesn't?"

IV.

No Man's Land

One

Of course I did not tell Polly everything I knew about Junior Quade, or about Garland's involvement with this scheme. Polly was holding on to the idea of the trip by a thread, and I knew she was only going for me. And if I entertained strange and ridiculous thoughts—that she would be healed and reunited with Garland, the man she loved—I kept them to myself. I was dying of curiosity about what exactly my mother and Garland had done to alienate Junior Quade, and possibly the whole town, but the solving of this mystery was second only to the saving of my mother's life.

Phoenix, who had returned to town with no explanation, was positive he was going with us.

"No way," Polly told me. "The weird boy and the mutt will be staying in Texas."

"But, Mom, he could take care of us!"

"He couldn't take care of a bird if you gave him a cage and a sack of bread crumbs. I'm not going to have him aggravating me on possibly my last car trip ever."

"He's been so good to us, Mom. How could you be so mean?"

"We'll be fine, just the two of us," she said. "Don't you worry about a thing."

Phoenix was beside himself when I told him. "But we won't be any trouble! I won't even say anything, not a thing."

"It's no use, Phoenix. I'm afraid if I push it, she'll back out of the trip altogether."

"I understand," he said sadly. "Although I don't really."

Slowly, Polly began to warm to the idea of the trip. She pulled out a bunch of old maps from the back of her closet and spread them on the kitchen table, her magnifying lens at the ready. "We'll take the 190 to Jasper, then the 96 North and pick up the 6 on into Natchitoches and then take the 117 down to Leesville," she decided. "I know a couple in Leesville. Joe and Estelle. Friends of the Captain's and mine for many years. Joe is a carpenter and a darn good one. He can make a raft for us in a day or two."

"Raft?" I said.

"Bethel is so remote, way back in the swamps. You can only get to it by river," she said, which was such a blatant lie I had to call her out on it, as I had spent many nights studying Bethel on the Internet.

"Mom, there is a road that runs right into Bethel."

She shot me a look. "Oh, I guess you've been looking on your fancy Internet and you know everything now."

Her tone foretold trouble. I immediately regretted challenging her. "I might have been mistaken about the road," I lied. "We can go by raft."

"Good. Because I want to take one last trip down the Whiskey Chitto River. My father and I used to float that river, way back when I was the brat and not the parent. Some of the happiest days of my life were spent there. I know it like the back of my hand."

"Fine," I said quickly. "Fine, fine, fine."

"Well then, that settles it. Your Aunt Rhea lives on the river. We'll land practically in her backyard in Bethel. I'll call her and tell her to expect us. And I guess I'll tell her I've got the Bear so she won't faint when she sees me. But I'm not gonna give her any more information about the river or this preacher or our plans and you better not, either. That woman's got a mouth as big as Texas."

"But why do we need to go to Natchitoches first?" I asked. "It's totally out of the way." I pointed at the map. "We could just take I-10 East—"

Polly slapped my hand lightly. "Whose trip is this?"

"Yours."

"And who's going along with it just because of her crazy daughter?"

"You are."

"Then don't ask so many damn questions. Natchitoches happens to be a town that holds some dear memories."

"And I'm guessing you aren't going to tell me why."

"Why start now? Now hush, and let me concentrate."

So I kept quiet as Polly continued. "So we're supposed to be at this nutcase preacher's doorstep next Friday at one? That doesn't give us much time. We'll have to leave on Monday. We'll put the raft in at Leesville and then ride the Whiskey Chitto River down

to Bethel. Should be a two-day trip, maybe three. We'll need supplies and provisions. Maybe I'll put a hook in the water while
we're at it." She was thinking, her mind racing a million miles an
hour. "Let's see, we'll need a kerosene lantern. And of course I'm
gonna bring my shotgun. Who knows what kind of varmints, animal and otherwise, are traipsing the banks of that river?"

I watched her as she again traced the route with her finger
on the map, noticing that her nails had been filed and polished
and gleamed her familiar fire-engine red. I caught a glimpse of
her short, new hair stubble in the gap of her scarf and wondered if I could dare to imagine Polly's natural hair restored
and dyed to be the flame color it once was, her body filling out,
the lines in her face that had appeared in the last few months
disappearing again. And no, I would never breathe a word
about Junior Quade and Garland, not until after Polly had received the blessing and the Bear had been pushed onward, mi-
grating to other organs in lesser people.

I heard her on the phone talking to Aunt Rhea.

"Yes, we're coming to see you. No particular reason," she
said. "It's just high time. Now, Devil Cat, I've got something to
tell you. I don't want you to go to pieces now . . ."

I didn't want to hear about the Bear, so I went to my room.

Our suitcases and knapsacks and fishing poles were stacked in
the driveway as Polly and I waited in the blossoming warmth of
an August morning. Phoenix was bent under the hood.

"I don't believe this," Polly mumbled under her breath. "That old piece of crap."

We had been loaded up and all ready for our trip, strapped in our seats, the morning paper canceled, and a local boy signed up to get our mail for us for a small cash payment, when Polly turned the key in the ignition and the car responded with a loud clatter and then silence. My heart sank. The entire time we'd prepared for our trip, I'd been afraid that she'd pull out at the last minute. And now this.

Phoenix pulled his head out from under the hood. "Well," he said, with the posture of a messenger about to beg not to be killed, "your timing belt has cratered."

"What does that mean?" she asked.

"You need a new one."

"And how much is that going to cost?" Polly sounded agitated. A grasshopper skated between Phoenix and us, bearing a quick, indifferent buzz from the universe.

"Several hundred dollars."

"Well, we don't have several hundred dollars!" Polly cried.

I sat down in the grass and put my head in my hands. "This can't be happening."

From the darkness made by the protective shadows of my folded arms, I heard Phoenix's tentative suggestion.

"I could drive you."

I raised my head.

"No, Phoenix, that won't be necessary," Polly said quickly.

"It's no trouble."

I leapt to my feet. "Mom, let him drive us! We're all ready to go!"

"The plan," Polly said evenly, "was for you and me to go down the river together on a raft . . . ," she glanced at Phoenix, "alone. Not with Phoenix and his damn dog."

"I'll tell you what," Phoenix offered. "I'll go as far as Leesville and help get you set up with the raft. Then you just call me from Bethel when you're ready to come home. After you're good as new. I'll come get you. Perfectly perfect."

"That sounds like a great idea, Mom!" I said encouragingly.

Her eyebrows were thinking it over. Twitching, rising, falling, pausing, debating, stalling, bargaining, as Phoenix rocked gently back and forth, a hopeful metronome. Finally Polly's eyebrows smoothed in grudging acceptance.

She sighed heavily. "I suppose."

"Great!" Phoenix cried. "Let's go!"

She looked over at her suitcase and then up at him. "Don't you need to go home and pack?"

"No worries," he said. He was already picking up our suitcases and heading toward his car. "I'll get a toothbrush on the road." He took me aside just before we left and whispered, "I forgot the muzzle with the lavender oil." He handed me a package of lamb treats. "Whenever Gravity looks like he's about to sniff your mother, shove one of these down his craw."

I held Gravity in my lap. Phoenix's entire car smelled of soap, in fact, and some kind of car deodorizer redolent of pine. And, miraculously, he had bought new seat belts that Gravity had only just started to chew and were still functional.

Phoenix had Polly's favorite classical music on low and was driving very carefully. I knew how he felt. Getting Polly in this car, on this trip, seemed equivalent to finding the face of Jesus in the random pattern of an Etch A Sketch. One shake and it could be gone. We rode mostly in silence past the familiar streets of our town, then onto the stretch of freeway, where the loblolly pines that lined the roads passed in a blur. It was near noon when we hit the I-45 exchange. A right-hand turn would take us to the dark waters of Galveston. A left turn would take us to Dallas, then Canada, then the North Pole. We went straight, toward Louisiana.

As the afternoon wore on, the highway narrowed into a comfortable country road.

"Watch out for the fuzz," Polly said. "I hear they're bad around here. Might stop and frisk you and throw you in jail for looking at them funny, much less speeding."

"I've got cruise control on, Miss Polly," Phoenix said cheerfully. "I promise you not a single fuzz will bother us."

In a way I wanted us to get to Louisiana and the cure as soon as possible; but I also wanted this agreeable present tense to go on forever: fields of cows on our right, crops of corn on our left, ditches full of yellow flowers, the heat of Gravity on my lap, Phoenix's calm bald head and steady driving, Polly's music and Polly herself. We would not need Louisiana, or miracles, or Junior Quade if we could just ride perpetually in this moment, with no more living or dying or growing up to do. I closed my eyes and let the sun warm my face. We were in the boonies now, tire shacks, rusting farm equipment, and endless stretches of pastureland filled with bundled-up hay. We stopped for lunch at a promising-looking roadside café called Rose's Diner. The restaurant was dim and quaint, with hubcaps on the walls and license plates from all fifty states. Phoenix slid into a booth on one side and Polly and I sat on the other.

"Look," said Phoenix, pointing to a bowl in the center of the table. "Peanuts."

"You can always tell when you're closing in on Louisiana," Polly said. "You got peanuts on the table and icebox pie." She opened her menu. "Aha!" she said. "Told you."

Phoenix and I spent lunch rolling through the songs on the mini-jukebox on the wall end of the booth: Patsy Cline, Elvis Presley, Hank Williams. Polly gazed around at the walls, at all the license plates.

"There are so many places I've never been," she said wist-fully. "Guess I never thought about it 'til recently. When I was young, I dreamed of going everywhere."

"We *will* go everywhere, Miss Polly!" Phoenix assured.

She gave him a look and went back to her catfish. Suddenly I heard an older woman's voice, crackly and heavy with a country twang.

"Pauline?"

My mother froze, a bite of catfish hovering on her fork in midair.

We turned to see a silver-haired old lady in a flowered dress, clutching a box of leftovers, and one hand resting on the arm of a much younger woman.

"You have got to be Pauline!" the woman exclaimed as Polly flinched. "That's you, isn't it?"

"Mother . . . ," said the younger woman in a don't-be-rude voice.

"Yes," Polly said, putting her fork down, her eyes on the old lady, searching as though trying to remember her.

"I knew it!" the old woman crowed. "I'd remember those green eyes anywhere. It's Myrtle. Myrtle Bowman."

"Myrtle Bowman . . . ," Polly said. "Yes. We were in high school together."

"Right! Remember sneaking cigarettes out by the coal bin in December? We had to smoke fast so we wouldn't freeze!"

Phoenix and I exchanged glances. I looked at him meaningfully and he read my expression and held his hand up to the waitress to signal "check."

Polly looked supremely uncomfortable.

"I remember," she said.

"Where do you live now?" Myrtle asked.

"Here in Texas," Polly said. "I've lived here over fifty years."

"Well, the folks back home will be gobsmacked that I ran into you! You're practically a legend, how you blew out of town and never set a foot back there, not even for your own daddy's funeral. . . ."

"Let's go, Mama," the younger woman said, pulling Myrtle's arm steadily, finally coaxing her toward the exit. Halfway to the door, Myrtle turned around and called, "It's like seeing Bigfoot!"

Polly looked shaken. She picked up her purse. "Let's get out of here."

"Hey, Miss Polly," Phoenix said, "don't pay any attention to what some crazy old bat has to say."

But Polly had already stood up.

Phoenix dug in his wallet for some change.

"I'll go calm her down," I said. I found Polly outside, leaning on the rail and staring out into the distance.

"What's the matter?" I asked.

She shook her head. "I shouldn't have come. Haven't even crossed into Louisiana and it's all coming back. This was a mistake, Willow. We're not even close to the border yet and people are coming out of the woodwork."

"It was one woman."

"If I keep going, it will be a whole town."

"The whole town is not going to turn out to stare at you," I said. "It's been fifty years. Half the people you know are probably dead."

The last word hung in the air longer than I meant it to. Polly glared at me. "I want to go home."

Phoenix came out carrying a box of leftovers. "Wait, why?"

"Because I'm tired! Can't you see that I am tired? I should be home in bed instead of answering to the whims of a teenager!"

Phoenix held the box out. "I had your catfish wrapped up for you."

"Well, what the hell am I going to do with it?" Polly answered.

"Good point, Miss Polly," Phoenix said pleasantly.

Polly got in the car slowly. "I am so tired," she said.

"How can I help?" Phoenix asked.

"Just drive."

Phoenix looked over at her. "Toward Louisiana, or back home?"

Polly sighed. "Might as well keep going." I let my breath out. We drove. Gravity sat on my lap, breathing gently. Polly had her head against the window, and I couldn't tell if she was sleeping or not.

We stopped at a small town near the Louisiana border for the night. Polly was still quiet, and that troubled me. During her treatment, I had quickly found where she kept her medical records, and thus had access to all the shenanigans of her failing body: blood platelet count, white cell count, insulin response, cytokeratin fragments. With the help of Phoenix, the Internet sleuth, I had known what turmoil lay beneath her skin. Now that the treatments were over, the screen had gone black, and this lack of information frightened me.

We drove through the quiet, dark streets. "Wow," Phoenix said, "there are a lot of churches in this town. We must have passed ten of them. Too bad it's not Easter Sunday or we'd at least get some bread."

"Try not to be blasphemous," Polly snapped. "The body of Christ is not for slinging down your gullet like a buttered roll. It's part of a service acknowledging his great sacrifice. Now I'm worried about the electricity from the lightning bolt that strikes you jumping over to me."

"I would protect you from the lightning God sent for me," Phoenix assured her.

Polly seemed spry, sassy, and I began to feel slightly better as we turned down a street, and then another, looking for somewhere to eat.

"Look, there's a burger joint that's open," Phoenix said.

"Over my dead body," Polly said.

"You don't like burgers?"

"I don't like chains, and I will not support them."

Finally we found a run-down shack called Crawfish D's. "That doesn't sound like a chain," I said encouragingly.

It was cool enough by now to leave Gravity in the car with the window cracked. A couple of rednecks were drinking beer out of long-necked bottles at a table out in front. They nodded at us, tipping their hats at Polly.

"Evening, ma'am," one said.

The sound of a hillbilly band poured out of the front door. Polly was no fan of loud music but she marched inside anyway, and we followed. People were dancing around, boots against a sawdust-strewn floor. A group of burly men were taking shots at the bar. Most of the tables were full, but one near the corner was empty. We headed for it as Phoenix found some menus. Polly had applied some blush and lipstick. She looked at the dancers, and just like the old Polly, she located the sleaziest woman first. "Look at that tramp with the skirt cut up to her hiney and both honkers about to bust out of her shirt. I shouldn't have my precious daughter in here witnessing such a thing."

"I'm a big girl, Mom."

"Seems to me I do remember a phone call from your guidance counselor about you getting in the family way, and not knowing who the father was, so I guess you're ready," she remarked.

I smiled. Her old wit was back.

Phoenix sat down and handed us the menus. "They serve until nine P.M.," he said over the music. "We're just under the wire."

Polly perused it. "Well, big surprise, they've got crawfish. 'Cept crawfish are out of season. I'd be wary of any fish that's out of season."

"I'm sure they're frozen, Mom," I said.

"Speaking of frozen, I'd sure like a margarita."

"Yes, yes, right away, Miss Polly," Phoenix said. He started to rise, but just then a waitress came by, dressed in a revealing spandex top and a miniskirt. She had long hair and dangling earrings and a big smile.

"Well, hello," she said. "What can I get you?"

"Frozen margarita!" Polly said.

"Well, we only have margarita on the rocks," the waitress said apologetically. "But that man over there . . . ," she pointed to a big redneck at the bar, "wants to buy you a drink."

Phoenix stiffened. "We can buy our own drinks."

"Phoenix," Polly said, "that's not very friendly. This gentlemen wants to buy me a margarita, let him buy me a margarita!"

"This isn't right," Phoenix muttered. "A strange man in a strange town. What does he want from you?"

"Would you like a drink, sir?" the waitress said.

"No, thank you," Phoenix answered. "I don't drink."

The waitress took our food orders—grilled cheese sandwiches all around—and disappeared. The big guy at the bar picked up a shot, looked over at my mother, drained it, and held the empty glass up in kind of a salute. Polly smiled and gave him a little wave.

"I'm glad I fixed your car," Phoenix said, "because you need me at times like this."

"You fixed it?" Polly asked.

He blinked at her. "I mean, I'm glad I couldn't fix your car."

Polly's eyebrows shifted. "Phoenix," she said severely, "did you do something to my car?"

He looked trapped. "Maybe," he said.

"Phoenix, *what did you do to my car?*"

He ducked his head. "I loosened a couple of the spark plugs so it would make a loud noise and sound like ass," he said. "But only because you and Willow need someone to keep you safe, Miss Polly! You're precious cargo. I couldn't let you go off alone to the middle of nowhere! I couldn't!"

He gave up talking and sat with his large head bowed in shame.

Polly rolled her eyes. "You're an idiot, Phoenix," she said. "But a well-meaning one."

"I think it's nice," I said, "that Phoenix wants to look out for us. Maybe we need protecting."

"Maybe *you* need protecting," Polly rejoined.

The waitress and the placating margarita arrived just in time. Phoenix, though, immediately grabbed it and took a swig.

"What are you doing?" Polly asked. "Getting your germs all over my margarita. You don't even drink."

"The drink could be drugged!" Phoenix exclaimed. "You never know what some redneck might slip into a pretty lady's drink when she's not looking. Then he'd tie you up and throw you in his truck bed like a deer."

"I'll take my chances," Polly said, and took several gulps. "Ah!" she said. "That's a damn fine beverage."

"It's quite tasty," Phoenix admitted.

Polly finished her drink in record time and we watched the dancers twirling around until the food came.

"Would you like another drink?" the waitress asked.

"I'm buying her a drink!" Phoenix said. "One more margarita. No, wait—make that two!"

Polly and I looked at him.

"Really?" Polly said.

"Why not?" Phoenix said. "You seem to enjoy them so much, maybe I'm missing something. Besides, I learned Dutch in two months during my marriage, and I can learn margarita."

"Margarita is not that difficult to learn," Polly remarked.

We ate our food and the waitress brought two more margaritas and Polly and Phoenix went at them. I imagined the Bear positioning himself under Polly's gullet: drinking her margarita and becoming gentle and mild as a result. Taming himself as his blood alcohol level rose.

"These 'ritas are strong!" Polly said happily.

The music was loud. I looked around at the bar's so-called decor: crab nets hanging from the ceilings, framed watercolors and retro calendars nailed to the wall, and any number of photos of people I guessed were famous country singers. Phoenix began telling Polly about the time his grandfather taught him to swim by tossing him into alligator-infested waters, his voice growing louder as the alcohol took effect.

A fiddle player joined the band and they began to play a bluegrassy tune. Polly's arm rose to direct the music and her leg bounced up and down.

"This music isn't bad at all. Reminds me of my youth. I was the best dancer in Bethel High School. I could cut a rug, that's for sure."

"I'll bet you could," Phoenix said admiringly. He threw back his head and finished the rest of the margarita in one gulp, the ice clicking against his teeth. He signaled the waitress. I noticed the big redneck who had bought Polly her first drink was on his way over to our table. He was an enormous man, even bigger than Phoenix, his body bulging out of the fabric of his T-shirt and jeans.

He stopped in front of our table, looking down at Polly. When he spoke, his accent was distinctly southern.

"Why, it just breaks my heart when I see a lovely woman sitting all by her lonesome with no one asking her to dance."

Phoenix glared at him. "She's not by her lonesome. She's with us!"

He held out his hand to Polly. "Madam, will you do me the honor of dancing with me?"

"Why, most certainly!" Polly accepted his big hand and he led her to the dance floor as Phoenix fumed. The waitress brought his drink and he slugged it as he watched Polly and the big man two-step.

"She's really good," I said admiringly.

"That big, fat fuck is going to crush her," Phoenix grumbled. "What if she trips and he steps on her? This is wrong."

Polly twirled and dipped.

"She's amazing," I breathed.

"I don't like the way he's slinging her around," Phoenix said. "I've seen my grandfather shoulder dead alligators with more tenderness."

I was having a great time. A redneck bar is the furthest thing possible from a hospital room. The swirling lights and the music and the volume were a welcome relief from all those weeks and months of quiet. The other dancers had begun to clear a space for Polly and her partner. The bandleader shouted, "You go, girl!" and the fiddle player broke into "Callin' Baton Rouge" as people stood up and began to clap along.

Phoenix and I rose to our feet to get a better view. I joined in the clapping but Phoenix stood with his hands clenched at his sides as Polly and her partner separated and began to dance freestyle, my mother kicking up her heels and twirling and bowing and shuffling in perfect time to the music, but as fast as the music went, it could not outrun my mother.

The scarf, which I did not love, but tolerated more than the wig, was tied a bit funny and the front of it flapped when she moved, but she had transcended the scarf, so much that it was nearly invisible.

"I'm going in there," Phoenix muttered as the song finally ended.

He lumbered his way through the tables and headed to the dance floor. I saw him say something to the big man, who looked annoyed, but backed away as another number started, and Phoenix and Polly began to dance. I had never seen anything like Phoenix's dance, some kind of mutant jitterbug, as Polly gracefully floated around him, somehow interpreting his random moves and integrating them into her steps. Even from across the room Polly's smile was electric, her dancing natural and ecstatic. Once again people clapped along, possibly for the two of them, but most likely for Polly's rescue of the wreckage of the dance through sheer determination.

The song ended, and everyone in the bar cheered and whooped, and Polly and Phoenix made their way back to our table. Phoenix was lumbering a bit unsteadily. But Polly didn't seem to notice. When they got to the table, Phoenix flopped down in the chair, tilting back, back, until he crashed to the floor.

"Phoenix!" I cried.

"All good," he said, but didn't move. He stared up at the ceiling, his eyes glassy.

The band stopped playing. A great collective hush fell over the room.

"Ah," said Polly. "I forgot he doesn't drink. We better go."

The brief silence ended and people were chattering and laughing at what had just happened, craning their heads over to our table. A group of men from the bar came over and tried to help, but Phoenix waved them all off. "I've got this. I'm perfectly perfect," he insisted, getting up himself with a great effort. We guided him out of the bar, Polly on one side and me on the other.

We trailed out into the cool night air, the sound of crickets around us, the moon bright overhead.

"That was a great time!" Polly said. Her voice was a little slurred.

Phoenix was struggling for balance. "I'm fine, I'm fine. One fine evening. Good times. It's okay, Gravity, Daddy's here."

"Give me the keys," I said. "You're not driving."

"Don't worry," he said. "I'm perfectly capable of—"

Suddenly he fell backward, like a great totem pole, and landed faceup toward the night sky.

Gravity went insane, so to avoid a scene, I let him out of the car. He immediately rushed to his master and began licking his face. I stood over Phoenix, inspecting him anxiously. His eyes were closed, and a faint smile played upon his face.

"Mom?" I said. "Do you think he's okay?"

"Oh," she said cheerfully, "he'll live. Let's go."

"Go? We can't leave him here." Gravity had finished licking his face and continued to his bald head, with tight, even strokes of his pink tongue, starting at one ear and working toward the other.

"Well, what are we supposed to do with him?" she asked.

"Watch me walk the curb, Willow. I have perfect balance!"

"Mom, help me get him in the car."

She laughed. "Get that big moose in the car? Hell, no. I'm not gonna pull my shoulder out of joint before our river adventure."

"Phoenix," I pleaded. "Get up!" I grabbed his arm and tugged, feeling a dead weight so profound it might as well have been a boulder.

"Told ya," Polly said. "We'll come get him and his little rat dog in the morning."

"Mom, get in the car. No, not the driver's seat." I opened the back door. "We are not leaving Phoenix."

"Of course we aren't. I was joking. I can sleep anywhere. In a car, leaning up against a tree. Did you see me dance?"

"Yes, I saw you dance."

I helped her into the back seat and then climbed into the front. The starlight came into the car.

I looked out the window. Gravity had resettled on his master's neck.

"This has been a great night, baby," Polly said from the back seat. "Are you having fun?"

"Sort of."

"Ah," she laughed ruefully. "You're just like your dad. So worried all the time." She reached forward and stroked my hair. "I had fun tonight. I used to have so much fun."

Two

We reached Natchitoches by eleven o'clock the next morning. Polly gazed out her window at the passing town square, the shops and the cafés, the churches that seemed to be everywhere.

"Have you been to Natchitoches before?" Phoenix asked her. It was almost noon and he was still speaking softly, no doubt because of the first hangover of his life. "Am I dying?" he had whispered to me in the parking lot, as dawn broke and I lifted Gravity off his neck.

Now Polly smiled faintly as she answered Phoenix's question. "Yes, many years ago, I came here with a gentleman friend. Just for a weekend, in the middle of winter. We stayed at a little . . ." Her voice trailed off, perhaps remembering I was in the car and not a good candidate to hear about a single woman spending the night with an unknown companion. "The whole town was lit up with Christmas lights and there was a great big banner across Main Street . . . Hey!" Something had caught her eye. "Stop, Phoenix. Stop here."

Phoenix hit the brakes and Polly looked out of the car. "I can't believe it. The theater is still here. Can you park, Phoenix? Can we go inside?"

The theater was largely empty at noon, and the teenager at the ticket counter let us go in. The screen was covered with velvet curtains and the glow from the row of lightbulbs at the stage guided us through the gloom. "Wow," Polly breathed. "They still have the old-timey curtains. But all the seats are different. They used to be made of wood."

She sat down and stared at the screen. Phoenix and I sat behind her. We both knew that this moment was important to Polly in a way that we couldn't comprehend. The minutes passed by. No one said a word. The theater smelled faintly of popcorn and old leather and Milk Duds.

Finally Polly spoke. "I was still so young last time I was here. Thought I was all grown up, but I was just a girl."

We reached Leesville, a town not far from the Whiskey Chitto River, in the midafternoon. Polly's friend Joe had a propane tank next to an A-frame house, a long graveled driveway, and flat fields that went on into the distance. A large patch of corn covered one end of the property, and a tractor was parked in front of it on the grass. He had a front porch full of wicker rocking chairs. Phoenix turned off the engine as Joe came out of the house. He was a small man, with a short, dark buzz cut and bifocals. His pants were wide in the legs and he wore a gold chain necklace.

"Joe!" Polly cried, and when he got close enough to get a good look at her, he could not keep the look of surprise and sadness off his face. We had adjusted to her appearance over the months of her illness: the hollow cheeks, the scarf, the way the skin had shrunk on her collarbones. But his eyes clearly showed how much she'd changed, in that unflinching way that instincts measure before graciousness kicks in.

"Polly Havens!" he cried, recovering quickly as he embraced her. "Good Lord, woman! How long has it been?"

"Sixteen years or so," Polly said as he lifted her gently off the ground, possibly a ritual that was done with much more alacrity when Polly was a younger, healthier woman.

"Oh, Polly," he said, setting her down and gazing at her adoringly. "You are still so beautiful."

"Oh, horse doody, Joe. I'm on my last legs." He flinched and she quickly changed the subject. "Last time I saw you was at Samuel's funeral."

I rarely heard my father called his real name and it sounded exotic to my ears.

"Ah, yes," Joe said to Polly. "Has it really been sixteen years?"

"Well," she said, "I was pregnant with this one . . ." She pointed to me. "And she turned a sassy sixteen a couple of months ago, so yes, at least that long."

Joe looked at me. "Well, hello. You look so much like your mother, and you have your father's eyes."

"This is Willow, my pride and joy," Polly said.

I held out my hand to him. Joe took it but pulled me toward him to hug me. He felt warm and solid, his aftershave musky and agreeable. When I had detached myself, Polly said, "And this is Phoenix, the neighbor boy. Shel's best friend and our driver."

"And our friend, too," I added.

Joe gazed up at the towering Phoenix as they shook hands. "Don't look like a boy to me, Polly. Looks like a man, grown up and more some."

"Oh," Phoenix said, "Polly thinks the kids in the neighborhood all stayed kids."

There was something still and quiet about the place that made me feel at home. As though time passed very slowly here, and that if we just stayed here, we could watch the corn waving and the tractor rusting and eat fried things and live in a bubble where bad news was absent and milk was fresh.

Joe led us into the house. "Estelle can't wait to see you. . . . She's in the shower."

"You have such nice friends, Miss Polly," Phoenix told her.

Polly nodded. "They are precious, and there are damn sure few of them."

❦

Estelle was small and willowy, with a lilting southern accent, and she and her husband were so lost in memories over the lunch they'd made for us that Phoenix and I could only listen. Polly was animated and girlish.

"Remember when we all went fishing down at the Sabine River?" Joe asked. "And we were going down that steep hill . . ."

Polly laughed. "And I said, 'Everyone be careful! Dig your heels in' . . ."

"And down you went," Estelle finished. "You ended up in the river, soaking wet."

We were all laughing now, even Phoenix and me. "We were worried that you'd been hurt," Joe said, "and when Samuel was scrambling to get to you, he almost fell himself. Then you surfaced hee-hawing about the whole thing."

"Lost my sunglasses," Polly said. "I'd paid ten dollars for them. That was a fortune, back then."

They kept reminiscing long after we'd finished lunch. I'd really never seen Polly among her true friends before: only fans, like Mr. Chant, and enemies, like her neighbors. She spoke in a tone of voice I'd never heard before, easy and familiar and girlish. Finally she said, "I suppose you want to know why I showed up here looking like death warmed over, wanting to go down that river again."

A short silence followed.

"You sick, Polly?" Estelle asked softly.

"Well . . ." She touched her scarf. "Guess it's ridiculous to try and cover it up."

I saw naked pain on the faces of Polly's friends.

"Cancer?" Joe asked.

"Well, we don't call it that around my house. We call it the Bear. Doctors chased it around with chemicals and then a scalpel but it's a wily creature. Funny thing is, since everyone gave up I feel better than ever."

"Gave up?" Joe asked.

A tear slid down Estelle's cheek. Polly put her hand on her wrist. "Just the medical folk. Other people round here . . . ," she gave me a quick, conspiratorial glance, ". . . apparently have other plans. You see, we're on our way to Bethel to see Junior Quade, and he's going to drum us up a miracle."

"You never know!" Phoenix chimed in.

"Who's Junior Quade?" Estelle asked.

"You haven't heard of him up here? Some fancy-pants preacher, cures the gout and arthritis and all kinds of things, so they say."

"Oh, Polly," Joe said.

"Well, couldn't hurt now could it?" Polly demanded. "There are things in this world that no one understands, least of all me. Besides, my girl was gonna nag me into an even earlier grave until I said yes."

Joe looked at Polly anxiously. "But are you sure you're up for this river trip? If you didn't have your friend along with you . . . ," he pointed to Phoenix, "I'd be seriously worried."

Phoenix shook his bald head. "Apparently I am not invited. Although I am available in case she changes her mind."

"That won't be necessary," Polly said sharply.

"You know," Joe said, "it wouldn't hurt to have a man along. Just to look out for you."

Polly would hear none of it. "This trip is about Willow and me and that's it. And don't you worry—I've got my shotgun and I know how to use it."

After lunch, Joe and Estelle took Polly to the river's edge to inspect the raft. It was clear that Phoenix and I weren't invited along, so we lounged against the car and waited.

"Well, looks like this is the end of the road for me," Phoenix said.

"Thanks for coming with us and everything."

"Of course. No worries. Perfectly perfect. You sure your mother won't let Gravity and me tag along? I mean, we could help. I could catch fish, and Gravity could scare off predators."

"She's made up her mind, Phoenix. It's just Polly and me."

Silence. The corn waved in the field.

"You think Polly will forgive me for screwing up her car?"

"Eventually."

"You're excited." There was a sad tone in his voice I could not place at first. "I mean about Junior Quade."

"Yes," I said. "I've done the research and he has a pretty good track record."

"But he hasn't healed everyone."

"I know that," I said, the irritation suddenly rising in my voice. "But I can hope, can't I?"

"Of course you can, Little Squirrel. But are you going to be all right?"

"Sure."

He looked uncomfortable. He swayed, his hands in his pockets, looking off into the cornfield, and it was hard not to imagine that both Phoenix and the cornfield were in synchronicity, moved by the same breeze.

"What I mean to say is, are you going to be all right, no matter what happens?"

"You mean if she . . . ?" I couldn't finish the thought. "No, Phoenix, I will never be all right."

His eyes met mine again. "But you have to be. You have to be, because you are Little Squirrel, and you will have to be Little Squirrel all your life. Right now it's Little Squirrel and Polly, but someday it will just be you. And that won't be okay for a while, maybe for a long time. But then out of the clear blue sky, you'll have a good day."

"I don't want a good day. I want her."

"She'll be part of every good day. No matter what. And someday, there is going to be a good day that we are all part of. I'm not sure where that is, or what it looks like, but I believe in that day."

I said nothing.

Phoenix looked at me sadly. "I had an uncle like you, afraid to go through life."

"What happened to him?"

"He went through life."

Polly and her friends came into sight, walking our way. Phoenix touched my arm. "I'll always be around, LS. Always."

The raft was loaded. Polly and I sat near the middle, getting used to the feel of the water. Our supplies had been transferred from the suitcases to various empty knapsacks. We each had a pole to guide us. The river was slow and wide and lazy. Joe untied the rope and threw it to me. I caught it and the raft began to move as Phoenix, Joe, and Estelle watched us from the wooden dock. They waved as we moved away from them.

"See you in Bethel!" Phoenix called. "I'll pick you up. Just call me! Unless you want me to come with you! I can make a fire! I am very good with fires!"

"See you later, Phoenix!" Polly called back, waving, but not as though saying good-bye, more like shooing away some smoke that's strayed too far from a campfire and is getting in her clothes.

"It's not too late to take my cell phone," he called. "How will I know if you're in trouble?"

"Cell phones are too twenty-first century," Polly rejoined and then our raft went around a bend in the river and we were alone.

"Always, Little Squirrel!" Phoenix's disembodied voice was growing fainter.

"They grew on me," I said wistfully. "Phoenix and Gravity."

"I know, baby. Phoenix is a good boy, but I'm glad not to have that yappy dog around."

The current was mild and the raft carried us along past scrub oaks and cypress and willow trees. White birds paused near the shallows, turning to watch us. The sun beat down and Polly took off her scarf, revealing the short stubble all over her head. She glanced at me, "You don't mind, do you, honey?"

"Of course not, Mom," I said. Her head seemed smaller than I remembered. She squinted and looked up at the sun. "Sun is out and means business." She rummaged through one of the knapsacks and found her enormous nylon broad-brimmed hat.

"Put yours on," she scolded. "Or you'll get burned."

I put on a baseball cap of Shel's. She eyed it. "Shel was good at baseball," she said. "There was a time when he was good at everything."

She stared out at the water. My brother's name hung in the air.

"I shouldn't have burned his father's boat," she said. "I thought it was the right thing at the time, but I didn't know how much it would affect him. I was afraid, Willow, that you would turn out like him. Lost and angry is no way to go through life."

She was folding her scarf very carefully, lining up the corners. "But anyway, I wish I could go back in time and take it back. Mothers regret their actions. But there's very little news coverage when they do."

The subject of her son had darkened her mood, sent her ruminating in a direction that I didn't like. It was too far from joy, too close to illness.

"Shel would like it out here," I said.

"Oh, yes," she said. "He loved the water." A current right in the middle of the river guided us so slowly along, we didn't even need to use our poles. She looked contemplative again. "You know, honey, when you reach the end of your life, all the fighting and the bad blood just seem so . . . well, quaint. You want to just go and find those people and say, 'I was wrong,' whether you really think you were or not."

"You haven't reached the end of your life," I said.

She glanced at me, a flash of annoyance crossing her eyes. "I knew that would be the part you heard, Willow."

"But you believe, don't you?"

"Believe what?"

"Believe that Junior Quade can cure you."

She sighed and spread her hands. "Don't make me talk about belief, sweetheart. I believe that this is what you want. And I'm going down this river. I am visiting a town whose front door I swore I'd never darken again. I'm doing this for you."

I persisted. "Suppose Junior Quade healed you, and you had another ten . . . twenty . . . even thirty years . . ."

She gave me a look. "I would clobber myself with my own frying pan if I lived to a hundred and four."

"But suppose you had some years left. What would you want to do?"

"I would want to go down a river, on a great adventure, with my beautiful daughter."

"Be serious."

"I am being serious."

"How about love?"

"Funny you should mention that Willow, 'cause I have a question for you." She peered at me. "That's right. *I* have a question for once. How do you like them apples?"

"Fine. Because I'm not the one always holding back information."

"All right, then. Why'd you run off that Dalton boy?"

I hadn't expected to hear his name out here, along this winding river on a day almost entirely without clouds. I had tried to put him from my mind, leave him back in Texas.

"Well?" Polly asked. "Cat got your tongue? You know, I don't think much of that boy's daddy, but I like *him* quite a bit. He's a good, kind person, and he's loyal . . . the way he kept coming back to mow my grass after you chased him away. I'm not saying you should marry him, I'm just saying you appeared to be slap-dilly crazy for him one day and done with him the next."

She studied me. "You're still slap-dilly crazy for him, aren't you?"

"Yes," I said at last.

"Then why?"

"He got in the way."

"Of what?" My shrug seemed to leave her slightly exasperated. "You know, Willow, you're allowed to have a life, too. During and after mine."

I suddenly felt exhausted, fighting against not only her death but also the very idea of her death for so long. A heron flew across the river and landed in the water near the shore. Polly gazed at it and seemed to deliver her next remark to the bird.

"I liked that boy."

Suddenly Dalton felt so immediate, as though he were sitting on the raft next to me, his posture so familiar, the faint scars on the sides of his eyes, his hair hanging in his face, the way he knitted his hands together. I wondered if Polly was healed and I came back for him, if he'd still be there, waiting for me, or if he would have moved on to someone else, some girl without my quirks or superstitions, someone normal and predictable and kind, whose mother could be counted upon to linger, hale and hearty, in the background.

"You can love two people at once," Polly remarked as if reading my thoughts. "Folks do it all the time."

The afternoon passed mostly in silence, Polly and I both lost in our own thoughts. Occasionally she would point out a sight—a screech owl or a snake swimming languidly in the shallows, but mostly we stayed in our own worlds. The river was blue and beautiful, vines hanging from the trees, trumpet flowers flashing orange near the banks, sparrows and finches and bluebirds and, over the tree line, vultures circling something unknown.

When the sun began to go down and the crickets began their song, Polly broke out our food supplies. Saltine crackers, Spam, grapes, and Vienna sausage. "Fit for a king!" Polly cried, breaking open two bottles of warm Coke. The raft got caught up on some rocks, but Polly just kept eating. "This is as good a place as any to spend the night. Tie us up."

I tied the raft to a tree limb that hungover the water and we finished our dinner as the shadows grew long around us.

"Plenty of varmints are out here," she remarked. "Bobcats, wolves, coyotes. Maybe even panthers. You know, they had black panthers in the woods in my day. Little ones, but they could still jump on you and gnaw on your head. People said they screamed like a woman."

"Quit trying to scare me." I chomped on a sandwich I'd made of crackers and Spam and washed it down with the Coke.

"Varmints don't scare you?"

"Only one. And he'll be gone soon enough."

"You never know, baby, what surprises the Lord might bring." I wasn't sure whether she was speaking from her own belief or just saying it for me, but I appreciated the words. She had seemed so energetic today, so much like her old self, that it was hard to remember that her strength was a ferociously empty lie.

"I've got to pee," I said.

She handed me the flashlight. "Take this. Step on that rock there and then the other one and then you can jump to the bank. Be careful. Watch for snakes. Don't go too far. And if something takes after you, just holler. I've got this." She patted the shotgun.

"Great," I said. "Shot by my own mother in the middle of nowhere."

"I beg your pardon," she snapped. "I used to shoot tin cans with my daddy with a .22. He called me Deadeye Polly."

"Good to know."

Polly grabbed onto a stump to steady the raft while I stepped off onto the rocks and clamored up the bank. I made my way through a copse of gloomy trees, my feet sinking into the soggy ground, the glow of the flashlight revealing rotted stumps and flowers with spidery tendrils.

"It's creepy here," I called to Polly.

"Then hurry up!" she called back. "I've heard of panthers catching people with their pants down in the woods!"

"Stop it, Mom."

I unzipped my pants and crouched against a tree. Nothing now but a trickling sound and the wind in the branches and the crickets.

Suddenly there came a fierce, high scream.

I gasped and lost my balance, falling forward on the flashlight and floundering in the weeds.

I heard Polly's laughter then, raucous and merry.

"Look out for yonder panther!" she called.

Annoyed, I collected myself and made my way back to the raft. "Very funny. You made me fall on the flashlight and break it, so I hope you're happy."

"Oh, we still have the lantern!"

"You're evil," I said. "The Bear is no match for you."

"Well, that's the smartest thing you've said all day."

We lit the old-fashioned coal lantern Polly had found at a yard sale and spread out our sleeping bags on the raft.

"Hope I don't wake up with a cottonmouth snake wrapped around my neck," Polly remarked.

"Now I know what I will dream about," I answered crossly.

Polly and I lay on our backs, side by side, staring up at the stars overhead. The crickets chirped, the wind moved the branches of the trees, and I decided I could sleep like this, a slow river beneath me, all the nights of my life.

"You know," Polly said, the red polish on her toenails shiny in the moonlight, "Joe told me the river has changed a lot in fifty-odd years. Indeed it has. It's changed course, winding where it used to be straight, and straight where it used to wind. But those stars hold fast to the very same place."

"Why was it just you and your dad on the river?" I asked. "Where was your mother?"

"Oh, Mother wasn't much into river rafting. She was quiet. Liked to garden and read. There's where I got my love of gardening. Daddy was fun. Always wanted a boy, never had any, so he made boys out of his daughters. Rhea loved going down the river, too."

The raft moved slowly beneath us. A cloud of fireflies hovered, glowing on and off. It seemed like a good time to ask again about the story of Garland, now that we were completely alone together and Polly was in an introspective mood. But my eyelids were closing. The fireflies fading. Polly's breathing steadied beside me and soon I fell into a warm, gently rocking sleep, and I was with Dalton in the back seat of some broken-down car, his body warm against mine, a Tom Waits song playing on the radio, and then the car was moving. Tom Waits was driving us down a long, lonely highway, his eyes watching us in the rearview mirror, his hand moving over to flick off the radio while he continued the song in his own deep and mournful voice . . .

I bolted awake, my heart racing. I heard it again, the sounds that had roused me from my dream.

Footsteps in the dark, heavy feet on dry leaves.

I bolted upright on the raft.

"Mom!" I whispered. "Mom!"

She stirred. "What's the matter, baby?"

"Someone's out there in the woods! I hear them!"

Polly fumbled for her shotgun. "Which direction?" she asked.

"That way!"

She peered into the darkness.

"Who's there?" she called in a clear, strong voice. "I've got a gun so you best not bother us!"

We listened. The footsteps were gone now. Just the sound of the wind.

"You sure your mind wasn't just playing tricks on you?" Polly asked.

"I heard something," I insisted.

"Well, could have been a varmint, could have been something else. But don't you worry. You go back to sleep. Your mama's here."

But I couldn't sleep now. I sat beside her, legs crossed, arms around knees, until the sun rose and the woods brightened and the river shone.

"Maybe it was a mistake," Polly muttered. "Bringing my baby girl out here."

"It was probably nothing." I felt calmer, soothed by the morning sun, as though bad things couldn't happen by the light of day. We had our breakfast—sliced cheese, dry bread, beef jerky, and eggs cooked on a tiny Coleman burner. Polly had not brought her coffee, and now regretted it. "Thought I could get by without it. But I suppose I'll be cranky now."

I untied the rope and we headed downstream. The morning was even more beautiful than the one before.

As noon approached, we passed a small johnboat with two fishermen in it.

"Hey," one called to us as we slowly passed, "that's quite a Huck Finn rig ya got there."

"We're going to Bethel!" I called.

"Bethel?" said the other one. "That's still quite a ways. You girls be careful now."

"Careful of what?" Polly asked.

"Well, we've got wolves in these woods. And you got to look out for the hunters."

"Hunters?" Polly said. "It's August. Hunting season's not 'til October."

The fisherman laughed. "Ain't no seasons for a redneck, ma'am."

The water was swifter as we moved into the next leg of the journey. We reached a calm stretch and put down our poles and had Spam and crackers for lunch.

After we ate, I began to take off my clothes.

"What are you doing?" Polly asked.

"I'm going swimming."

"Have at it. But don't dive in. Jump in. Don't want to cart a cripple around the rest of the trip."

"How dumb do you think I am?"

"Most of the time, not very. But it just takes once."

Wearing only my bra and underwear, I slid into the cool water, which went up to my shoulders before I touched the silt of the river bottom. I stood there, gently buoyed by the current, enjoying the chill of the water against my skin. Then something caught my eye, moving near the bank behind us. A figure glided between the trees, easing into the shadows.

I looked back at Polly. "Mom," I whispered, "someone's watching us."

"What do you mean?"

I pointed. "There. But he's gone now."

"He?"

"He, she. I don't know. But someone, definitely."

"Well, get back on the raft, and let's get out of here." She pulled the shotgun closer to her.

I clamored back on and dressed quickly. We grabbed our poles and urged the raft along faster. Sweat poured down our faces.

"You sure you saw someone?" she asked me.

"Yes, I'm absolutely sure this time." I kept looking into the twisted trees and the bushes.

"Maybe it's that Calhoun boy, back to haunt us."

"No," I said. "Phoenix would never sneak around and scare us."

After a few miles, I stopped looking behind me. My sense of dread receded and I began to enjoy the river again. According to the map, we were making excellent progress.

"Look!" Polly said. "There's the old Waverly Bridge." It was a rusted bridge over the river, no longer in use, whose shadow darkened our faces when we passed under it. "We should be in Bethel by tomorrow morning," she continued with a hint of anxiety. "No going back now. I just wonder if—"

She fell silent. Two men wearing camouflage and holding guns on their shoulders were standing at the water's edge, in a marshy clearing full of high grass. They were rangy and sunburned, with full beards. They were frowning, as though we had trespassed on their private river. I waved at them. They didn't respond. Just watched us pass by.

"I guess those good old boys were right," Polly said. "There *are* hunters out here. I never would have agreed to go if I knew we'd have this kind of company."

We floated a little further down the river before it began to narrow. Stumps hit the bottom of the raft.

"We might have to get out and wade for a bit," Polly said. "The water's not more than a couple of feet or so."

We jumped off the raft and I took the rope, guiding it along as we waded.

"Careful not to slip," Polly said.

"Are you okay, Mom?"

"I'm fine." But she looked tired, and worried.

We reached a place where the river curved, and a large shrub pushed into the water.

"Keep away from that shrub," Polly warned. "Never know if a snake might be tangled in the—"

We stopped. The two hunters were standing out in the river in front of us, facing us. They said nothing, but began to wade over.

A shiver of fear ran through me.

Polly reached for her shotgun.

The men watched her with hard eyes.

"That ain't too friendly now, is it?" said one.

"What do you want?" Polly asked. For now, she had the gun pointed into the water. She was waiting to see if the mood warranted the barrel's raising.

"We'd like some food, for starters," the other man said.

"Fine," Polly said. "Take whatever you want."

"Why, thank you," said the first man. He splashed up to the raft, snatched our bag of food, and threw it to his friend, who caught it one-handed. "That's awful nice of you. What are you doing out here alone?"

"We're not alone," Polly said. "My husband and son are in a kayak about half a mile behind us."

Both men laughed. "Ah," the first one said. "We know that just ain't true."

"What do you want?" Polly asked again.

"You sick, lady?" asked the man. "What's under that hat? Old sick lady and a nice young girl might need some help."

"She's not sick," I said. "Leave us alone."

"I don't think so," the first man said. "I don't think we're gonna leave you alone."

A terrible feeling came over me that the dominoes were falling, and nothing could stop the tumbling, not even out here when time had slowed. I looked to my right and my left, hoping to find an escape route for my mother and myself, knowing in my heart it was hopeless. My mother was going to have to shoot them. And they didn't seem to believe it.

The hunters moved closer. The second man tossed our bag full of food away and it made a splash and sank in the water.

Polly leveled her shotgun at them. "If you try anything with my daughter," she said, "I swear to God I will shoot you."

"You're not gonna use that gun," the first man said. "You're shaking so bad, you can barely hold on to it."

The look on Polly's face was steady, and determined and fierce, but the rest of her body trembled. The shotgun looked like it was about to slip from her hands.

"We don't want you," the man continued. "We want the girl."

"Go now," Polly answered, "or I'll pull the trigger."

The other man made a sudden move toward me, and Polly's gun went off. The explosion echoed loudly through the forest. The men looked shocked to find themselves still alive and whole.

"Well, I'll be," the first one said to Polly at last. "Are you that senile that you'd load your gun with blanks?" He looked at me. "You comin' here, girl, or are we coming for you?"

"You touch my child," Polly said, "and I will claw your eyes out and I will rip out your skin with my teeth and I will kill you with my bare hands." She readjusted her hands on the shotgun until she wielded it like a club.

"I'm tired of playing," the second man said, and again moved toward me in the water.

"Willow!" Polly shouted, and then the man gasped and grabbed his arm. Blood seeped out between his fingers. He stared down at it.

"What the hell?" his friend exclaimed, and then the water kicked near him.

"Who's there?" the wounded man shouted into the woods. "Hey, hey, don't shoot! We weren't serious! We're hunters!" The blood covered his arm now, dripping into the water.

"Let's get out of here!" the other man exclaimed, and the two floundered to shore, where the wounded man fell to one knee, holding on to his arm.

"Get up!" his friend shouted.

"It hurts too goddamn much! Bone is splintered!" he replied, and his friend gave him one last look and fled into the woods.

Polly dropped her useless shotgun into the water and we helped each other scramble onto the raft, poling furiously as we left the wounded man behind, still kneeling motionless on the bank. We were both shaking all over: stunned by what had happened, bewildered as to who had saved us. We said nothing, just pushed the raft along frantically for what seemed like forever.

Finally I stopped to catch my breath. I looked at my mother. She seemed exhausted, but kept jabbing the pole in the water determinedly.

"It's okay," I said. "They're gone."

I took the pole from her hands and she gave me a helpless, defeated look.

"Polly Havens," she murmured. "Stupid old woman." She sank down cross-legged on the raft, her head bowed.

"It's okay."

She looked up at me fiercely. "No it's not! I could have got you killed, or worse."

"But you didn't. Someone saved us."

"Phoenix?" she asked.

"I'm guessing Phoenix would have shot both of them through the head. Then swam over to say 'I told you so.'"

"Then who?"

"I don't know." But I wondered if he'd come back to her. Come back after all these years, an old man now but one with river sense and a steady hand.

Garland.

❧

We wanted to keep going as the sun went down, because we were afraid to stop again. And yet, a layer of clouds hovered above us, blocking out the starlight and darkening the river.

"Can't see trees nor stumps nor branches," Polly mumbled. "We'll have to just tie up somewhere and wait for dawn."

I felt oddly serene, given the circumstances.

"You know what, Mom?" I said. "I don't know who it is out there, but someone is protecting us. We're going to be okay."

"I hope to hell you're right, baby," she answered. But just the same, she didn't light the lantern, and we crouched together in the dark. Our food had been taken by the two men, and we drank the last of the water. "Not too much further to go once dawn breaks," Polly murmured. "So we'll be okay without drinking from this river. Who knows what's floating around in there."

She seemed agitated and distracted, and so I asked her, "Tell me more about your daddy."

She had an arm around me, as though someone or something was going to rise out of the river and try to grab me at any moment. "Oh, he was a funny man. When a fly would come into the house and buzz around our food, he'd pretend to grab it and wring it out over Mama's tea. I can still hear his laugh."

A branch creaked nearby, and she stiffened, listening.

"It's nothing, Mom," I said, but the tension didn't leave her body. When she spoke again, I knew why.

"You know," she mused. "All that happened back then made my daddy stop laughing. I didn't see him very much after that. I married the Captain and we moved to Texas and my daddy died of a heart attack that next spring."

I said nothing.

"I know you want the story. And maybe it's unfair, keeping it from you all these years. And here we are, together on a river in the middle of nowhere, and if God is willing and we arrive safe in Bethel, you're gonna find out anyway."

I felt calm and ready, as though the story was a lost balloon I'd chased for years and now it was slowly, as though of its own accord, drifting down into my hand. "You have so many secrets, Mom. You know everything about me—how would you like it if somehow I could keep myself from you? My first tooth, my first step. What if you got none of that? How would you feel?"

She sighed. "It's just ugly, Willow. And I was trying to protect you from ugliness. But, as I found out earlier today, I can't always do that. Besides, I want to give you the truth before you hear a lot of rumors from the busybodies in Bethel, if they're still alive, that is."

"Garland." I said his name into the gloom.

"Yes, Garland." I could hear her voice change. A wistfulness and a sorrow.

"Tell me."

Finally, after all these years, she began.

⌒

"Wish I had a cigarette. It would help me know where to start. Ah, hell with it. I'll start when I met the preacher."

"The preacher?" I asked.

"I was just eighteen. Was working in the library. Daddy had lost his job at the electric company to a younger man and was pushing mowers around people's yards trying to make money, and Mama was taking care of babies for a quarter an hour. You think we're poor now, Willow. Well, that was poor. Anyway, there was this preacher in town. Name of Robert Lee Webb. His wife had run off on him and left him with a little boy. He was quite a bit older than me. He was nice and he bought me things. He wasn't a rich man but he was richer than me, for sure. There I was, living with my folks and barely getting by."

The clouds had moved. A bit of moonlight came down on us. I hung on her every word. A panther could have swum to the raft and I would have quietly knocked it on the head with my pole, so as not to interrupt my mother.

"Everyone in town felt sorry for Robert Lee, that poor abandoned man. It affected his sermons. He'd start off soft, kind, talk a lot about loving your neighbor, but then he'd get mad. He'd scream and wave his arms and quote Bible passages about hellfire. I reckoned a lot of that was over his wife running off. But he scared me a little, when he went on like that in church.

"My folks were proud that a preacher was courting me. And I loved his little boy, with his sweet blue eyes and long lashes. I thought I was gonna be a preacher's wife, and I guess I thought that was okay by me. I was still working in the library. There was a young man in charge of periodicals, 'bout my age but from the next town over. Name was Garland."

"Ha!" I cried.

"Yes, you're a sharp one, Willow. Now can I finish? Garland wasn't too much to look at, not at the time. He was kind of skinny and long legged and droopy-eyed. But something about him struck me. I guess like how the Dalton boy struck you. He wore Wildroot Cream-Oil in his hair, and that scent on other men always reminded me of him. Of course, that made me feel guilty 'cause I was promised to Robert Lee. I tried to put Garland out of my mind. But I have to tell you, every time I went to work I was happy because I knew I'd see him.

"A few months passed, and I began to know a different side of Robert Lee. He would make me tell him every single place I went to in a day, who I'd talked to, and what about. I had to call him from the library right when I got there, and right when I left. Had to call him again when I got home. He made me wear long skirts and no lipstick. Made me study the Bible. He said I wasn't good enough to be a preacher man's wife yet, and I had to be trained, lest I run off just like his first wife. Well, time passed and Robert Lee got worse. Suspicious I was fooling around on him. He'd make me pray with him and his little boy for hours and work himself into a rage. Then he'd go out to the woods behind his house, always to the same place, and he'd talk to the ground. I know it sounds crazy but that's what he would do. Once when I knew he was at the church I went out there, and there was a patch of ground there that was a few shades lighter. It looked like a grave. And I began to wonder if Robert Lee's first wife ran off at all."

"But, Mom," I said, "this doesn't sound like you at all. Why didn't you just leave him? Or clang him over the head with a skillet?"

"Willow, I know in this day and age it sounds really easy for a woman to leave a man or give him a good wallop with a cooking utensil, but things were different back then. Different in a way I hope they never are again. A woman was more like a man's property, and being a beloved preacher gave Robert Lee a certain power over the town. And I wasn't quite the woman I became later. Wasn't so tough. Wasn't so sure of myself. And I was very fond of his beautiful boy. The boy had the most striking blue eyes I'd ever seen."

I wondered to myself, could this same boy have grown up to be Junior Quade? But I kept silent.

"Sometimes I'd make Robert Lee angry and he'd really fly off the handle. One day, when I was reshelving a book and the arm of my sweater pulled up, Garland saw the bruises, and he asked what they were from. And I tried to lie but I had lied so often that by then I just told the truth—that Robert Lee had grabbed me there.

"Garland was a very kind and sensitive young man, but his eyes blazed when he heard that, and he said, 'He had no right to do that, Pauline. He might be a preacher, but he's not God.' Garland had his hands on my shoulders when he said this. We were behind the stacks where no one could see us. He pulled me close to him and kissed me on the lips, so gentle and sweet, and I knew then what I should have known a long time ago, that I had fallen in love with Garland."

I gave a little gasp and put my hands over my heart. "That's so romantic!"

"If you don't stop interrupting, I'm going to push you off this raft. Garland told me I had to get away from that man. I told him I couldn't, that I was afraid. He said he would protect me but really, what could he do? Robert Lee was ten years older and a lot bigger and stronger. 'Tell your daddy, then,' Garland said. 'Your daddy will help you.'

"But I couldn't. My family went to Robert Lee's church, and to be quite honest with you, Robert Lee was helping my family with money from the church fund in times of great need. I worried that if I left Robert Lee, the money would be gone, too. And by then, I was just plain scared of him.

"Late in the afternoons, Garland and I would find little quiet places in the library to talk. It was our secret, being in love around all that knowledge, but not a single book could tell me how to get out of the situation I was in. I was afraid Robert Lee would hunt me down, or worse, hunt down Garland. And so that's the way that fall passed. The miserable life I had with Robert Lee and the secret one I had with Garland.

"So, coming up on Christmas, I went to Natchitoches for a library convention. Robert Lee couldn't go with me because of his tent revival going on that weekend.

"I borrowed my daddy's old truck and I went to Natchitoches. Garland met me there. But I didn't go to the convention at all. Instead we spent the weekend in a cheap hotel on the outskirts of town."

"Did you . . . ?" I whispered.

"None of your damn business, Willow. But no, we did not. We slept in the same bed, though, with our arms around each other. Early in the morning we walked to a café—neither one of us had much money so we split breakfast. We walked around all day, looking at the different stores. That night we went to that little theater on Front Street and watched a Jimmy Stewart movie—can't remember now which one it was. The theater was packed but we were alone together. I'll never forget the feel of his hand. So cold outside but his hand so warm, and his only good jacket across my shoulders, and the smell of his hair cream and the cologne he'd put on for me. I wished the movie would never end—so that Garland and I could stay there forever.

"The day after we got home, I was at the library and got a call from Robert Lee. He sounded mad as a hornet. He said to come to his house right away. I told him I couldn't leave work and he began to scream so loud that Garland could hear him on the phone.

"'Don't go,' Garland said. 'It's not safe.'

"'He'll calm down,' I said. 'I don't know what he's angry about.'

"When I got to his house, Robert Lee was waiting for me out in the yard. Before I could speak, he grabbed me by the arm and pulled me inside. He said a friend of his had seen Garland and me together in Natchitoches. He called me all kinds of names and began to hit me with his open hand. Not on the face but so hard on my head that I felt dizzy. I tried to get away but he was bigger and stronger than me. He hit me again, this time with his fist, and I shouted at him to stop but it did no good. I thought I was going to die.

"Just then the door flew open and Garland rushed in. He started fighting with Robert Lee. Robert Lee punched him in the face and blood ran out of his nose and I screamed for Garland to get out, that Robert Lee was going to kill him. But it was too late, Robert Lee threw him to the floor and got on top of him and was beating his head against the floor, and I was screaming and screaming and trying to pull Robert Lee off him. And then all of a sudden, Robert Lee fell sideways on the floor. The handle of a pocketknife was sticking out of his side and blood was shooting everywhere. I ran out of the house with Robert Lee's blood on me, screaming for help from the neighbors. When we got back to the house, Robert Lee was dead. The sheriff pulled up and arrested Garland, even though I tried to tell them he was trying to save me."

"Oh, my God," I whispered. "Mom, that is terrible."

"No one wanted to listen to me. Even my own folks didn't know what to think. I told the sheriff to go digging behind his house for the grave of his first wife. The sheriff said he sent some men out there and didn't find anything, but I don't believe they even looked.

"Robert Lee's little boy went to live with his grandma, and Garland got fifteen years in prison. I tried to visit him but he wouldn't see me. I wrote him letters telling him I'd wait for him forever, that it was my fault what happened. As far as the town of Bethel was concerned, I had gotten a holy man of God killed and left their church without a leader. Back then, you see, not too much of what happened behind closed doors escaped into the world. No one had ever seen him when he went crazy, and no one believed me. And the man I loved was locked up in Breezeway Prison in Baton Rouge.

"And that's when the Captain came in. Samuel Havens, your daddy. He was in town with a bunch of boys—before they went on to Corpus Christi, where he was stationed. I met him in the post office when I was mailing a letter to Garland, and he was kind and handsome and thoughtful and not from anywhere around here. He'd heard the rumors about me, but he didn't care. He began to court me, and I went along with it because I wasn't sure what else to do. The Captain asked me to marry him. I told him that I couldn't, that I was waiting for another man to get out of prison. He wouldn't take no for an answer, and said that I could start over new with him in Texas, where people didn't stare or whisper.

"I wrote one more letter to Garland, telling him about the Captain's proposal and begging him one more time to let me wait for him. He wrote me back a letter. He said he didn't blame me for anything, that he would love me forever, and that he loved me enough to let me go. It was his final decision, and I couldn't change his mind. He said it would be best for me to start over, and that I deserved a good life. And he really meant it. I wrote him five more letters after that, and he returned each one unread. And so I did what I thought was right. I married the Captain. He treated me well and we had a very good marriage, Willow, a very fine love, even into the last years when he hit the bottle more than I'd like."

"And that was the last time Garland wrote you?"

"No," she said carefully. "No."

The river was suddenly quiet but for the wind in the trees and the crickets and the locusts and the occasional frog.

"He wrote me just after your father died," she said at last. "He told me a little about his life. He'd been pardoned by the governor after eight years. He went back to a little town just south of Bethel and married a woman in his church and worked at the paper mill. And he never forgot me, but like me he was married and faithful. They tried to have kids, but couldn't conceive. His wife died in 1985. A few years later, when the Captain had also died, word must have gotten back to Garland. Probably your nosy Aunt Rhea. He wrote me a letter saying that he still loved me, and invited me to come back and marry him at last."

"Well? Why didn't you go?"

She hesitated and so I answered for her.

"You found out you were pregnant with me."

"I didn't want you to grow up there, in that tiny little town in the middle of nowhere. And Garland was a country boy. He wouldn't have been comfortable in our world, with neighborhoods and freeways and high-rises. I sent my regrets."

"So I ruined your chance at love."

"Don't be silly, Willow. You gave me the chance to love one more child. You were a gift from God."

"He sent you roses a few months ago," I reminded her.

"Yes, he did."

"What did the card say?"

"That he still loved me. But it was too late for all that. He's already had one wife die in his arms and he doesn't need another."

"You are not going to die!" I insisted. "You are going to be healed and then you can do anything you want. You can marry anyone you want! You can have love! True love!"

"Honey," she sighed, with a rueful smile that tried to form

and then faded, "you spend too much time trying to set my life up the way it is in your dreams. Mind your own dreams."

"But I don't understand!"

"It is not your job to understand, and it is not my job to make you understand. Even if I were a healthy woman, there are some doors that are best left shut. Garland and I have led different lives and it's been more than fifty years since we saw that movie. More than fifty years since I held his hand. It's like that little town of Natchitoches. It tries to be the way it was, but it's changed. Parts have died off, been replaced. Time has passed."

Three

Aunt Rhea did not hide her shock at my mother's appearance when we finally docked not far from her back door late Thursday morning, river worn and sleep deprived and weary, but safe at last.

"Dear God, Polly!" she cried, throwing her arms around my mother's bony frame. "You are skin and bones!"

"I'm all right, Rhea, unless you manage to squeeze me to death right here and now." Polly struggled out of her grasp.

"What were you thinking, going down the river, sick as you are, and dragging that poor girl along?" she scolded, grabbing me and holding me tight. "I should call the authorities on you, Polly!"

"Oh, hush. We're alive."

"Barely," said Rhea disapprovingly. "You two hungry?"

"Yeah," I said. "We were almost murdered on the river by two rednecks who stole our food."

❦

Aunt Rhea's kitchen had pale green walls, an owl clock, a plaster of Paris sculpture of praying hands in a frame, and a cat calendar. We sat at her oval table and ate eggs and grits while Polly told her the tale of the men on the river who had tried to attack us and paid for their mistake. Aunt Rhea kept punctuating Polly's story with *Oh, my God* and *Dear Lord* and an occasional *Shitfire* that made Polly stop and raise her eyebrows in warning.

"Wow," Aunt Rhea said when the tale was over. She shook her head. "I knew he'd protect you." And then, realizing what she'd just said, she clamped a hand over her mouth as Polly swiveled her head to stare at her.

"You knew *who* would protect us?" Polly demanded.

"Oh," said Aunt Rhea, "wouldn't you like to know? Well, how's it feel to be on the other side of a secret? Not too fun, is it?"

"Maybe I'll throw you down and sit on your head until you cough it up."

"That worked when you were ten and I was five and had asthma, but now I outweigh you by a good fifty pounds and you're sick and you look like crap, so have at it."

Polly glared at her. "Regardless, we've got to call the sheriff and tell him what happened."

"Uh, no, best not to involve him," Aunt Rhea looked nervous all of a sudden. "You don't want to get your Good Samaritan in any kind of trouble, trust me."

Aunt Rhea was watching my mother with undisguised worry. "Well, at least you're eating," she added. "Now tell me, why on earth are you back in Bethel? Shouldn't you be looking after that Bear of yours?"

"That's what I'm here for," Polly said. "The cure."

Aunt Rhea snorted through her nose. "Well, if you think the cure can be found in Bethel, you must be pretty hard up for sure."

"I don't need a doctor," Polly said. "The doctors have given up."

"Oh, Pauline," Aunt Rhea whispered, her eyes filling with tears. She reached her hand over to Polly and grabbed her thin wrist. "Oh, my dear sister!"

Polly patted her arm. "Don't get Willow all worked up. That's all I need is a bunch of waterworks. I'm here to see Junior Quade."

She let go of Polly's wrist. "Junior Quade?"

"Surely you know him."

"Of course I do, but do *you* know who he is?"

I managed to shoot a warning look over to Aunt Rhea just in time. She met my eyes. I shook my head very slightly.

"Who is he?" Polly asked.

"Well," she said, catching herself just in time. "He's a preacher. He's famous for performing miracles. Some people say he's a fake. But an old woman who volunteers with me at the nursing home swears he cured her slipped disk good as new."

"Well, I need more than a slipped disk miracle," Polly said. "I need him to kick a Bear in the balls."

"How did you find him?" she asked.

"Willow rustled him up behind my back. Then threw a fit

and ran away and acted like an absolute crazy girl until I agreed to come here."

"Good for you, Willow," she said admiringly. "Can't believe you got your mother home after fifty years. I never thought I'd see the day she'd set foot in this town again, after . . ."

Her voice trailed off.

"Willow knows the whole story," Polly said. "I told her on the raft coming down here."

"Well," said Aunt Rhea. "I'd be curious to hear which version of the story she heard."

Polly raised an eyebrow in warning. "You leave it be. She's heard plenty."

"You know he'll want to see you, Pauline."

"I don't know who you're talking about."

"Oh, stop it. That man has loved you all your life and God knows he's suffered for you. You owe him a face-to-face meeting, at least."

"I'm not gonna show up in his life just in time to croak on him," Polly said firmly. "I'm here because I promised my daughter I'd see Junior Quade. I didn't say a word about Garland."

Later, when Polly was napping, Aunt Rhea stole a moment with me on the porch. The rail was covered with jasmine vines, and out in the front yard, birds flew around a birdbath made of a hollowed cedar log and two old cultivating disks.

"So she doesn't know who Junior Quade's daddy is?" Rhea said, keeping her voice low.

"No," I said. "She would never have come if she knew that, I'm guessing."

"Damn straight about that. Well, you're a smart girl to keep it from her."

"One thing, though, that I don't understand. Robert Lee's last name was Webb. Where does the name 'Quade' come from?"

"Well, after Robert Lee was killed, Junior went to live with his grandma, Josey Quade. After he became a preacher, he took that name for himself."

Out by the fence, yellow butterflies rode on a cluster of red flowers that were swaying in the breeze. The chain on the flag-pole out near the mailbox clanged.

"She's going to find out who he is soon enough," I said.

"Oh, she's got a few surprises in store for her, honey." She put her hand on my shoulder. "But tell me something. How did you ever get Junior Quade to agree to heal your mother? He hates her. You know that, right?"

"Well, now I do, since she told me who his father was. I wrote Garland to tell him my mom was sick. I guess he went over and convinced Junior Quade to heal Polly."

"Well, that must have taken a lot of convincing. Half Junior Quade's sermons are about how his beloved daddy died and how he's spent his whole life wanting revenge."

"His daddy sounds like a terrible man."

"He was. But no one wants to believe bad things about their daddy."

"What if Polly finds out who he is and refuses to be healed?"

Aunt Rhea stared out into the distance, out to the pond

where the ducks swam. "I've known your mama a long time. A more stubborn woman God never invented. The fact that she's come this far is proof of how much she loves you."

⁓

Polly looked tense as Aunt Rhea drove through the town the next day. Every time we passed someone she would duck her head.

"My God, Pauline," Aunt Rhea said. "It's been more than fifty years. That church Robert Lee preached at burned to the ground back in '75. You act like some kind of posse has been set up all this time waiting to beat you with sticks. Now just look around and enjoy your visit home. Take a walk down memory lane and what have you."

"It looks pretty much the same," Polly said, her voice wistful. "There's the park we used to play in. There's the old railroad tracks. And the museum. Looks like they added a wing but I swear that's the same coat of paint."

"Remember the old Coca-Cola bottling plant?" Rhea asked. "Now it's a law office."

Polly's mood seemed to improve as we drove. By the time we arrived at the Bethel Baptist Church, she seemed to be in excellent spirits.

"All right, then," she said, getting out of the car, "let's go see this preacher."

Aunt Rhea and I exchanged anxious glances. The three of us went down the gravel walkway, bordered by crape myrtle trees, to a plain-looking church with a large wooden cross on the roof. The plexiglass sign near the entrance said: **HOW STRAIGHT IS YOUR PATH?**

Inside, the church was deserted. We looked up and down the hallways until we came upon a small office with a thin, serious-looking man working the desk.

"I'm here to see Junior Quade," Polly said.

"Yes ma'am," said the man. "He's expecting you. You will find him in the sanctuary."

We went back to the other side of the building, where we found the sanctuary, which was sparely decorated, with folding chairs instead of pews, small square windows, and a raised platform with a podium on one side and an organ on the other. A wooden cross hung on the wall at the front of the church. On the edge of the platform, head down, a man sat, his hands folded. He had slicked-back dark hair and the straightest part in it I'd ever seen. He did not move as we walked up the aisle toward him.

Polly stopped a few feet in front of him and waited. No one said a word. Finally Junior Quade raised his head and looked at Polly.

"Way-ull, if it ain't you yourself, in the flesh. Amazing, ain't it? The way Jesus works. The things he commands of you. The sacrifices he expects you to make. He's a man whose scalp still aches from the thorns, hands punctured from the nails, his side opened up from the spear. Hard to say no to that."

Polly looked confused. She held out a hand. "It's nice to meet you, Junior Quade."

Junior Quade rose to his feet. He didn't take her hand.

"Nice?!!" he thundered. "Nice?! Nice! What in the Hay-ull are you talking about? You mock my torment, woman!"

Polly looked confused. "Torment?"

He began to pace the floor. "I've hated you, you see? I've done hated you all my life. Hatred burnin' in me when I was but a tiny little keed, sitting in the bathwater at my grandma's, an orphan."

"Hated me?" Polly said. "How can that be? We've never met."

He stopped pacing and stared at her.

I could take no more. "She doesn't know!"

Her head snapped at me. "Doesn't know what?"

"Who his daddy is," I said weakly.

Junior Quade turned on me, eyes blazing. "*Was.*"

"Did I know your daddy?" Polly asked.

"Know him? Hay-ull, you got him kilt!"

Polly froze. His eyes seemed to have pinned her down, weakened her knees. I grabbed her arm but she shook me off and straightened. "Robert Lee's boy," she murmured. "I remember you. I'd know those eyes anywhere. You were the most beautiful boy in the world."

His voice softened. "I remember you, too. You bought me taffy."

"I did."

"I've been wanting to ask you all these years. Why did you take my daddy away? What did he ever do to you?"

Polly looked lost for words. "It was an accident," she whispered.

"Then why did a man go to jay-ull for it? Tell me that. *Why?*"

"I'm sorry," Polly said at last. "I don't know how my daughter found you, but . . ."

"She didn't find me. The feller who murdered my daddy found me. Garland Monroe."

"Garland!" she gasped. "But that can't be. He didn't even know I was sick!"

"Well, that ain't my jurisdiction, lady, putting the puzzle pieces together for you." Junior Quade sounded hostile again. "All I know is, you're here and so am I."

Polly's lips had started to quiver. "This was a bad idea, Reverend Quade," she said. "I'm sorry for wasting your time."

She turned to leave.

"Wait," Junior Quade said. "Turn around, sister."

To my astonishment, Polly obeyed.

"God is a funny man," Junior Quade's eyes glowed. "A very funny man. He don't get a lot of press for his humor but he's got a funny bone long as a string of stars. You see, I kept telling him I'd gotten over my hatred. That I was free of looking for justice for my daddy, free to live my own life. And then God said to me, *Let me see how free you are. I'm gonna have the two people who kilt your daddy come to you for help. And you are gonna help them, not because you are your daddy's son, but because you are my son.* You see how funny God is?"

"You don't have to try to heal me," Polly said. "I'm only here because of my daughter."

"And I'm only here because of my Lord. And I have been commanded to heal you. And so it will be done. You are almost at the end, sister. The sickness in you is everywhere. Comes out in your sweat and song. You're all but done for. But here's the gift. Not for my glory, but his. Not my wishes, but his. You will be healed Saturday afternoon at the revival. You will be set free. And I will be healed. I will be set free. Because I can't live for my daddy all my life. That makes my life not worth much. That's God's message to me."

"I don't know if I can accept your gift," Polly said.

"You got to. You got to."

"You've got to!" I echoed.

He glared at me. "I don't need no help, heathen." He suddenly took Polly's hands in his. "Come to the tent on the fairground tomorrow afternoon. Accept the blessing. I'm tellin' you, it's your only hope."

∾

A highly agitated Polly drummed her fingernails on the dashboard as Aunt Rhea drove us back through town. "Tell me again, Willow," she said, "exactly how this happened, if you can keep track of your lies."

Aunt Rhea shot me a sympathetic look in the rearview mirror.

"Phoenix helped me track down Garland," I said miserably. "I sent him a letter asking for his help. Then Garland went to Junior Quade and asked for your healing. Then Junior Quade sent me his number and I called him."

"And it never occurred to you that it might be important to me to know who Junior Quade's daddy was?"

"I didn't know until you told me the story on the river."

"What a terrible thing to ask that boy, who lost everything because of me! And now he has to oblige me as a man of the cloth? Well, my promise was based on a lack of information, so I'm taking it back. I'm not going."

"Mom! You have to go!"

"I don't have to do Jack squat," she shot back. "You're not my boss, so shut up!"

"Now, Devil Cat," said Aunt Rhea. "She's just a girl."

"And you," Polly said severely. "You knew what was going on, but you just stood by."

"I didn't know you were seeing Junior Quade 'til just yesterday," she said. "Then I thought it best to keep my mouth shut, so sue me."

A brief, angry silence. Polly's arms were crossed tightly.

"I was just fine with dying and never seeing this town again and never reliving these memories. Some things are not meant to be disturbed again. They just cause more pain."

She was silent the rest of the way back, just looked out the window as we drove through town. Aunt Rhea turned on a country music station with a high swinging beat. Polly turned it off. Aunt Rhea turned it on again. Polly turned it off.

I sat miserably clutching my stomach. Polly hated me. And if she refused to attend the healing, everything we had gone through was for nothing. Maybe I should have warned her about Junior Quade earlier. Found a way to soften the blow.

"We need to stop for gas," Aunt Rhea announced, pulling into the Chevron station.

"You still have half a tank left," Polly said.

"This your car, or mine?"

The pumps were set up next to a little Quick Mart store. Aunt Rhea fished out her credit card and handed it to Polly.

"Go give them my credit card, will ya, Devil Cat?" she asked in a sweet voice.

Polly kept her arms folded. "No," she said. "I'm tired."

"Come on, Pauline, don't be like that."

"You don't need gas and a preacher just told me he hated me and I got a fat Bear big as Kansas living inside me and I'M TIRED! I'M TIRED! Why don't you ask my daughter to go give them the credit card? She seems to be in charge of all other areas of my life."

"You are just as childish as can be," Aunt Rhea said.

"Give me the credit card," I said.

I just wanted to get the gas and go back to Aunt Rhea's and sulk on the porch and plot my next move. I grabbed the card from her hand and headed inside. The store was jam-packed with everything one would need at the last minute: ice cream and canned goods and beer and hats and magazines and fishing lures. The man at the counter, tall and bearded, with long black hair, was ringing up some groceries for a man in a plaid shirt and Wrangler jeans with holes in them. The cashier reminded me a bit of my brother. His smile, the way his hands moved as he counted change. And I remembered what Shel said once: *I look like a thousand men all around the world. I'm just a copy, Willow; I can be found in more noble form again and again. . . .*

As I approached the counter, still looking at the man, I heard what he was saying to the customer: "I'm at the age where what I say to the mirror is both nonproductive and inflammatory."

I turned around and ran out the door, up to the car where Polly sat with the window down.

"Mom," I said. "Come inside right now."

Four

I'll never forget the look on Polly's face. Shock, relief, joy, and sorrow. She stood a few feet away from Shel and watched him as he straightened a box of matches at the counter. He hadn't seen her yet. He hadn't seen me. We were the only ones in the store now, the three of us.

"I can't believe it," Polly murmured. "My boy. My baby boy."

He looked up and their eyes met. It was hard for me to read his expression. He came out from behind the counter and walked toward my mother. He was thinner, his face more gaunt, his gaze steadier. His jeans hung down around his hips and he wore an old Metallica T-shirt.

He reached his mother, put his hands on the sides of her face.

"Ma," he said. "You're so thin, Ma."

They embraced as I stood there watching. Shel raised an arm toward me, offering me a place inside the reunited family, and I joined them, feeling the warmth of our bodies together. Finally Shel broke away. "What were you thinking?" he told my mother. "Going all Huck Finn down that old river! You and Willow, all alone. I could have told you those woods were full of creeps and rednecks."

"You were there?" Polly asked, astonished.

"Of course. Who did you think it was—the Montessori twins? We followed you all the way from the second bridge in a kayak."

Polly gave him a look. "We?"

"Yes, we. That would be my good friend Phoenix and myself."

"I knew it!" I cried.

"What did you think he was gonna do?" Shel demanded. "Let some sick old lady—"

"You watch it!"

"—and my little sister traipse off down the river alone? Hell, no. Soon as he heard the plan, he drove to Bethel to investigate. Where he ran into Aunt Rhea, and then she led him to me. I met Phoenix at Joe's three days ago and we followed you down the river, then we got a lift back to Leesville. Phoenix went back to Texas, and I just got back here. I've barely slept."

"Wait," said Polly. "Joe and Estelle were in on this, too?"

"Hey," a man said by the counter, holding a Snickers bar. "Can we get a cashier over here?"

Shel glanced at him. "Just take the damn Snickers bar. It's on me."

"And you shot that man on the river?" Polly asked.

Shel's eyes darkened. "That's right. I did. Never thought I'd have to do something like that. Been having bad dreams about it. But I had to, didn't I? There was no other choice."

He looked over at me. "Jesus, Willow, you're all grown up."

"She's a teenager," Polly said bitterly. She was looking at him again. "But why . . . How did you end up in Bethel?"

"Had to go somewhere. And I had Aunt Rhea here. That was something."

"Rhea knew you were here all along?"

"Of course."

"Why, I'm going to give her a piece of my mind," Polly said. "Not telling me a thing all this time while my boy was here right under her nose!"

"Calm down, Ma. This is no time for you to go all banty rooster on everyone. What I want to know is, what are you doing here?"

"Phoenix didn't tell you?"

"No. He said maybe it wasn't his place."

Polly laughed ruefully. "So that Calhoun boy sticks his snout in my business at every turn and this one thing isn't his place?"

"Tell me on the way to my house," Shel said. "I have something to show you. Something I think you'll actually like."

Another customer came through the door.

"Sorry," Shel said. "We're closed."

We were all piled into Aunt Rhea's car, Polly riding shotgun and Shel next to me in the back seat. He was arguing with my mother, urging her to go back to Houston instead of trying her luck with Junior Quade.

"There must be something else the doctors can try," he pleaded.

"They tried everything, son. Almost killed me in the process."

"But Junior Quade! He's just some whack job, redneck charlatan. He's come into the station a few times. Believe it or not, Jesus doesn't fill his tank with gas for him."

"It's worth a try," I said grimly.

Polly turned around from the front seat. "Just let it be, son. Couldn't hurt, could it?"

Shel let out his breath. "Shit, Ma."

"Watch your language."

We had crossed the railroad tracks and were headed down a narrow road with great swaths of deserted farmland and a few clusters of mobile homes on either side. Rhea slowed down and turned onto a short dirt lane that led to a single, lonely unit.

"This is home, Ma," Shel said. "Not much to look at, you know."

"Ha!" Polly said. "You should see the shack back home. Falling down around us."

Rhea parked the car.

"Just give me a minute, Ma." Shel got out of the car and went inside.

"Well," Polly said to Rhea, "I suppose you think you're very clever, keeping news of my son from me."

"Yeah," said Rhea, "it's terrible, these secrets we keep."

"I'd appreciate you not teach my daughter any more sarcasm. She has much too much al—"

She stopped and stared.

The door to the mobile home had opened, and Shel was coming out, followed by a young woman with olive skin, black hair in braids, and a baby in her arms.

"Oh, my," Polly breathed.

We all got out of the car and gathered around the young family.

"This is Rosalie, Ma," Shel said. "My wife. And this is your grandson."

Polly looked stunned. "Really?" she whispered. Rosalie smiled and put the baby in her arms. Polly held him close, gazing down at the chubby cheeks, the dark and knowing eyes, the tuft of black hair at the crown of his head. I drew in my breath. I was so amazed that I even forgave the baby and its fat, healthy face, juxtaposed against my mother's and what that said about life and death and continuity and the natural order of the world. I was no longer the last one. There was one after me; there were more of us. I had come to Louisiana dreading loss and now the tables had turned. I had my brother back. And I had gained a nephew.

I reached out and touched the baby's cheek.

"He's half Creole," Shel said. "And all Havens."

"Nice to meet you," Rosalie said. She had a friendly voice and a hint of an accent, not quite southern, not quite French. "I have heard so much about you, Polly."

"Lies," Polly mumbled, still clearly overwhelmed. She didn't want to let go of the baby. "What's his name?" she asked at last.

"Michael Winslow Havens," Shel said.

"A big name for a little man," Polly murmured. She finally collected herself. "You planning on more?"

"Good God, Ma!" Shel laughed. "This kid is only two months old."

∽

"I knew he'd come," Aunt Rhea remarked. We were looking out the window as a car pulled into the driveway. Polly had gone back to bed late in the morning. She had not gotten much sleep the night before after all the excitement with Shel and the baby.

"Garland?" I asked.

"You know anyone else dumb enough to court your ma for fifty years?"

"Did you call him?"

"No, but he knew your mother was coming to see Junior Quade, and he knows where I live. He's an old man but he's pretty good at math."

I pressed my face to the window. After all these years, I was about to meet the one whose mystery had loomed so large. The car door opened and out came a tall, slender man with pure white hair, wearing a beige linen suit. He closed the door and put on a hat. His posture was straight and his movements were graceful as he stepped onto the porch.

I opened the door before he could knock.

"I'm Willow," I said.

Up close, I could see that his face was very handsome, and

that his suit was perfectly pressed. He took off his hat and held out his hand.

"I'm Garland," he said in a beautiful southern accent. "And it is my pleasure to meet you, Willow."

Aunt Rhea appeared behind me. "Hello, Garland."

"Hello, Rhea. I hope you don't mind me dropping in unannounced?"

"Oh, don't be an idiot. Come on in."

She went to fetch Garland some lemonade as I sat down next to him in the front room, near a window that spilled a large amount of August light and framed a giant magnolia tree.

"How is your mother?" Garland asked me.

"She's doing okay. But it's hard to tell sometimes. She's very proud. She doesn't want people feeling sorry for her."

He nodded. "I understand."

His smile was warm. Instantly I felt drawn to him. Comfortable in his presence, as though he were my grandfather by blood. "Willow," he continued, "I can't thank you enough for writing me. I know it might sound absurd, but I do think Junior Quade has a certain gift, and could possibly help your mother."

I nodded. "We're desperate," I said, tearing up. "We'll try anything." He reached over and placed his hand on mine.

"Of course you will."

"It's not time for her to go." I wiped my eyes. "She just found her son again. She's just come back home. What kind of God would take her now?"

Aunt Rhea came in with two lemonades and set them down

on the coffee table. "Right from the tree outside. Kidding. Straight from a carton."

"How was your meeting with Junior Quade?" Garland asked me.

"It went okay," I said.

"Junior Quade hates Polly," Aunt Rhea piped up. "He looked like he wanted to strangle her then and there."

"He is not fond of me either, to say the least," Garland said. "It's understandable. Things that happened when he was just a little boy had a lifelong effect. But she's agreed to the healing?"

Aunt Rhea shrugged. "She still seems up for it, mostly for Willow's benefit, if you ask me."

"Well," Garland said, "if you can get her to the revival this afternoon, I pray that God will take care of the rest." His accent was from the deep woods but he spoke in a precise manner, his grammar perfect. "May I see her now?"

"She's in the back room, resting," Aunt Rhea said.

"Oh," he said, his face falling. "Perhaps I should come back another time."

"Let me see if she's up and willing." Aunt Rhea disappeared from the room and returned shortly, looking resigned. "She's playing possum. Lying there with her eyes shut tight while I'm talking to her like an idiot. Sorry, Garland. Looks like she's not ready."

"It's been over fifty years!" Garland said.

"Yeah, well, she's afraid she's gonna die in your arms."

"I was hoping she would live in my arms," Garland said. "At any rate, I understand."

Shel couldn't bring himself to go to the revival with us. "I don't want to watch Ma get her hopes up at the hands of a nut job," he'd said. But he had at least promised not to interfere. Aunt Rhea's old car rattled through the town streets. It was a Saturday afternoon, and the town was quiet as we headed for the fairground.

It had not been easy getting Polly into the car. The earlier part of the day had been marked by many fights, bargains, and changing of her mind. I felt exhausted, slumped against the back seat, the victor for now, but at a tiresome price.

Polly had on her scarf and a shirtwaist dress Rhea had taken from her knapsack and ironed for her. "This is a bad idea," Polly mumbled.

"Oh, quit your bitching," Aunt Rhea shot back. "We've been through this a million times."

"Everyone's going to be judging me," she said.

"From where, the graveyard? Let me tell you something, Pauline. Fifty years have passed. There's a few people who know the story, yeah, but in general it's like the recipe for homemade soap—no one cares anymore."

"Easy for you to say," Polly said. "You've lived here all your life and stayed under the radar. No one points at you."

"Sometimes small children point at my butt," Aunt Rhea said. "But that's just on account of all the fried chicken."

I had fought so hard for this trip, and now that it was coming to an end, I felt anxious and uncertain. I had tossed and turned the night before, unable to sleep. I was out of ideas. This miracle I had pushed for was my one dry match. And what if it didn't work? The trip home with Polly, full of regret, brimming with Bear, was too horrible to imagine. What would become of her? What would become of me? I had fooled myself all along with the idea that the desperation of my journey somehow affected the fate on the other end, as though fate were a prize given at the end of a swim or a battle, when in actuality I had simply been moving, at top speed, toward a destiny that would never think to consult me.

I wished Phoenix was here, calming me with his Zen smile, and his peaceful eyes, his dog my comrade in desperation and raw need. Phoenix would have said, *All good, all good, LS. Everything will be perfectly perfect.* And he would have some insane quantum theory, some unleashing of the principles of physics, to tweak this situation into something manageable.

A man on the side of the road worked on his truck. A loose dog ran down the sidewalk. Three red balloons waved from the fence in front of a used-car dealership. I began to feel ill and put the window down. A warm breeze came into the car, as well as the faint sounds of distant singing.

"That's them," Aunt Rhea said.

Polly listened. "I heard that song so many times during Fifth Sunday sing-alongs," she said wistfully. "It was Mother's favorite song, too. Stop the car a minute."

"Now, Devil Cat . . ."

"Stop the damn car!"

Aunt Rhea pulled over. Polly rolled down the window. "It's

my favorite hymn," she said. "I just want to listen to it here, in the car in privacy."

And so we listened.

> *Yes, we'll gather at the river*
> *The beautiful, the beautiful river,*
> *Gather with the saints at the river,*
> *That flows by the throne of God!*

❧

By the time we entered the tent, the healing was in full swing. Hundreds of people were crammed on metal benches, two organ players and a man on a guitar at the front, and Junior Quade, wearing a black suit, holding court as a line of people, some in wheelchairs, some leaning on canes, waited to be healed. The ushers looked like members of a local biker gang, decked out in leathers and bow ties. One of them sported a giant tattoo of Jesus' face on his bulging muscles.

The congregation seemed to be composed of the entire town—the old and young, and everyone in between. We took a back seat on the last bench as Junior Quade ranted on, dipping and twirling, working the stage, roaming back and forth, moving into the congregation, pointing at the ground as though talking to Satan, often turning his head up to the canvas ceiling of the tent to address God. Whispering and pleading and roaring, sometimes crying, he was a sight that no one could tear their eyes from.

"Yay-us, Jesus went into the desert and YAY-US, Jesus was a MAN! Subject to a man's temptations. He had flesh and blood, ALONE! His sword and his staff, brothers! And Satan came to him in many forms. Betrayal and temptation, and sins of the earth. There were probably some whores around, too, folks! Harlots and tramps circling Jesus, a-prancin' around him. You see, Jesus was a MAN! I am a MAN! It takes a man to heal the world, but first that man has got to heal HISSELF. AMIRIGHT BROTHERS?"

The men clapped and hollered.

"AMIRIGHT SISTERS?"

The women clapped and hollered.

"AMIRIGHT HARLOTS?"

Silence.

"That was a TEST! Ain't no harlots in a house of God, better not be!" He turned to the first man in line.

"Brother, what ails you?" Junior Quade demanded.

The man spoke shyly into the microphone. "I am going deaf."

"Is it your woman? Does your woman scream in your ear? I'm pulling your leg, brother! Humor is welcome in the house of the Lord. And now, with the full measure of God my Father, I am telling you, devil of deafness, LEAVE my brother NOW!"

Junior Quade's face was full of rage. His eyes sparked. He leapt forward and grabbed the man's shoulder. The man dropped as though shot, into the burly arms of two of the helpers, as Junior Quade stood over his prone body, yelling: "Leave him, Satan, for you are welcome NO MORE in the body of this man! LEAVE HIM, affliction of deafness! And REJOICE, brother, for you DONE BEEN HEALED!"

They lifted the man up as the congregation went wild, whooping and shouting. The organ started up, the guitarist began a riff that sounded more rock and roll than hymn. The man looked dazed.

"CAN YA HEAR ME!" Junior Quade thundered.

"Yes!" said the man.

"And how 'bout now?" he whispered.

"Yes!" he said.

The congregation clapped again.

"Go up there, Ma," I urged.

"It's a circus!" she whispered back.

"Come on! It only takes a minute. Go! Go!"

She sighed, stood, and began making her way to the front of the church. The music was still playing, Junior Quade and his helpers still dancing around in jubilation. I suddenly noticed a familiar figure standing near the front, and off to the side. It was Garland, dressed in a silver suit and looking dapper, following my mother with his eyes.

Junior Quade noticed Polly coming toward him. He stopped dancing, stopped smiling. "Quit the music!" he ordered.

The congregation murmured in confusion. Junior Quade was staring down at Polly, his eyes full of venom—for the Bear or for the woman herself, I wasn't quite sure.

He held up his hand for silence. I was standing now, unsure of whether to stay in place or run to help her. Garland was gliding his way closer to the front, his shoulder brushing the side of the tent. It was then that I noticed a familiar figure rise on the other side. It was Shel, and he, too, was moving toward the front.

"This tent is full of JESUS!" Junior Quade pronounced. "And Jesus is only truth. So this tent is only truth today! So I am gonna TAY-ULL you the truth." Junior Quade got off the stage and walked toward Polly until they were just a few feet apart. The congregation was transfixed. I held my breath. Aunt Rhea took my hand. Her fingers were icy in mine.

"Sit down!" someone whispered behind me.

I turned around. "That's my mother. And I will not."

I looked back at the preacher and Polly, their eyes locked on each other as Junior Quade began to speak.

"When I was born, my mama run off and my daddy had to raise me. Now, some of you knew my daddy. . . ."

Some of the old people clapped. He held up a hand and kept going, never taking his eyes from Polly, who stood calmly, hands at her sides.

"For those of you who didn't," he continued, "this man was the kindest servant of God that ever walked the earth. Never hurt nobody, only wanted to spread the word. And then along came . . . a *Jezebel*."

My heart began to beat. My fists tightened.

I looked at my brother. His face was a mask of anger. He edged closer to the stage.

". . . and my daddy fell for this woman. Maybe he lost his way. And this woman got my daddy kilt."

An old man in the congregation wheezed, but that was the only sound.

"And I went to live with my Granny Quade, and I didn't have no daddy nor no mama neither. All my life, I have had hatred in my heart. I have wanted revenge against the man who killed and the woman who got him kilt. But you know, Jesus will put your worst sin to the test. And my worst sin was hate. Just pure, old-fashioned, burning hate."

He was staring holes into Polly's eyes but Polly's back remained straight, and she did not turn away. I wanted to run forward, to save my mother from this spectacle, this judgment, but I was too afraid that I would be saving her from her last chance for a miracle cure.

"You see," Junior Quade continued, "all my life I've lived for my daddy. Lived in his shadow. Lived to revenge his early and unfair departure. Lived to right that wrong. But Jesus—way-ull, he had other plans for me. He wanted me to set down my daddy's torch, 'cause it was burning me. And so he struck down this Jezebel I hated all my life with a terrible illness, and now he commands me to heal her, and only by this can I set myself free."

The congregation suddenly sprang to life, cheering and shouting "Praise the Lord!"

"So I will do this, not for me, not for MY glory, not for my DADDY'S glory, but for the glory of the Lord and the glory of the TRUTH."

My brother looked like he wanted to rip Junior Quade's head off.

"Because the truth—"

Junior Quade stopped, looking surprised.

Polly had taken the microphone. She spoke into it.

"I killed your father."

Junior Quade's mouth fell open. The congregation made a great whooshing sound that faded into silence. Meanwhile, I quickly made my way to my brother, and we stood there together, listening as she continued.

"I didn't just get him killed," Polly announced. "I killed him with my own hands. My suitor, Garland, removed my fingerprints from the knife when I ran for help, and added his own. That's the truth."

"Jesus," Junior Quade whispered, "why are you doing this to me? Why are you testing me?"

Polly kept going, her words tumbling out. "Garland took the blame for what I did. I tried to tell the sheriff, but no one would listen. Garland spent eight years of his life in prison. And your daddy wasn't quite the saint you made him out to be, Junior Quade, as long as we are telling the truth. Your daddy used to beat me."

The congregation muttered. Someone from the back shouted: "Liar!"

Polly paid no mind. "In fact, he was beating me when Garland interrupted us, and they began to fight. He was gonna kill Garland, and so I stabbed him to stop that. I had no choice at the time. I know I did wrong, loving another man when I was promised to your daddy. But there's enough blame to go around, and that's the truth."

Junior Quade's face was beet red and sweaty now. A reservoir of rage seem to break in him and he lunged for my mother and they both went down, as Shel and I dashed for the stage and the congregation erupted into chaos. I tripped over people, getting elbowed and elbowing back, screaming at them to get out of the way. When we reached the stage, Polly was on the floor and Garland was rushing toward her from the other side.

"Demon! LEAVE NOW! I command you, demon!" Junior Quade howled just as Shel's punch caught him in the side of the head and the preacher fell over, my brother on top of him. They wrestled as the congregation roared like a lion, on their feet, now, pushing in on us.

Garland cradled Polly's head on his lap.

"Mom!" I shouted. "Mom! Are you okay?"

Polly opened her eyes. Garland helped her to sit up, his arm around her protectively. She turned her head and locked eyes with the man she'd loved for so many years, as finally a group of men separated Junior Quade and my brother, who were still straining against their captors and trying to get at each other.

"WHO THE HAY-ULL ARE YOU?" Junior Quade demanded. "WHO THE HALE ARE YOU?"

"DON'T YOU EVER TOUCH MY MOTHER!" Shel screamed back. "You damn hillbilly!"

"Mom," I said. "Say something."

She blinked. A look of utter wonder crossed her face.

"It's gone," she whispered.

Five

Around Aunt Rhea's table, a debate took shape over the following days: Polly and I thought that Junior Quade was banishing the devil from Polly. Shel and Aunt Rhea seemed to believe that Junior Quade thought Polly *was* the devil. And Garland, who sat at the table next to her, was content to stay out of the fray, as long as he had his Pauline back.

And back she claimed to be, swearing that the moment Junior Quade seized her, she felt the Bear leave her body. Indeed, she had the beginnings of a rosy glow on her face, and her green eyes were brighter than they'd been in a long time.

"I'll believe it when you get back to Texas," Shel said, "and have some tests."

"I'm not taking any tests, boy," Polly snapped. "I'm never gonna go to a doctor again as long as I live. I'm telling you, I feel fine."

And as for my brother's demons: I did not know their status, but he did seem to be a man at peace. He came over every day to Aunt Rhea's house to see Polly, often with his wife and baby, whom Polly could not get enough of holding and bouncing on her lap. And Rosalie, who was witty and kind, seemed more than a match for Shel, who let him go on about politics or religion only so long before cutting him off in midrant with some gentle teasing, steering him toward some topic of conversation that would leave him less red in the face.

"She knows how to handle that boy," Polly said admiringly. "I think he chose wisely, and it's gonna lead to a lot more peace and quiet for the rest of us."

Around Aunt Rhea's table, the fragments of our family, which had been drawn together again, had a feeling of serenity, and the days passed slowly, one after another, hot and calm, Aunt Rhea cooking and Garland coming every day to visit, hat in hand.

"What are you going to do about Garland?" I asked my mother one night before we went to bed. "Is he coming back to Texas?"

"Oh, Willow, I can't answer that. Who knows? We just found each other again."

And for once, I felt content with that answer. Some hole inside me had been filled, some kind of uncertainty had steadied itself. Somehow, through all the adventures a bit more of myself had emerged. A bit more of Willow.

I was me.

A week into our stay, I made a call. Aunt Rhea's phone was the old-fashioned kind with a whirling dial and a cord I had to stretch across the kitchen and into the laundry room, where I shut the door and sat down against the dryer, which was warm and trembling with its load of sheets. I dialed the number and my stomach clenched as I heard the ringing.

"Hey, it's Pete, whatcha got?" said the voice on the other end.

"Hello, it's Willow." My voice was shaking.

"Well, hello Willow! How've you been? Your ma still in this world?"

"Oh, yes," I said. "Absolutely."

"Well, like I'm always telling my boy, no one can kill that woman. Want to talk to him?"

"Yes."

"Hold on, then."

I held my breath.

"Hello?" Dalton's voice still had that boyish yelp in it when he answered the phone. He hadn't quite grown up yet.

"Hey," I said.

"Willow?"

"Yes," I whispered. "It's me."

A silence. The time it takes to beat an egg or thoroughly rinse a plate.

"How are you?" he asked.

The dryer hummed warm against the back of my head. Sunlight streamed into my lap. And I was tired of waiting, the seconds going by, and the minutes and hours and days. Tired of strategizing, sacrificing. Holding back. Living for someone else.

"I love you," I said.

∽

Two weeks after we departed on our river journey, Phoenix came to get us. Polly and Garland were sitting in lawn chairs, hand in hand, and Aunt Rhea was in the kitchen. I came out on the porch and waved.

"Phoenix!" I shouted as the engine died.

He waved back at me and opened the door. Just then Gravity leaped out and came running into the yard. My heart froze. The little dog was headed straight for Polly, who, deep in conversation with Garland, their fingers entwined, paid no attention.

I ran down the steps and across the yard, arms pumping, legs churning, heart beating fast, running at top speed, intending to intercept the little dog, but he was dodging me, moving around me, tongue lolling out of his mouth; he was a streak of furred agenda, he was fast but I was faster. I turned and cut him off and picked him up just before he reached my mother. He was hot and fuzzy in my arms, shivering with the sudden action and the new adventure and the sights and smells of this moment, this moment that was one of a series of moments that would take us to the end of our lives.

Perhaps I should have just let it be, let the scene play out, but I couldn't help it.

I am Willow and I have a story, this is my story, and it is perfectly perfectly perfect.